BOOK I

BATTLEFIELD PRAYER

DESERT WARRIOR

Maureen Hartson and Shannon Coe

Published by Market Refined Publishing,
An Imprint of Market Refined Media, LLC
193 Cleo Circle
Ringgold GA 30736

marketrefinedmedia.com

Cover and Interior Design by Nelly Murariu at PixBeeDesigns.com

Manuscript Edits by Market Refined Media

Print ISBN: 979-8-9855797-3-4
Digital ISBN: 979-8-9855797-4-1

Library of Congress Control Number: 2022912951

First Edition: July 2022

DEDICATION

To the Most High,
Thank you for never forsaking us.

To our husbands, children, their spouses,
all of our grandchildren,

We will fight for you through prayer
until our final breath.

To every woman who has prayed at her kitchen sink,
while nursing in the midnight hours,
at stop signs, on her knees in the bathroom,

Thank you for coming to the aid of your sisters in Christ.
May your eternal reward be great.

ACKNOWLEDGEMENTS

We cannot adequately express our gratitude to so many who supported and encouraged us in the process of writing Battlefield Prayer.

Our simple words of thanks seem so small in comparison to what you gave us.

To our husbands and our children: for all the times you sat and tried to keep up with the ideas, plots, biome developments, dark descriptions (we are sure some of this had you worried about us!), praise moments, we thank you. For seven years you listened to our story take shape, in cars, on beaches, in our homes, gathered at the table, and you encouraged us. You were our first experiences with intercessory prayer, and for every moment that drew us to fight for you, on your side, in a battlefield, we thank you.

To our friends and family who painstakingly read our chapters as they very slowly rolled out, in their unedited form (how painful that must have been), you encouraged us. Every single chapter, you encouraged us. Your pushes to keep going kept us going. We may not have ever seen our story in book form had it not been for you.

For the team that sat in cars, praying with us at the same time, in different states, in seedy districts, with our children in back seats while we each prayed scripture over women we did not know, we thank you. We learned together to sharpen our swords and fight for others through prayer. We will never forget our stakeouts complete with coffee on the dashboards, sometimes donuts or a pizza for dinner, while we took turns watching the surrounding areas and praying scripture.

To our sister who is still on her battlefield, we remain with you, swords raised in battle and sometimes raised in praise, until the end. Always. Thank you for including us. It will forever be an honor to come when the shofar blows.

For all our little grandchildren, who let us share our love of storytelling and reading books to them, you are our joy and all of the picture books we have read on repeat, have deepened our love of a good story. For our littles who have left us early, we love you, we remember you, and we trust the battles we fought in prayer for you were heard and the tears we shed for you are in safekeeping, maybe lined up in little glass bottles strung like beautiful twinkly lights.

For our team at Market Refined Media, we thank you for capturing our vision and sharing it with us. For the long hours each of you invested in our work, thank you. As you saw from our rough drafts, we could not have done this without your help!

To our readers, although we may never meet you in this life, be assured, when the shofar blows on your behalf, we will be there.

With lifted swords after good battle and good prayer, join with us as we cross our swords and say "clink-clink"!

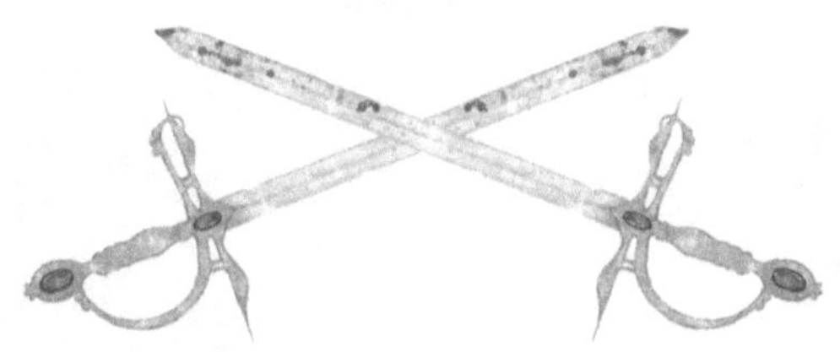

*"Take the sword of the spirit,
which is the word of God ...
and pray."*

Ephesians 6:17-18 (NIV)

Table of Contents

CHAPTER ONE

She took shape and form after coming through the portal and stood in a pile of hot sand.

She stretched out one vertebrate at a time, rolling her head up. Her eyes remained closed the entire time. She needed one more minute, one more moment to gain a last ounce of strength. Taking advantage of the darkness, she listened.

The air was dry with a stench of something rotting. She had nothing with her but the sword given to her at her second birth. Drums sounded in the distance, and her heart pounded to the beat. She was unnaturally still and to the Watchers she looked bored. She had been here many times before. She kept coming back to this place and couldn't seem to leave it once and for all.

She gave a low-toned whistle. There was no bounce back, which told her the battlefield was wide open. She was transported in and was vulnerable and exposed. Not good. But she was ready.

She opened her eyes and felt blinding pain. The brightness of the sun costs her valuable time, and she was disoriented. Maybe she should have come through the portal with her eyes wide open. Her vision came back slowly as the heat pulsed over her body and adrenaline, that elixir of bravery, shot through her veins. Sweat beaded on her upper lip and she hadn't even started killing yet.

Here they were, close enough to hit with arrows that she didn't have. She needed to wait until they were closer. Her sword was not the only weapon in the armory, but it was always the one she had with her when she arrived on the battlefield. She was promised she would never be without a weapon, but an upgrade would be nice. She smelled them now and knew that they might likewise smell her and the distinct odor adrenaline leaves on a body.

She counted fifty Corgs, the stupid, vile linemen of the Enemy. These expendable, filthy demons were as countless as the geckos in this desert. Their high-pitched squeals alert that they'd seen her or smelled her. Or both.

There was hardly any place to find cover or shelter on this battlefield, and she hoped she wouldn't have to stay here long. Her job was to get transported in, fight a battle, and leave. She was always a victor- proving the truth that just showing up and arriving is the most important part of winning.

The Corgs screamed now with their high-pitched pulsing squeals. They'd sensed an invader, and they knew the victor's status belongs to her as she walks towards them. They knew their end was near.

Sword ready, eyes on the Corgs, she closed in on them without making a sound. The worn leather boots, covering her knees, represented years of battles and made no sound as she ran.

She hoped she looks like a mirage to them as she moved closer to the enemy. The Corgs didn't see well, but often in vague, blurry images. If they didn't move in the next few seconds, she *would know that she entered the battlefield and successfully caught them off guard.*

But that was not to be, for the heavy one in front saw her and knew her to be real. They all ran away from her. But still they met. She grabbed the first filthy Corg she could reach by his hair and sliced his throat. As several turned and came towards her, she dropped the dead Corg, thrusting her sword behind her into another Corg and her hand was plunged, alongside the sword, deep into his chest. When she pulled out both hand and sword, maggots came out as well. Two down, many more to go. The sandy earth was soon littered with dozens of demon Corgs, but the fat one, running further than her eyes could see, escaped.

The battle continued for half an hour. Although it was seemingly swift work, tomorrow she will show up on this same desert battlefield and fight more of the same disgusting demons. But she was not thinking about that now. She was thinking about the latest battle. She won today. She won because she showed up. She beat the Corgs. But her desire wasn't just to slaughter Corgs. What she wanted, what she needed, was a final victory, an answer to her prayer.

The sounds of the diner filled the room as coffee drinkers and big breakfast eaters went about the business of enjoying the most important meal of the day. The counter was lined with working men who shared their plans for wells that needed to be drilled, trees that needed to be cleared away from power lines and potholes that needed to be filled before the day is over.

One booth was filled with church ladies, the kind that know everyone and everything. Complete with makeup, ironed dresses, and hats, they were finishing their second pot of tea. Men in business suits planning acquisitions and a few tables of moms with children rounded out the scattering of tables and booths. Evie knew every one of them, what they liked in their coffee, or how they liked their eggs. She remembered which kids were allowed hot chocolate and which kept to juice or water for breakfast. She knew them, and loved them, every one. She could stand there all day and remember a thousand and one memories of these people. Her people. If she had but one moment left in life, she'd close her eyes and recall a few of these good memories, of families she grew to love, of women who became friends, and putting good food on welcoming tables. But lately, when she remembers, it was only bad memories that flooded her mind.

Although she'd rather be behind a restaurant counter creating new dishes and plating food that seemed too beautiful to eat, she's waiting tables in a diner because she was a single mom, trying to pay the rent and put food on her own table. She gratefully pocketed any tip left on the tables and gave thanks for every one of them. She valued every penny given and needed every penny enough to treat it like gold.

As the morning rush wound down, checks paid and goodbyes said, she finally had a moment to stop and give attention to her friend booth, as she called it. Her friends sat there while they waited for the rush to slow down. They didn't get their coffee filled as often as everyone else, but they got to hold the booth for as long as they want.

Sam sat there now, in the booth. With her jet-black hair cut short, and a silver nose ring, she sipped the same cup of coffee she had almost a half an hour ago. Without even looking, Evie knew she had headphones in, and was tapping her foot, hidden by the table, to the music.

Evie breathed a sigh of relief and knew she could let down her guard and relax for a few moments. She stopped at the friend booth and refilled Sam's coffee.

"You have been very patient, and I think this calls for... Sam?!" Evie tapped the coffee carafe on the table to get Sam's attention. The table was covered with Sam's phone, headphone case, and a tablet propped up next to her open laptop, and Sam was seemingly focused on every device at the same time and with the same degree of intensity.

"Oh, Sam!"

"Oh hey, Evie. Any chance I can get coffee...or food?"

"There's a chance, but where would I put it? It can't possibly be good for you to eat with all this...stuff, sitting here. I'm sure it gives off radiation of some sort," teased Evie.

"How about you don't worry about that? What is good to eat here?"

"You eat here almost every weekday morning," laughed Evie. "You already know what is good to eat here. But if you need a reminder, the bacon. The bacon is very good here!" Evie knew Sam would appreciate the taunt. Sam refused to eat meat. Not that Evie hadn't made every effort to tempt her otherwise.

"Funny. Really, funny." Sam replied sarcastically. "I'll have the egg white omelet with cheese. And coffee...park the whole carafe right here." Sam pointed her finger in front of her cup.

"Don't you ever get bored?" questioned Evie. "You have every single new electronic gadget that comes out but eat the same egg white omelet every single day!"

"Yes, I get bored," Sam said dryly. "I get bored with telling you I don't want bacon. I get bored with explaining these are not gadgets, these are my connection to the outside world. I love them." Sam said with adoration, laying her hand over her heart.

Evie sat the carafe down. "You really are weird. No one likes you but me."

"I'm not weird. You know I'm bad." Sam grinned and Evie immediately remembered Michael Jackson's catchy hit.

Bursting out laughing, Evie replied, "Ok, I walked into that! I'll get your food; you clear your space. Do you want me to throw something together for Jack?"

"Yes, he'd love that, thank you," answered Sam.

"We single moms have to stick together." Evie said, as a sad look crossed her face.

A few minutes later, with the diner now quiet, Evie delivered Sam's order and slid into the opposite side of the booth. She watched as Sam quickly bowed her head and gave thanks for the food before demolishing her egg whites and toast in record speed. There was quiet and silence, not the usual volume of their frequent meetings. Usually there was small talk, talk about faith, and lately, whispers of hopes and dreams. But the silence hung heavy today and even though Evie's body said "peace" her essence emitted "stress".

"You okay?" asked Sam.

"Sure, I'm okay. Why wouldn't I be?" Evie quickly replied with the gentlest of smiles.

"I don't know. That's why I asked."

The playful banter was gone, replaced with a seriousness. Evie and Sam had known of each other for some time but had only been close friends for a few months. Sam knew that silence from Evie usually meant something. She never knew exactly what, but it meant something, and she gently pursued her friend.

"Listen," said Sam, "I know you. I know you well enough that I can see something is on your mind. You're joking like you, but you're not... you."

"That is so...profound. Me, but not really me."

"Exactly. So, you look tired. Want to talk about it?"

"Look tired?" gasped Evie, while lifting her eyebrows. "Tired, how? Tired like old lady tired? Or tired like you are sick tired, or tired like you should have spent more time on your makeup tired?"

"No... not any of those kinds of tired. More like sleepy tired. Kids good?"

Evie sighed. She knew that Sam was relentless. A dog after a bone. She won't stop, she'll keep talking and talking until she wears you down and you just spill everything that had ever bothered you. She also knew she was one of her very best friends. If she needed to talk, she could talk to Sam.

After a long pause of internally weighing what she wanted to say, she responded with the tiniest bit of information she was willing to let out, "Yes, I'm a little tired."

"That's it?! 'Yes, I'm a little tired?' You really shouldn't say everything all at one time. I need a little time to process all this information. I may need to enter this into a document so I can be sure not to miss any of the details," Sam said, reaching for her notebook.

"Okay, okay..." Evie stopped her.

Sam knew that to get information from Evie, she needed to ask the exact right question at the exact right moment. With time, she learned it was not that Evie didn't trust her, it was just that she needed time to figure out she needed help. She watched as the battle over the right words was real on Evie's face.

"Here's the deal...I've been praying," Evie said as she closed her eyes, taking a calming breath.

"Praying, praying? Like... 'battlefield praying'?" Sam asked, while making air quotes.

"Yes, exactly like battlefield praying."

Sam let out her breath. "Oh, crap. Have you been alone?"

"I have been, but I think it's time I admit I need some help."

Sam's mouth dropped open, and she asked, "Have you been there more than once?"

"I've been there a few times. I'm not sure what I'm doing wrong, but I haven't got an answer yet, and I'm worried this might be bigger than I first thought," confessed Evie.

"You know I'll help. Is it the kids?"

"Kind of," Evie paused. "I mean, well, yes, it's the kids. And Bryce.

"Bryce!" Sam nearly shouted. "Bryce, as in your ex, Bryce?"

"He's not my ex. And don't shout."

"What do you mean, he's not your ex? I specifically remember asking you about where Bryce had been, and you said, 'He left, and we're divorced.' You said divorced. And I'm not shouting." Sam's eyes blinked as her voice raised.

"I mean, we're not officially divorced. I said divorced because I felt divorced, and I didn't want to talk about it. And yes, you were almost shouting. Practically shouting, which is the same thing."

Exasperated, Sam lowered her voice to just above a whisper. "What do you mean you're not 'officially' divorced?" she said through her clenched teeth.

"Why do you keep repeating me?" Evie huffed back. "We're not divorced. So that means we're technically still married." Evie quickly leaned back and crossed her arms over her chest.

Sam was quiet for a moment. That wasn't lost on Evie. Sam was never quiet. Evie was the quieter one of the two. Maybe not as quiet as some of their friends, but quieter than Sam. Of course, everyone was quieter than Sam. Evie's mind seemed to be going in a million directions at once.

"Ok, walk me through this," Sam brought Evie's attention back. "We've been best friends for months now. I've watched you go home every single night with your children, alone. Since you told me you 'We're divorced'," said Sam as she madly used air quotes again, "You haven't mentioned One. Single. Word. about Bryce and your 'feelings divorce' and now you're telling me that you're still married to him!"

"You are getting slightly off track," Evie said as she avoided eye contact with Sam and nervously adjusted the carafe.

"Off track? I'm getting 'off track'?" Sam couldn't stop air quoting.

Evie and Sam both were suddenly aware the diner was quiet. Too quiet. Everyone who was talking before was not talking now, but rather listening to their own conversation.

Evie whispered, "See what happens when you shout? Everyone is listening. And you should consider sitting on your hands. Now I have to go talk to them all, to get them to forget what they heard."

"'No problem', 'I'll wait'!" Sam whispered in a furious tone using her final air quotes.

After cashing out most of the customers and leaving a few older men with their own pot of coffee, Evie returned. She slid in the seat across from Sam and when she exhaled, her shoulders slumped as if the weight of the world rested on them. Sam stared at her. No foot tapping, no headphones, no tapping on the computer. She was fully engaged.

Sam broke the silence, asking in a sugary sweet voice, "So what is it exactly about your husband, Bryce, that has you going into the battlefield, Evie?"

Evie knew letting Sam in, asking for help, meant she had to share some things she hadn't shared previously. She had thought about it before. She'd weighed all the possibilities and had decided it was better for her to handle this herself. It wasn't a trust issue. It was just that she thought she could handle it. There was no need to involve Sam. It wasn't meant to be hurtful, although she knew some explaining was needed, so that it wouldn't feel hurtful to her friend. But there were some battles you are meant to fight alone. And for several months, that's what she had been doing.

But it wasn't working, and she knew the time had come to ask for help. Even asking just one friend could make a difference; she would no longer be fighting alone.

"I'm sorry I didn't share all this with you or Vicki before," started Evie. "I didn't want to involve you or anyone. I really didn't think it would come to this, but it has. And it's obvious to me that I need some help."

"Since I have no idea what you're talking about, in fact, I just found out that you're still married, I'm going to have to ask that you give me just a little more information." Sam said, still in a sweet voice.

After another long pause, and a tap-tap of Sam's foot, Evie answered. "I have Kendall and Janey. I thought he was gone. I mean, he left, and it's been six months." Evie lifted her hands and dropped them to the table. "He said he wouldn't come back. And I wanted to believe him. At the time, I didn't have the money for legal filings, and I thought I could do it later. I thought it was over and everything has been so good. The kids are good, I'm doing good. I think I'm doing good, don't you?"

Sam, still trying to piece together what Evie was saying, "Do you know where he was? Of course, you're good. Never better."

"That's what I thought too! Ok, I don't have time to go into all of this now. But I do need some help."

Evie pressed her palms to her tired eyes. Her throat felt thick and coarse just speaking these words. "I'll tell you the rest later, but right now I can just say that he's coming back. He wrote me, and he says he is coming back," Evie paused, "and he thinks we're getting back together."

Sam knew Evie had to be scared to share this much. She instinctively knew this was bigger than Evie let on, and that there was no way she could battle this on her own. She needed to know more, but before that and more importantly than that...she felt that familiar press. She knew what it was. They needed to pray together, side by side, and pray now.

CHAPTER TWO

*T*hey arrived on the battlefield back-to-back with eyes closed. The blast of intense heat washed over them both as they pulled in the first breaths of sulfuric laced air. Sam opened her eyes first and, in her usual loud manner, shared her thoughts about the battlefield.

"Ouch!" she howled the moment her eyes opened and burned from the glaring light. "Why didn't you warn me?"

"You didn't ask. You just started praying. And can you quiet down? I can smell the Corgs. That means they're near." Evie opened her eyes slowly, carefully letting the light in, wanting to avoid wasting precious minutes for them to adjust, like Sam would have to now.

Fifty yards away was a small scouting group of Corgs. The cluster of demons stopped to stare at the passageway to the realm that was forbidden them. They'd heard tales of what was on the other side, but no one they knew had ever made the crossing. No one had even tried. It was a discussion around many fires, but that's all it was, talk and superstition.

Occasionally, when more than one prayer warrior transported through the prayer portal, the ground would vibrate and give an advantage to the enemy, alerting them that they were coming. The smartest Corg, if there is such a thing, could figure out the area where the warriors might be entering. No one said war was fair. Because the Corgs were the most expendable demons, they seemed to be the fastest. Sam had just enough time to see shapes take form before they were within fighting distance.

This time, the Corgs weren't running away, but rather just the opposite. And three, two, one....

Evie pulled her sword from her sheath and steadied herself for the coming impact. Sam, her life without crisis at the moment, eagerly ready for good hard battle, reached for her own long sword from its sheath. She held the hilt of the sword in her hands and put the blade to her mouth for a quick kiss. No sooner was the kiss blown away by the desert wind, than the first of fifty Corgs were upon them. Sam and Evie both managed to evade the jagged fingernails that swiped out at them. Evie grabbed the wrist of the first Corg and pulled him close, thrusting her weapon through its throat.

The goal was to shut their filthy mouths, preventing their screams from warning the bands that might be roaming on the other side of the dune. Pull, stab, drop-both women worked efficiently, each energized from the other's presence.

Not every Corg made this easy and several fought back with an unholy vengeance, as if there was a chance for escape. But the prayer warriors wouldn't let them escape-they couldn't. Once you entered the battlefield, there was to be no peace or agreements or covenant with any enemy.

Evie and Sam were in no need of a reprieve yet, and they wouldn't stay there long. They entered the battlefield from the portal that developed near them when they bowed to pray. And the portal began showing itself once again. The waves of air were pulsing and shimmering like waves of heat. The Corgs may have thought it was a heat pulse, but only the warriors who came through the portal could see and hear the sounds from beyond in the natural world. Seeing the portal return this early meant that this battle was over. But until you had your prayer answered, it was unfinished business. Sam and Evie will be back, fighting and battling until God led them to a specific place and an answer was revealed. But they won't get their answer if they don't show up.

Evie sheathed her small sword on her hip while Sam wiped her long sword on her leather-covered thighs to clean off the slop of Corg blood. She spat on the sword and, after one last wipe, put it into the scabbard on her back. Each woman raised her hands to her King, open hands without a weapon, leaving her vulnerable for dangerous moments. But that is how they ended battles together. Remembering the words of David in the Psalms, they shouted to the Lord, saying,

"Blessed be the Lord my strength, which teacheth my hands to war, and my fingers to fight!"

The air pulsed as they transported through the portal and nobody in the diner knew that while they sat in a booth, these two women went to war. They also didn't know the entrance to the battlefield could be opened from anywhere while doing anything.

"Amen," said Sam.

"Amen. And thank you," said Evie.

Sam smiled, "I got your back, you know that. So, what happens now? Have you seen him?"

"So far, we've just talked. I'm supposed to be meeting him today. He wants to see the kids."

Sam let out a low whistle. "Moving kind of fast, don't you think?"

"Well, yes and no. I mean, legally, he has every right to see his kids and can enforce that if he wanted. So, I need to decide if I make him enforce it, or if I try to work with him."

"And what about you? What do you want? I mean, do you really want to do this?"

Evie was quiet while Sam waited her out. After a long breath, Evie said, "I don't know. I guess I thought when he left that it didn't matter what I wanted. Now I don't know. I know what I always wanted was my family together. Now I want answers. I think when I see him it will be easier," she said while taking another deep breath.

"Really? You think somehow when you see him this is going to get easier?!" Sam said, narrowing her eyes.

"Not easier in that it's all going to be fixed, but easier to know if this is a door opening or door I need to lock, dead bolt, stick a chair under and pile the furniture in front of."

Sam laughed. "Okay. I get it. Not really, I'm still wrapping my mind around this. But I'm here, with a chair and a couch, ready to pile it in front of if needed. Will you call me and let me know how it goes?"

"You betcha."

A few hours later, Evie clocked out from the diner and knew she had enough time to get home, get cleaned up and still have enough time to meet Bryce at the coffee shop on time.

"A coffee shop," she muttered to herself. "Of course, a coffee shop. Probably has all exposed brick walls and black shelving and chrome espresso machines and little perfect white espresso cups."

Coffee was a weakness for Evie. Coffee and coffee shops. She loved them. Little, quiet, quaint rooms with little cubbies to hole up in with a good book and sip sweetened nectar from tiny little cups. She loved the little pastries behind polished glass. She loved the diner, but it wasn't a coffee shop. And Bryce knew that. He knew her. Or at least he used to. He'd only been gone physically for months, but in his heart, he had been a million miles away for years.

Looking back, she knew the changes in him happened so subtly that at first she barely recognized them. But eventually her happy, easy going, take-it-in-stride husband gradually became so discontent with everything-their house, their cars, their jobs, their faith. It wasn't long before he dropped out of church completely, working as much overtime as he could. Despite that, she loved him, and until he left, had not given up on their dreams and ambitions. He had the advantage. He knew her, but she didn't know him anymore.

"Stop trying to figure it out," she reminded herself. They needed to meet if they were going to work something out with the kids and she agreed with him that the diner wasn't the best option. It had too many people, too many friends, too much noise. The coffee house outside of town was just far enough away to make this easier. After her first email from him, she knew she'd end up here. To ease where this was going, she'd started bringing him up to the kids. He hadn't been gone so long that they'd forgotten him; they just missed him. She'd purposed in her heart to not speak badly of him because she knew if there was ever any chance of their family being whole again, it would only make it more difficult for them.

She didn't tell them he was back. They would have wanted to see him right away, but she made sure she brought him into the conversations a little more. Things like, "I remember the first time your dad and I did…" or, "Janey, you've got your dad's grin on your face right now!" They were too young to pick up on her intentions and seemingly accepted her explanation that their daddy had been on a big secret trip for work. She knew they would need more information eventually, but this story bought her time. The fact was that she didn't know what to tell them because even she didn't know the answer to where he had been. Either way, good or bad, this meeting was happening, and she needed to figure out what to wear.

Exactly what do you wear when you are meeting a husband who, after months of growing struggles, just didn't come home? Does one dress like a nun or dress like you want him to pay? Did she want him to pay? Or did she want to be a nun? She paused.

"Ok, no nun," she said to herself. "But no leg either. Jeans are good. No-they scream comfortable and I'm not comfortable. Jeans and tall boots. That's totally different.

Or jeans and a sweater. Shoot! Comfortable again!" Evie was rifling through everything and wondering why was it that all she had was comfortable? "When did this happen?" she thought. "Probably when I was raising two kids all by myself when he was who knows where." Evie was too good at compartmentalizing. Anything she didn't want to look at or didn't know what to do with, went in little boxes in her mind. She'd look at that box later and just deal with whatever is front of her now.

That's where Bryce has been, in a little box, inside her mind. She'd known he was going to leave and was not surprised even a little when she came home, and he was gone, with a few of his personal items. She was surprised, however, that nothing of hers was gone. Not her jewelry, not their pictures, not their kids. She later felt guilty for that. Obviously, she had misread everything. The fear she had of him taking the kids was exposed as being an ungrounded fear. He'd never said it, never even implied it. In the end, he left everything. He didn't even take the car.

"And now he's back and I have nothing to wear." She talked to herself, "This is not a date. I'm not dating my husband. That's ridiculous. This is two adults trying to find a way to work out how to take care of two little people."

In the end, it was a long red maxi skirt, with a gray t-shirt knotted at the waist. "Comfortable, but with myself. Red for the non-nun. Soft gray t-shirt for the kind of make you pay." Evie was comfortable in her own skin, and she knew she looked good. With her long, light-brown hair in a messy bun, and natural makeup showing off her flawless skin and chestnut-colored eyes, one would never suspect the stress she had been under. She carried her tall frame confidently and knew Bryce would like the way she looked.

What she didn't know was how many mental boxes she was going to have to peek into after today. Kendall and Janey were in a box. They were in the box with her heart. So far, those were all intact and regardless of what Bryce had in mind, that's how it was going to stay.

The coffee house was just as she remembered it. She said a prayer to steady her nerves as she got out of the car. She thought she'd gotten there in time to get her little cup of espresso and find a place to sit and wait for Bryce. Old Bryce was never on time, and Evie was never late. It always drove him nuts that she viewed appointments as commitments, and it dove her nuts that he viewed it them as general guidelines.

A soft bell tinkled when she stepped through the wooden door. The room was cozy, quaint, lovely. She didn't even have to scan the room. Bryce was already there. He was in a booth against the far wall, facing the door, and he looked straight at her. She knew she'd be nervous, but she didn't anticipate the surge of adrenaline or emotions that flooded her the moment she saw him. He looked her up and down, met her eyes, and grinned.

That ticked her off. How can he grin? Grinning isn't allowed. That's not part of business plans. Grinning is what friends do. They weren't friends anymore. Maybe never had been. The reasonable part of her thought, "Of course, you were. You made two babies. Probably because of that stupid grin." Pushing back her emotions, she kept her face neutral, gave him a brief glance and stepped to the counter to order her double Americano. She knew they'd bring it to her, so figured there was no time like the present to do this. Taking a deep breath, she walked over and slid into the seat facing Bryce.

"Hey," she said.

"Hey," he said softly. She resisted the urge to roll her eyes and concentrated on keeping eye contact.

"You're early," he said in his old, easy-going manner.

"I'm always early," she replied stiffly. "Did I get the time wrong?"

"Nope. I was just anxious to see you."

Evie felt like she was being baited and wasn't sure what the hook was, so said nothing.

After what felt like a very long moment of awkwardly looking at each other, he said softly, "You look really good."

Bait. Long pause. "Thank you, so do you."

His laugh filled the room and took her by surprise. She hadn't expected that. He did look good. He looked… healthy. His golden-brown hair looked like it'd recently seen some sun. He looked relaxed. She couldn't remember the last time she had seen him look relaxed. She hadn't heard his laugh in even longer and it made her heart clench. "Keep it together, girl," her heart whispered. Thankfully, the barista stepped around the counter with her Americano and gave her a small distraction. She could feel his eyes on her as she busied herself with stirring her black coffee. When she looked up, she knew he was amused. She felt irritated that he seemed so relaxed but still smiled back.

"How've you been?" he asked.

To herself she said, "What a load of crock. How do you think I've been?" But to Bryce she said, "Great, how about you?" She probably said it a little too quick, thinking, "I'm good. Move on. Nothing to see here folks! No train wreck, no broken bodies, no tortured survivors. Keep it movin'!" But in just the 10 minutes she'd been here, she felt like the box was shifting front and forward and up to the top of the box pile.

"Evie," he offered, "I'm not trying to make you nervous."

"I'm not nervous."

"Okay, if you say so. But in case you were, that's not my intention."

"Really? So, what is your intention, Bryce?" He was still looking at her, relaxed, beautiful hair... stupid hair. "And it's about to get real here now," she thought to herself.

"I miss Kendall. I miss Janey. You and I both know I could just set up my visitation rights, but I was hoping, I intended, that we could open this door together."

"Why?"

"Why? Don't you think it'd be easier for them? Don't you think it'd be easier for both of us?"

Evie was usually the reasonable one. Bryce was the unreasonable one. So why was he being reasonable? "And why am I suddenly so suspicious of reason?" argued Evie with herself.

After a pause, she said, "Yes, I do think it would be easier. But it's not that simple."

"Why can't it be simple?"

"Are you ignoring reality?! You've been gone for six months! I've been paying the mortgage by myself for six months. I've paid for groceries, electricity, shoes, the tooth fairy, all of it by myself!"

"Who lost a tooth?" Bryce grinned.

Exasperated, Evie said, "Who do you think lost a tooth? Kendall, of course. He's six. A parent starts paying the tooth fairy at five and six. We pay mortgage, groceries, light bill and tooth fairies!" she said as she ticked them off on her fingers.

Bryce just looked at her. "I'm sorry. I'm sorry I left. I'm sorry I missed that. I did try to check in and let you know what was going on, I…"

Evie interrupted, "An email once every couple of weeks that says, if kids need anything, this is my number, isn't letting me know what's going on!" Evie thought she saw a tightening in his jaw. Then back to relaxing.

"I know. I should have contacted you more. I didn't have a way. I know that sounds crazy, but I did not have a way. That's why I'm here now. I know…and I'm sorry. I needed time. And help."

Bryce never needed help. Or at least he didn't think he needed help. "What kind of help?" she asked.

Bryce, who was always so quick to speak and be heard was now quiet. "Listen, I want to do this right. I want to do this together. I miss my kids. It took some time without them to know that. I thought about them every day. I just wasn't any good, Evie. I knew it, you knew it. I went someplace out of town, away from here, that helped me," he paused, "A…shelter."

"What do you mean a shelter? You told me you were on a job." Evie asked leaning her arms on the table. "Which is it? A job? A shelter? A friend's house, or what?"

"Ha, not a friend's house," Bryce snorted. "Kind of like a rehab center, I guess. I checked in and stayed, figured some things out. But what I couldn't figure out was how to do this part. But I thought, if you'd meet with me... maybe you could help me figure out how to do it. If you would. I can't go back in time. I can't fix what happened between us. But maybe you could help me start over, at least with them. Do you think you could do that?"

Evie prayed silently, "Lord, I didn't see this coming. But it doesn't add up. What in the world do I do now?"

CHAPTER THREE

*W*hen the portal shimmered and hummed near her bedside in the midnight hour, Vicki knew she wouldn't be going back to sleep anytime soon. It was going to be a battle in the dead of night-her favorite kind of battle. It meant someone was in trouble, suffering enough that Yahweh was waking people up in the middle of the night. She could not stand for people to suffer, and if it meant staying awake all night and fighting demons to help a sister, she would gladly do it. The shofar that just sounded had a chilling effect when it was heard in the utter blackness of the hour.

She closed her eyes and her spirit rolled away from her body, leaving the warmth and her husband behind. He would never even know she was gone.

"Please, let it be a warm battlefield this time," was her thought as she stepped through the portal.

"Welcome to Miami!" she thought as she stood on a dune. Vicki's eyes weren't affected or delayed by the blinding sun because her Chanel sunglasses were in place. Her perfect blonde locks were in place, as well. Her leather halter-top and pants were of the softest camel color available and if it wasn't for the heavy blonde highlights in her caramel-colored hair, she would not have even been spotted against the dune. But her hair and the metal rings and buckles from the dual sword belt reflected the high sun. She may have entered quietly, but she also entered sparkling and shiny. This was not good.

The Ventars had small heads, but their eyes worked exceptionally well. They caught the shiny reflections coming off Vicki and knew someone had accessed the battlefield. They'd been waiting since the inept Corgs had failed at keeping the enemy from entering the portal. If it hadn't been for a fat Corg they caught and persuaded for information, the Ventars wouldn't even have known where the portal had been. Storek, leader of the Ventar battalion, would need alerting. Jangis, in charge in Storek's absence, ordered the cluster of demons close and whispered the command to one Ventar named Balid to summon their leader. Storek's been waiting for a good fight and would welcome the news. Now, to cross the sandy drifts between here and that lone enemy. Then they could feast.

Vicki saw the ripples in the sand approaching. They might be Jaders or Ventars. They are the only demons she's met that can travel under water and under land.

"Please be Jaders. Please be Jaders," she said as she pulled both swords from their sheaths. Her wrists twirled them with the same ease she rotated her batons back when she was young. They spun round and round, ready to be used for what they were made to do. Someone was in need. Time to meet the enemy. She ran towards the ripples and jumped as high as her long legs could lift her. When she landed, she stabbed down into the sand, driving her right sword into the sand all the way down to the hilt. Her left hand kept swirling its sword even as she pulled back out the now bloodied weapon. She heard a scream, but *from a Ventar. Of course. Why did she expect anything else on a midnight raid in enemy territory?*

Other Ventars rose quickly from the sand, emerging from the ground while sand slipped off them like water. One of their companions was dead. The Ventars, while they will never know or understand love, were still a strong knit group, comprehending war and unity against their enemy. A death of one of their own enraged them. But you would never know it by their smiles they wear or their twinkling eyes. You know it by their raised swords and their screams. Those screams compete with the Shofar for most eerie. Vicki stopped her twirling and engaged the closest of the four Ventars. She wasn't looking for a pile of bones just yet. She needed information, because somewhere in this sandbox, someone she loved was in need. A Ventar needed to talk, or she'd never find her loved one. She needed to spare two of these demons, if only until she got the intel she sought.

A Ventar moved close and swiped at her with his long arms. His nails and his teeth were his weapons and if he grabbed her hair, he could pull and bite her to her death in an instant. She wished she could enter the battlefield with a choice of her hair in a bun or a skull cap, but when the shofar blew, she came just as she was. Vicki jumped back and slashed with her sword at the same time. The diseased and filthy hand that reached out to snag her fell to the ground, and the Ventar fell to his knees. The pool of his own blood should keep him mesmerized and well fed for a little while. She only needs to hinder one more to have the advantage.

The sound of the Ventar gnawing and gorging on its own stub drew the lust and the eyes of the Ventar beside him. Vicki only needed that second where this Ventar was distracted enough to drive her sword through its throat. With a quick slash, followed by the gurgling and gushing of fluid, the Ventar was undone. It was quite easy.

Just don't bleed first and you won't be eaten.

That leaves the biggest one. Vicki and Jangis stared at each other, and Vicki realized this must be a ranking Ventar because he hadn't even flinched from the desire to feast. Jangis controlled his breathing but also his eyes, not even looking at the dead Ventars. But his hunger for blood still burned and the only way to prevent himself from toppling over this enemy to begin eating and feasting on his fallen troops was to flee. Storek would want to know what he had seen. Jangis knew where the deep holes in the sand were. He lunged to get near one. But his enemy was quicker than him, dropping one of her swords and seizing him by the tuft of hair on top of his small head. She held him tight, and with his hands and arms buried in the sand from his leap, he only had his teeth to aid him, and he could not reach her.

"Where is he?" Vicki demanded.

"Who?"

"You know who. Give me a location or I'll draw your blood and your hungry brother will come chew off your head."

"What did it matter?" thought Jangis. Storek would be here soon, and he would find her wherever she was at. "North."

He pulled so hard down into the sand Vicki's body slammed onto the ground, nearly falling into the hole. Her left sword, staked into the ground, was the only thing that prevented her from falling in after him.

The sound of a Ventar eating the last of his brother just about made Vicki sick. But when she saw he'd started consuming and slurping from his own wound, she knew she needed to get out of there quickly. The only way to stop this horrible feast was to kill them all, but this demon was too strong and intoxicated with his own blood lust to be faced in a battle. She spun both her swords in a fluid and beautiful motion and returned them both to their sheaths on her hips. She took off running north. Someone was still in need.

Vicki heard clanging of swords as she crested the dune. It was always at this moment where the rush of adrenaline was the highest for her, caused by the anticipation of finding out who it was who needed prayer and help.

But she felt a kick in the gut when she saw it was Evie, battling sword to sword with a small band of Corgs. Evie? Dear Yahweh, what happened to Evie that pulled her into battle at midnight? She wasn't doing so well, even against the rather unsubstantial Corgs. The Corgs were usually like a warmup crew that got you all stretched out, preparing for harder and longer battles to come. But by the looks of it, Evie's been coming here before and still wasn't getting very far-a warning sign that Vicki would muse on later. No one noticed her shininess now as she drew near to help her friend. She ran down the dune, pulling both swords from their sheaths and twirling before piercing two Corgs through the back at the same time. She gave a savage cry that matched her pounding heart. At least she now knew who she was fighting for. She'd worry about the reason for it later.

Evie, who had been struggling on her own, felt invigorated, shouting, "Yahweh!" as her thanks for bringing help. Between the two women and the weapons between them, the demons now fell easily. As soon as the Corgs fell, maggots come out of their wounds and began consuming them. It was no wonder Vicki rarely woke up hungry.

"*Evie, are you ok?*" *Vicki asked as her back was to Evie's back, slowly circling the area to make sure no demon was going to pop up out of the ground to catch them unawares.*

'Yeah, yeah, I am. I was just a little tired there. I got scared and cried to Yahweh. I'm so glad He sent you. You're the best in the night," she said as she squinted into the sun that blazed at irrational times.

"I just fed a bunch of Ventars a mile south of here. One got away. No telling when and where they will come back."

They both heard the hum of a portal being made. Scanning in each direction, Vicki saw it at the top of the next dune. She nudged Evie and pointed at it with one of her swords. They set off, side by side.

Neither spoke. It was not the time. Evie knew Vicki would want, and deserved, an explanation of what she had been doing here. They reached the top of the dune, and turning around to look one last time, they were startled to see a half-chewed Ventar only two feet away. But Sam appeared, and he never saw what was behind him.

In a blink of the eye, they watched their fierce and noiseless warrior-sister grab the Ventar's hair and slice off its head.

The demon fell to the ground, and Sam spoke to the two women, "Hey there, Malibu Barbie! And Evie! I see how it is! If it wasn't for Yahweh, I would have missed the party! Maybe I just misplaced my invitation?" Aside to Evie, she said quietly, "You know I'm going to need an explanation, right?"

"Thank you for answering the call. Was it the Shofar?" Evie asked.

"Yes," answered Sam.

Vicki sighed. "You know I love the sound of the Shofar."

"Shall we?" Sam asked as she bowed slightly and extended her arm to the portal in a polite offer to go last.

But before they stepped through, Vicki performed one last twirl of the swords and sheaths them. She took the hand of each sister and raised them to the sky. Words from the Psalms poured from their lips.

"Blessed be the Lord my strength, which teacheth our hands to war, and our fingers to fight!"

They stepped through the portal. Vicki's spirit slid back into her own skin, and she rolled over to spoon along Steve's back. She kissed his neck, breathing in his smell and whispered. "I love you."

It was a typical Saturday morning for Evie. Cartoons blaring with no one watching them, and kids giggling, running back and forth between rooms. A load of laundry was already started, the washing machine sounding as if was near its last load. She peeked in the laundry room, but quickly closed the door again, deciding that it was best to just let it work itself out.

Her hair was up in a bun, and she was still in her pajamas and fuzzy socks. "Fuzzy socks rock," she said to herself, and stepped into her kitchen. She loved her kitchen. It was the place where she became her own kind of artist. She loved eating food, but she loved cooking food more. She loved watching people she loved eat her food. She loved how it looked on a plate, and how it looked all chopped up and ready to be thrown into whatever dish she had chosen specifically to be the holder of said food. She loved her jars full of spices and oils. She loved the scratches on the counter, the little step stool that Janey stood on so she could reach to help stir a replica of whatever Evie was making, and Kendall's own little mortar and pestle he used to "grind grass stuff".

What she didn't love was dirty dishes. She hated those. Because it was Saturday, and because a group was going to be here for her turn to host their weekly Bible study, she decided the kid's "help" was not needed after all.

"Okay, you two, as you were, no need to run to help. I got it!" she hollered into the other room with a touch of sarcasm. Before she could even get it finished, they tumbled into the kitchen.

"I was coming to help but Janey needed me." Kendall said, almost as if he believed it himself.

"Nuh-uh! I din't need you, Kenal! Mom I din't need Kenal!"

Evie laughed at Kendall's seriousness and Janey's suddenly offended expressions. "It's all good. I was just playing! I need you both to go get dressed before everyone gets here and move your toys from the living room to your bedrooms."

"I don't have any toys in the living room," said Kendall.

"Good, you'll have more time to help your sister."

Janey was already off and running while singing her latest favorite song at the top of her lungs, offended expression gone.

"Mom, one day she's going to have to pick up her own toys."

"Yes, I know. And I'll cry. So, if you don't want me to cry today, then maybe you can help your sister?"

With that, he was off.

"Don't make him grow up too fast," she reminded herself.

Evie struggled with knowing if she was doing everything right. Was Kendall so serious because he was serious or because he hadn't seen his dad had in six months? He was young, but he was old enough to know his dad wasn't here. And with that, her thoughts moved to Bryce. Evie knew what today was. Today was reckoning day. The day that her friends ask their questions with no interruptions, expecting, and needing, the truth. After last night, she was surprised Vicki hadn't been on her front step before she even woke up. Evie hadn't spoken with Sam since the diner, other than a text Sam sent last night to confirm that Evie was not, in fact, drugged and held hostage in a musty room outside of town. Sam's mind often went to crazy places when worried about someone she cared about.

Evie's reply of, "I'm home, I'm good, will talk later" was met with skepticism by Sam, who couldn't accept it was actually Evie sending the text. After a brief text battle, Sam would only accept it was Evie when she was able to accurately name what Sam believed to be the icon for all 1980s songs. No covers. One guess.

Evie rolled her eyes while typing and replied, "Bohemian Rhapsody, Queen".

Sam texted, "See you on the battlefield tonight."

Today they would be here, and ready for answers. And then there was tonight. "I can't even go there right now," Evie said to herself, shoving that thought into a box in the back of her mind. "One thing at a time, girl."

Evie had just the right amount of time to finish up her to-do list and get the coffee going. But before she could pour a cup, she heard a knock on the kitchen door. Out came the kids, running to answer the door before Evie. They knew who was on the other side of that door and stopping her children from getting to Sam and Vicki was like stopping a moving train.

Over the past six months, these women who had previously been mere acquaintances in Evie's life had become friends, sisters, and warriors to and for her and aunts to her babies. Her kids loved them, and Evie loved them for loving her kids. They'd fought some battles together, and shared dinners, pedicures, massages, chick flicks, bonding more than Evie thought anyone could. But even though they were close, she hadn't shared the truth that she would share with them today.

She'd held Bryce close to the vest. She thought she could battle on her own, making the right decisions, finding open doors, and walking through them on her own. She didn't think that anymore. She was weary and instinctively knew the battle was just heating up.

After the kid's show-and-tell, hot coffee was poured, and the kids ran off to play video games only allowed on Saturdays. The room was finally quiet. Even the washing machine had settled down. Evie motioned to the kitchen table where they could sit and have their inevitable conversation.

"So, I see it's just the three of us?" said Evie after an awkward pause. Sam and Vicki exchanged glances.

"Funny thing," said Vicki as she pushed her always-perfect blond hair over her shoulder, "I spoke with Mrs.

Taylor this morning and whaddya know? She was kind of busy today."

"Really?" said Evie. "How odd. She's never missed a group meeting before!"

"I know! I think I said that same thing. How odd. Given her antiquity, I didn't want to pressure her, so I said not to worry, you'd understand. She says hi. And she's praying for us."

Sam, who had been watching the exchange like watching the Wimbledon, spoke up, "And speaking of prayer...."

"Great idea, Sam! Let's speak of prayer." Getting serious, Vicki continued, "That was no bedtime prayer, Evie. That was a battle. And judging from the scene, I saw you've been hanging out there for some time now. In fact, it looked a lot like you were getting tired. I can piece together that Sam had an idea to be there. But what I can't piece together is what in the world has been going on, and why am I just now hearing about it?"

"Here we go", thought Evie. After letting out a breath, the words began to tumble out. She'd reached the point where she couldn't keep them back any longer.

"Okay, I'm not sure how much you know about the kids' dad, so I'm just going to pretend like you don't know anything and go from there." Evie could hear the kids laughing in the other room and the bouncing of Sam's knee. She could see that Vicki had settled into her patient look. A calm enveloped her despite Sam's annoying knee, and she knew the skeletons about to jump out of her closet would not scare either of them away.

With a deep breath, she started, "As you know, Bryce left just over six months ago. For about two years before he left things with him went downhill. At first, he was just distant, like, quiet. He became very discontent with everything we had or didn't have. Then he started spending more time away in the evenings working extra hours. It didn't matter what I said, or didn't say, he just said he had extra work he had to do."

She told them how she thought he was seeing someone, at least it seemed like an obvious possibility to her at the time. She had tried to find some clue, anything that looked like it could be another woman. She hadn't known where to start so she when she finally asked him, he looked at her like she'd grown horns.

"He told me there'd never been another woman," she continued. "Never. He said it like it was the truth and I wanted to believe him, but it wasn't adding up with how much he was working, or how quiet he had become. I'd watch him when he did manage to be home before the kids went to bed and he'd look at them like they were the most beautiful things he'd ever seen. But he'd see me watching him and then he'd just get angry. After a while, he was either gone, or he was here and angry. There wasn't any in between anymore. I started wishing he would just be gone until I was in bed. It was easier than tiptoeing around him and living with a stranger. Then one night he didn't come home, and I thought, this is it. He's left and it's finally over. But when I got home from work the next day, he was there again, acting like it was the most normal thing in the world. We fought all night long. I thought for sure that Kendall would be scarred for life. I wanted to know who he'd been with and all he would say was that he couldn't tell me, and somehow that was supposed to be a satisfying answer?! Finally, he told me, 'Evie, I know it doesn't look like it anymore, but I love you. Everything I do is for you, for us.' And he promised me that it will get better. I remember laughing. I couldn't cry anymore. I felt like I'd lost Bryce to something or someone so long ago and this wasn't even him anymore."

"Invasion of the Body Snatchers," whispered Sam. Vicki stared at her with a blank look. "You know, the old movie where aliens invade the bodies, but their bodies look the same, only they act a little off?"

Evie laughed, "Exactly like that. I thought maybe he was on drugs. But it seems like I'd see money missing or some signs of addiction. But nope. Bank account had direct deposit and I could account for every penny being spent. I knew he was still working because I'd drive by his work and see his car. But by the end of the year, we never saw each other. If he came home, he'd come home after I was in bed. I didn't know what to do. I didn't have any real friends. Bryce didn't have any friends that I knew anymore, and we hadn't lived here long enough to be in church. Then finally, he just didn't come home at all. I didn't get too worked up about it until after a few days. I know that sounds crazy, but I figured at first that he'd probably been here and left early until I noticed there weren't any wet towels from the shower or change of clothes. I started looking at his things and nothing was gone. He just didn't come home. I was getting ready to call the police and then I noticed that I had an email from him. I stared at the inbox forever. I didn't even know he knew my email. But there it was, and it said, "I can't come home for now. If you need anything, email me at this address." I responded and asked him what was going on and where was he. His only answer was, "I need a break." That was it. No explanation, no nothing.

"That was six months ago. From then until a month ago, I'd get one email a week. At first, I sent emails every day. Long emails. I begged to know where he was. I begged him to come home. I told him I was praying for him, told him his kids missed him. Eventually I told him not to come home, that we didn't miss him anymore and that I'd be filing for divorce, and he needed to do the right thing and just stay away. Every week he'd still send me an email. He couldn't come home. He said he understood how I felt, and he wouldn't fight me on a divorce. Could I email him a picture of the kids? Just random stupid meaningless stuff. At first, I planned to file, but I didn't have the money and there didn't seem to be a rush. Nothing was changing for me, and I thought I could save some money and do it later. I'm so sorry I lied to you both and said we were divorced. It was stupid. I felt paralyzed and I didn't think I could talk about it. Then I just got used to how it was."

Evie stopped to take a drink of her now cold coffee. It felt so awkward with Sam and Vicki just staring at her. Sam's knee had stopped bouncing, and the expression on Vicki's face was unreadable.

Finally, Vicki broke the silence. "I just can't believe you were going through this alone. I can't believe you didn't say anything. Why? Why wouldn't you say something?"

"What was I supposed to say? It was already over, and I planned on telling you, but there wasn't anything to tell yet."

"Nothing to tell? I don't know how you handled it. I can't imagine how much you must have been hurting, and you didn't tell a single person!" Vicki looked like she'd just thought of something. "Is this what you were helping her battle, Sam?"

Sam sat perfectly still, looking at the floor. When she did look up to answer Vicki, there were tears in her eyes. Her voice was hard with anger as she replied, "No. No. I didn't know. I found out part of this yesterday." Turning to Evie, she said, "Why is he still around? Why haven't you changed your email and why have you not gotten a restraining order?"

"What do you mean, around?" asked Vicki.

"He's back, and she met with him yesterday," Sam informed her.

Vicki, the patient one, couldn't hide her shock over this news. "You actually met with him? Are you crazy?"

"I don't know if I'm crazy! He started emailing every couple of days, just over a month ago. Said he was done with what he'd needed to do. He knew he needed to talk to me first, but he wanted to see the kids. I was too shocked and scared to answer immediately. But then I started getting handwritten letters. He said he understood how I felt but he was coming back soon and was hoping he could meet with me to talk. Just talk. He said the job he'd taken was finished and that he wanted to work out visitation with the kids. Now I don't think he was on a job after all."

"Have you considered that it might not be safe to have him visit?" snapped Sam.

"Of course, I have!! That's what took me to the battle-field! I needed answers. I needed a clue as to what I was supposed to do! But I still don't have a clue! I have been in that stinking desert for over a month now and nothing!" She paused, taking a breath. "I'm sorry I didn't tell you sooner. I didn't think out that far in advance and now that it's here, I'm scared."

"You should be scared! He's a psycho! A man doesn't say 'I need a break' and then disappear for six months and send you letters like everything's okay! That's the definition of psycho! You should never have met with him. If I'd known all this, I would never have let you go alone!" exclaimed Sam.

"I'm not scared of him! I'm scared of doing the wrong thing. Or saying the wrong thing. Or reading it all wrong."

"Okay," interrupted Vicki. "What happened yesterday?"

"He called and asked me if he could meet me. I hadn't had any direct answer to prayer, so I agreed and went to Beckville and saw him."

"He was there?"

"Yes, Vicki. That is what happens when people meet!" said Evie.

"You're smirking!" said Sam.

"I'm not smirking!"

"Yes, you are! You started talking about your meeting and you smirked!"

"Oh, good grief. It was a reassuring smile. Not a smirk."

Vicki interrupted, "Just tell us what happened. Exactly."

Evie took another deep breath, looked at them and thought, "In for a penny, in for a pound." Out loud she said, "When I got there, he was already there, early."

"Creepy," said Sam.

"And we got coffee and talked."

"Coffee? Like at a...coffee house?" said Vicki, looking at Sam. They knew how much she loved coffee. The exchanged glances weren't lost on Evie.

"Of course, in a coffee house. What's wrong with a coffee house?!"

"Nothing's wrong with a coffee house. Just seems a bit contrived to meet you at a coffee house, don't you think?" questioned Sam.

"Of course, it was contrived! But where were we supposed to meet? The diner? The house? I couldn't bring him here yet!"

"Yes, the diner! That would have been safer for you! How do you know he's not on drugs now?" said Sam. "Wait! You said you couldn't bring him here yet?? What is yet?!" Sam's voice was getting louder. She was quietly passionate about her friends until she got loudly passionate. It was starting to look like the quietly passionate and protective stage had passed and they were moving full force into the loud stage.

"If you calm down, I'll tell you!" Evie said with frustration. "Ok, we talked. Just talked. We talked about the kids. We talked about visitation."

"Did you talk about where he'd been?" asked Vicki.

"Of course, we talked about where he'd been! I specifically asked him where he was. Job, friend, shelter? He said he'd been to a kind of rehab."

"Nailed it!" Vicki exclaimed with a fist pump, which was almost humorous because rarely, if ever, did you see Vicki fist pump. Both Sam and Evie stared at her in surprise before responding.

"He didn't say what kind of rehab. He said rehab-kind of."

"Doesn't matter. People go to rehab because of a drug problem."

"Actually," said Sam, "there are all kinds of rehab. They have rehab for hoarders. And people with strange addictions, like glass eating. You can't just quit eating glass. You have to go to a rehab and get help for it."

Now it was Evie and Vicki's turn to stare at Sam. "My friends are weird. Really weird," thought Evie. "And yet here they are here, because they love you," she reminded herself. She suddenly noticed them both staring at her, Sam's suspicious eyes squinting while Vicki's eyes were wide with anticipation.

"What did he look like?" asked Sam.

"What did he look like?? What does that have to do with anything?"

"What. Did. He. Look. Like" repeated Sam, slowly.

Evie didn't really understand where she was going with this, but figured, whatever. "He looked like Bryce. He looked like he used to look. He had a shaggy hair, but it was cut. He looked like he'd been in the sun because he was all tanned and he had highlights in his hair. He was wearing jeans and a t-shirt. And a belt. And boots."

"You have got to be kidding me!"

"What?" Evie shot back at Sam.

"Sam didn't ask you what he was wearing, Evie," Vicki said, gently.

"She didn't? Oh. Sorry. Does it matter?" Evie was getting a bit annoyed with the looks they kept giving each other.

"You don't think you were played at all?" asked Sam.

"Played? I'm not stupid! But played? No. No, I wasn't 'played'. Would it have been better if he looked horrible? I admit it! He looked great! And it made me mad! He shouldn't get to look great, but he did! It doesn't matter, anyway! He's not back to see me. He's back to see his kids. And as far as I can see, I don't have a lot of legal choices in this, do I? I know I need more information. I need to know what he's been involved in. I'm not letting him take them for any weekend until I get some answers from him."

The room was quiet again before Evie continued. "Look, I know I messed up by not telling you both about this before. I didn't mean for it to be like this. I really thought I would just end up at the courthouse filing papers and then the problem that was Bryce would just go away. But it didn't. I don't know why. But now he wants to see his kids and even I know I can't stop that if he wants to. Nothing is happening on the battlefield, so I think it's safe to say I keep on this path for now. I told him he could stop by tonight." Evie dropped the news.

"Holy Moly, Evie! How do you know he's not a serial killer?" asked Vicki, who usually never thought badly of anyone.

"He's not a serial killer. He's not! But just in case, I'm telling you now that he's coming over tonight, so you know."

"Not funny. Not funny at all," said Sam. "I'm sure we could hook up some kind of camera. I don't know how to, but I can look online."

"I'm sure you could, Sam, but maybe we can talk through that one later?"

"What are you going to tell the kids?" Vicki asked.

It felt like the air had just been let out of the room. Evie said in a whisper, "I don't know yet. I've been saying things here and there. Janey doesn't seem to get it. She's four. How do you get this at four? Kendall though. He just gets quiet and looks at me with those big eyes and I know he's thinking something, but he doesn't say what. I told him last night when we prayed before bed that I thought it was time for him to start praying for his dad again. He asked me why and I told him I thought he would be back soon, and that I was sure Bryce missed him, and will want to see him. He didn't say much, and he didn't pray for Bryce. I didn't push it. I texted Bryce and told him I didn't know if it was a good time for the kids."

"What did he say? And you're texting now? Isn't that kind of personal?!" challenged Sam.

"Only you would think texting is personal, Sam. He said there was never going to be a good time now, after it's been so long. And then he said he'd take it slow. He wasn't trying to take them out to the park to play ball, he just wanted to see them."

Evie wasn't sure when she got choked up, but she did. And she felt like a dam inside her was about to burst. She wasn't ready for that. Pandora's box wasn't open quite yet, so she stopped and gave herself a second to get herself under control again.

"Why do you do that?" asked Vicki softly. "Why do you hold it all together? You know it's okay if you just let yourself feel this, right?"

Evie held up her hand to stop her. "I know. I just can't. Not yet. I'm mad. I thought I was done hurting, but it's hurting anyway. It's not fair. Not to me, not to my two kids in there. But I can't think about that right now because if I do, I'll cry. And I'm afraid if I start crying, I won't stop for a really long time."

After a pause, Sam got up from her chair and knelt by Evie. When she wrapped her arms around her, Evie felt Vicki join. And from those two silently kneeling by her and wrapping their arms around her, Evie felt strength. And peace. The tears were gone, and instead she felt loved and comforted.

Unfortunately, the peace only lasted until they heard a car pull into the driveway. Not a car. A truck. A pickup truck. "Oh no," thought Evie. "Why is he here already?" But before Evie could even react Sam and Vicki both jumped to their feet and literally dove to the window.

"Are you kidding me? He's here!" came Sam's loud whisper.

"Why is he here?" came Vicki's equally loud whisper.

Evie just stood staring, frozen, not from fear but disbelief. "Bryce is here. Too early," she thought. She wasn't ready, hair still in a bun and outfit complete with fuzzy socks. She snapped out of her stupor when she saw her friends rushing for the door.

"No!" came Evie's panicked whisper. She moved so fast she slammed into their backs and if they hadn't all three hit the wall, they would have hit the floor.

"Really, Evie? Is this necessary?! We were just going to try to look. Why is he here?"

All three were still leaning on the wall, Evie's arms wrapped securely around them.

"You can't go out there! He can't be here yet; I have to talk to the kids!" Evie whispered.

"It seems pretty obvious that we should go out there and tell him this is not the right time," muffled Sam.

"No way are you going out there. I'll do it.", whispered Evie.

"Maybe you could just get off of us?" squeaked Vicki.

"I'm not letting you go until you promise to stay inside while I go outside."

Sam's voice came still muffled, "This is ridiculous! Let me go!"

"Not until you both promise!"

"Fine!" came Sam and Vicki's agreement.

Slowly Evie removed her arms, still expecting them to bolt. They just stared at her.

"I'm going out. You two stay in here and keep the kids away from any windows. They are in the basement playing video games," she said as she backed away. All she could find were her bunny slippers, and she didn't dare leave Sam and Vicki to go find her shoes. She peeked out the door window and could see Bryce had gotten out of the truck, leaning against its closed door. Thank God he didn't seem to be coming towards the house.

"Okay. I'm going out. Alone. And you two are staying here. Together," she repeated and turned to open the door.

"And stay away from the windows." With that she slowly opened the door just enough to let herself out giving one warning look to them as she stepped out. She hadn't even heard the door close before she heard them running to the living room window. She slowly walked out towards the truck.

Bryce's slow smile wasn't lost on her as he took in the bunny slippers. "Aww. You didn't have to wear the bunny slippers just for me," he said.

"What are you doing here, Bryce? We agreed on seven."

Bryce ignored her irritated tone, and said, "I know. I tried calling you and texting you to see if it was okay if I came earlier but you didn't answer, so I thought I'd just stop and see if it was okay to come now?"

Evie just stared. So many thoughts were swirling around in her head. Finally, she answered, "I was busy, and didn't see you called. If I don't answer your text, it's because, like I said, I'm busy and no, it's not a good time. I think it's safe to say I need to be able to trust when we make an agreement that you don't just go and change it on your own, like showing up eight hours earlier than we had planned. So, seven is good. Now is bad."

Bryce wasn't smiling anymore, but she could tell he wasn't angry either. His expression softened, and he spoke quietly. "I know you don't trust me, Evie. And I'm sorry I did that to you. The wait to see them is killing me. But still I should've waited for you to call me back." He paused like he wanted to say something more and thought better of it. "I'll be back at seven unless you call and tell me differently." He pushed himself off the truck and stood before her with his hands in his pockets. She had her arms wrapped around herself, her weight on one leg. "Your friends are going to fall out of the window if you don't go rescue them."

Her head snapped to the window in time to see the curtain fall and two heads disappear.

Bryce had turned and opened the door to the truck. "See you tonight. Your shirt is buttoned wrong," he said, with a smile. She looked down at her shirt. It was buttoned wrong. "Crap, crap, crap!" she thought.

She turned and stormed back to the house as if the buttons were meant to be that way. She heard the truck pulling out and didn't bother to look back as she entered the house.

When she closed the door, both friends were standing in front of her, waiting.

Vicki broke the silence. "You left out that he was gorgeous."

"He looked at you like you were a jelly donut," Sam said, bluntly. Evie slumped in a chair, feeling spent and undone.

Vicki spoke up, "This is some battle. I'm in."

Sam stepped forward, "I'm in, too."

There was a long list of questions Evie didn't have the answer to right now. But the question of how she would fight this battle alone was no longer one of them. Together, they answered the call to pray.

CHAPTER FOUR

Gratitude and confession, as well as a fight itself, allowed one to step through the portal. Evie, Vicki, and Sam entered the same desert as before, but this entry was more peaceful than the last few times. The portal appeared wherever Yahweh decided, whether in the middle of a horde or in a solitary place. With no Corgs or Ventars on the horizon, the women kept their weapons sheathed, instead joining hands and raising them in praise to Yahweh. There was much to be thankful for, blessed as they were with this time to be together to pray. For once, the battlefield seemed beautiful.

After the three warriors offered their prayers of thanksgiving, the return portal did not appear like they expected. Vicki and Evie exchanged knowing looks. The need to hurry back was always the strongest for them, while Sam would stay on a battlefield forever if she could. She preferred the fight with demons than with her own flesh and blood. The longer she stayed here, the less she fought there. She led the way, walking up the high and rippled dune.

The brown of sand was no longer the only color to be seen and when the women stood at the top of the dune, they were awarded with a vision of beauty, a gift from Yahweh Himself. The stretched thin and rippled clouds hung low, their underside colored with fuchsia and magenta with purple highlights. It was breathtaking, and Evie and Vicki might be willing to stay longer if this spot was always so gorgeous.

"Why do you think He's kept us here longer this time, without a battle?" Sam asked. "There has to be a purpose. There's always a purpose."

"I don't know, and right now I don't need to," replied Evie. "There is sand, there is sun, and there is a desert to be explored. The more we learn and know about this place, the more advantage we'll have when we come back." Evie was never one to waste time, and if she was going to be in the spiritual world for any longer than she had to, she wanted to make it count.

"Well," observed Vicki, "I know we'll burn here if we don't find cover. Ask me how I know. I'll tell you how I know. I burned to blisters in the arctic zone on my last battlefield. That much cold should not produce that much sunburn. So, I am guessing it's gonna happen here too." Vicki shielded her eyes from the sun and looked out while scouting the horizon. "Do you think there is an oasis? What about a stream in the desert? I bet there's one here." They took off in a slow run.

As the women moved, they used their swords as walking sticks and stabbed deeply into the sand occasionally, hoping they would hit a Ventar or two. Some Ventars were sent as scouts, and they were able to creep in tunnels and paths made under the sand. Their keen hearing allowed them to travel deeper than other demons. Even individual body parts could be sent through the sand to relay messages. For now, they moved undetected and were able to keep pace with the warriors as they moved through the desert. The Ventars would lose their targets temporarily when they reached the end of the dunes and came into the hard and parched desert ground. They hoped to Hades that the women would keep talking or sweating so they could find and follow them once again.

"I'm just gonna attack the big, pink elephant in the desert," said Sam. "Bryce has to be the reason we're here. We heard the Shofar blowing and understood we were being called to pray at the same time that he showed up on your doorstep. I am pretty sure if you send him packing, we'll be able to finish up here without any casualties." Sam clapped Evie on the back and kept walking, not noticing that Evie had stopped walking altogether.

"Woah... seriously?" Evie replied, loudly enough for Sam to hear. Sam stopped and turned, immediately noticing the distance between them. They'd never stood this far apart on a battlefield before. She hurried back to Evie, both for protection and so they wouldn't have to yell, their voices a clear invitation to any foe in the area.

"Good grief," Sam whispered, "Keep it down! Every Tom, Corg, and Ventar will hear you."

"Hang on!" answered Evie. "You don't know that we are here to fight off Bryce and that I am supposed to send him packing! How can you possibly know that? I don't even know that! And I didn't force you to come! If you are somewhere you don't want to be, find a portal and go home!"

Vicki jumped in between the women and placed a hand on each woman's shoulder. "Hey, girls! How about we just take the tension down a few notches here, okay? Let's enjoy this beautiful sunset and be still enough to feel that warm desert breeze. Just breathe in," breathing in deeply herself, "And now exhale...there. Girls. We are in prayer. What does it mean when something distracts us from our purpose of prayer in this battlefield?" She turned her head back and forth to each friend, waiting for them to answer. It took a few moments for them to remember, but the answer was finally clear.

Sam was the first to pull her sword from the sheath on her back. Evie's small sword was out and ready for use. The enemy was close.

The irritation they felt with each other a minute ago escalated too fast to be irritation alone. A demon, or demons, was involved. After a few minutes of calm, it was clear that their enemy wasn't going to make themselves known. The demons must not be looking for a fight. Each woman knew how close they had come to turning swords on each other. They've heard of it happening to other saints, but never had they ever been tempted until now.

"Yahweh, please, we need refreshment. Would You guide us to an oasis?" was the whispered prayer of Evie. Vicki and Sam both whispered their agreement, "Amen".

The three women stood back-to-back with weapons drawn, surveying the desert as far as their eyes could see. Heat pulsated off the ground in waves and one had to be careful not to be tricked into thinking a mirage was the oasis they needed. They knew if they waited and kept watch, He would send them a haven to heal and recover.

"There." Vicki nodded her head to the east. Looking for any vertical structures on the horizon, she saw something else instead. They ran towards it at a gentle pace, knowing it was better to get there with strength than not at all. Soon, a grove of palm trees was visible to them. They ran, now with abandon, and reached the oasis. Sheathing their weapons, they collapsed onto the lush grass, demonic irritations forgotten for a moment.

They rested on the ground, enjoying the cooler temperatures that washed over them. Looking up at the palm leaves, Evie felt it was as good a time as any to clarify the confusion began by the demons.

"So, I just want to say that I'm truly thankful you both are here with me. I am. But you need to know that I don't think this is about getting rid of Bryce. It feels like it's about my family, but I don't know if that includes him or not."

Sam remained still while Vicki rolled over onto her side and faced Evie.

"We don't need to know until Yahweh tells us, but I'm going to say, for now, we may need to disagree. We are united in prayer. We are united in support of you, and on your side. But we're just not sure what side Bryce is on." Vicki voice was full of emotion.

They all felt the peace and calm of the oasis.

"I understand," replied Evie. "But until we know for sure, can we not make decisions about him? Keep an open mind? It may sound like a lame question, but I have to ask."

Sam avoided eye contact with Evie, but she said the words Evie needed to hear. "Sure. We'll wait for Yahweh to reveal why we are here. Just remember our loyalty is to Him. If facing Bryce is part of that, we'll do it together, all three of us. Agreed?"

"Agreed," Vicki and Evie nodded.

Sam asked Vicki, "So, how did you spot this oasis?"

"Oh, I just saw birds flying nearby, and birds stay close to water. Speaking of which..."

They began exploring the oasis, looking for water or anything that would give them an advantage should they make their way back here again. The oasis was large enough to spread out, but still hear if anyone cried out for help.

It was Vicki who stumbled upon something. She clamped her hand over her mouth in shock, keeping in a scream. But she couldn't prevent the heaving and gagging that inevitably came. Sam heard her first and sprinted to her side. She gathered Vicki into her arms and turned her head away from the pile of carnage so grotesque and base that it looked like a scene from a horror movie. "Great," she thought." Laying right there in the water supply."

The ground was covered in piles and piles of demons, beheaded, quartered, and disemboweled. Corgs, covered in the maggots that came out of their bodies, were feasting on their own bloated flesh and the pieces of their bodies were swelling and expanding with each bite. The visible pieces of Ventar demons were black, which meant they fought as hard as they could before dying. Other hairless and gray demons suffered a unique mutilation. Known as Snappers because of their long necks, those very necks had been chopped into bits, not with a clean swipe and slash, but apparently by hacking and chopping. A few of the elusive and high-ranking demons called Jaders were strewn about in this mass of blood and maggots. They must not have fought long, as their bodies hadn't yet started mutating as they do when their own blood was drawn. The creatures had instead died quickly and painfully, their red intestines dumped over the demons of lower rank, and the maggots were hard to distinguish from the guts of the Jaders. The maggots didn't care what rank of demons they were eating. The sounds of slurping and chomping added to the horror of the moment.

Evie came over before Sam or Vicki could stop her. Her face turned gray, and she trembled. "Dear God. Someone else is here."

"Someone strong," said Sam. "This is the work of someone strong. Very strong."

"I think you mean powerful," said Vicki when she finally stopped gagging. "We're in the middle of an oasis. Who was here, sitting in this peaceful haven, that was such a threat that a whole horde of demons were sent to attack them? And here, on our battlefield? Who else knows about this? I thought it was just the three of us. Evie?"

"I don't know. I haven't told anyone."

Each one turned around and pulled out their weapons. Back-to-back, shoulder to shoulder, they scanned both the oasis and the outlying desert land. Their unity restored, they now faced something much worse than the evil they normally battled in spiritual warfare. They faced an unknown. Friend or foe? You couldn't tell by the pile of blood and guts left nearby.

But they were ever so thankful when the hum of the portal began to sound, and the shimmer was less than ten feet away.

It was six o'clock and Evie felt like she was going to throw up. "Maybe I'm getting sick," she thought to herself. "I've heard there's something going around. This is probably it." She busied herself with puttering around the house. Dinner was finished, the kids had helped clean up and the evening was going as planned. She wanted it to be calm and relaxing before Bryce arrived. But now she didn't feel calm, she felt sick, and nervous, and agitated. She'd been in prayer with Vicki and Sam earlier, and although she didn't find the answers she was looking for, she believed she was following the right path. She prayed as she worked, calm and rest quietly restored.

She'd spent some time with Kendall and Janey this afternoon, preparing them for their dad's visit. Although she hadn't expected fear or apprehension, she realized she wasn't quite prepared for their visible excitement. "Your dad coming to see you after being gone for nearly six months shouldn't feel like Christmas," she begrudgingly thought.

In truth, she'd been preparing them for this over the last few weeks. Janey took it in stride. But Kendall, sweet and serious Kendall, couldn't help himself. He beamed at the news. He hadn't said a lot over the last few months of his dad's absence, keeping his feelings quietly to himself. Evie had begun to wonder if Kendall even missed Bryce, or if he was angry since he'd said so little about him being gone. But today's breathtakingly beautiful smile both warmed Evie's heart and caused pain like a knife to twist. She admitted it. It felt like a knife to the heart when Bryce left. He walked out and left. And now when he finally comes back, it's a big-fat-giant-celebration for her kids.

These feelings tonight were not new feelings for her. She'd had a little time to get used to them, get acquainted with them, and even cozy up to them a bit. She knew it was a mixture of concern, fear, bitterness, and even some jealousy. Her heart had been broken and had just begun to heal, but it felt like it was healing with big, ugly scars. She hoped that she could detach her emotions, doing what she needed to do in a good, healthy way, but she also knew that too much detachment could lead to bitterness taking hold of her heart. All her emotions, fears, and feelings be examined and reexamined again, but now she wanted to focus on Kendall and Janey. Bryce wanted to see them, and it seemed like they wanted to see him, too. About this, she felt peace. Nervous, yes. But still peace.

But now she had to figure out what to wear. After this morning's bunny slippers, the cozy look was off the table. What does one wear when you don't want to be frumpy, but you don't want to look like you planned your outfit? "I want to be present, but not be noticed," she told herself. "Stop. It's ridiculous. I'm ridiculous."

She was just putting away the pile of rejected clothes after choosing brown suede leggings and a cream fisherman sweater when the kids barged in.

"You look pretty, Mommy!" Janey exclaimed as she crawled up on the bed.

Evie froze. "Pretty??" she squeaked. "I didn't mean to look pretty!!"

"You always look pretty, Mom," said Kendall, ever the diplomat.

Evie relaxed, as she knew Kendall was trying to put her at ease. "Thanks, Kendall," she smiled. "You look quite handsome tonight yourself. Except you forgot to wear your dimples!"

"No, I didn't!" He grinned.

"Mommy, did I wear my dimples?" asked Janey, suddenly serious.

"Well, let me see," said Evie as she slid closer to her on the bed. "Maybe if I get up real close, very, very close and look..." She grabbed her feet and pulled her to her as she tickled her tummy and chin. Janey's giggles were contagious as all three began to fall in a pile of tickling and laughter.

"Yes, you most certainly wore your dimples, sweet Janey!" Evie snuggled her and as Janey settled into her lap, Evie breathed her scent. Soft hair, pudgy neck, she could feel her little arms around her own waist. Even Kendall enjoyed the quiet moment. "Thank you, Lord," Evie's heart whispered. Of course, it would be in this moment of serenity that she heard his truck. She carefully sat up and gave the children a big squeeze.

"Okay, I think it's time for our special visit!" she made herself sound as cheerful as she could.

"Is my dad here now?!" bounced Janey in her spot on the bed. Evie looked at Kendall, who didn't even show a flicker of doubt.

"Janey, he's my dad too, not just yours," reminded Kendall.

"Yes, he is here and yes, he's both of yours!" Evie squeezed one more quick tickle in before she made a forced-casual exit from the bed.

She knew he was walking to the door, and she felt the symbolism of her walking towards the same door. "Lord, you see us. Please be near," she whispered one last time before she reached the barrier between them.

He reached the door just as she was opening it. She could tell by his expression that he knew how important this moment was. He wasn't flashing a grin; he wasn't looking amused. She allowed herself to relax, just a little.

"Thank you," he said. He stood on the steps, humble, his hands in his pockets. "I mean it, Ev. Thank you."

Evie held his look for a moment before opening the door to let him in.

"They're excited to see you," was all she could say as she watched him step through the kitchen door of the home from which he had walked away so many months ago.

She saw his gaze take in the kitchen. He looked at the refrigerator plastered with crayon-colored drawings. She watched him observe the lopsided pottery bowl, filled with fruit, that she made at a pottery class he had gifted her for their first anniversary. He looked at the wooden kitchen table, picked out together, around the time they found out she was expecting Kendall. She saw him breathe in the scent of the home they had once shared. She could tell he recognized the warm smell of the kids' favorite cookies she had made earlier and a trace of her sandalwood candle. His eyes closed for just a moment, and the muscles in his jaw tightened as he swallowed back his emotions.

She couldn't look away. She knew that for this moment, these feelings were real. Before she could even remind herself to get a grip, the moment exploded, replaced with the sound of running feet and the noise of two voices yelling at the same time.

"I get to go first because I'm the oldest!"

"Nuh-uh, I go first because I'm the lady!"

The oldest and the lady stopped as they burst into the kitchen. For Evie, time stopped with them. She saw it all. Their faces. His face. Janey's awe and Kendall's wide eyes. She saw Bryce open his eyes and see them as they entered. She watched him slowly bend down to his knee and get on their level. She knew when the day ended, and this meeting was all over, the kids would be in bed and she would be alone in her room, replaying this scene over and over, that it really happened quickly. But right now, it felt like watching slow motion. Janey was in front of Kendall and bouncing in place.

Bryce finally said softly, "Hi, Janey." Before he could say anything else, she was running. Blonde hair, dimples flashing, a ball of energy. Evie wasn't even sure her feet hit the floor. She crossed the kitchen as if she were flying and then launched herself into his arms. Bryce's arms closed around her, and he buried his face in her baby fine hair. They knelt there for just a few moments when he looked up and saw Kendall still standing in the doorway. Moving Janey to sit on his knee, he stayed kneeling.

As Bryce smiled at Kendall, Evie watched that exact same slow grin of his spread across the face of her son. She felt her heart clench as she saw Bryce hold out his arm to their son. Kendall paused, but only for a moment. Then he joined Janey as he ran across the room and into his dad's arms. It looked like one big, giant hug, Kendall and Janey with looks of pure joy on their faces. Bryce's eyes were closed tight. His mouth moved in silent words as he took their little bodies and held them to himself.

It was then that Evie noticed that she was standing alone. Alone in her home, an observer of this beautiful scene between this man, who'd become a stranger even while so familiar, and her children.

The knife in her heart twisted a little more. Her own eyes filled with tears. She loved her children. How could she, for one second, deny them this moment of joy? This was joy for them. Janey's joy was clear from her arms around his neck that she had. Kendall, her beautiful boy who never complained, never questioned, seemed desperate as he clung to Bryce. He seemed afraid to let him go. And there was no denying that Bryce seemed desperate for them as well.

Evie suddenly felt awkward. Like she didn't belong here, like an intruder of special moments. Not knowing what to do, she figured she'd turn to busy herself at the counter.

That was when Janey noticed her.

"Momma, do you want to hug my daddy, too?"

If it wasn't awkward before, it was now. "Thanks Janey, thanks so much," she thought.

And there it was. That grin. Bryce, keeping Janey on one knee and his arm around Kendall, turned to Evie and just grinned. There was Janey in her innocent smile, there was Kendall in his matching grin, and there was the man she'd let in the door, grinning.

The tension of all the emotion seemed to bubble up and Evie couldn't help herself. She laughed. She laughed at the joy of children, the innocent invitation of her daughter, the matching grins of son and father. Their faces just beamed back at her.

"I think you two are doing a very good job of that all by yourself! Why don't you take him to see the pictures you drew for him today?"

"Okay," said Janey. To Bryce she said, "You wanna see my princess?"

"You could probably see my lion first, since she always loses all her stuff. Because she never puts it away," said Kendall.

Bryce, standing up, still smiling, said, "Still my messy Janey, huh?!"

"I'm not a messy Janey!"

"Well," said Kendall, "actually she is, but mom said we can't call her that anymore because it doesn't help anything."

Laughing, Bryce said, "Okay. I won't call her that either. I'll look at all of them, whichever ones you can find."

Evie watched as he followed them into the living room. She could hear them talking, running back and forth to gather everything in sight to show him. She didn't really know what to do with herself. "Do I stay in here and give them space?" she thought. She was opening and closing cabinets, looking for something to do, when she heard him speaking.

"You don't have to stay in here, you know," she heard Bryce say.

She turned to look, and he was leaning in the doorway into the kitchen. "Me?" asked Evie.

"It's your home, Ev. You can be wherever you want to be," he said softly.

"Yeah, I know!" she said brightly. "I was just making something. Coffee. You still like coffee? I mean, it's okay if you don't. I just won't make much." "Shut up already," she told herself.

Bryce laughed, "Yes, I still like coffee. Thank you. Again."

One of the kids called him and in a slow, easy way he pushed off the doorway, walking back into the living room.

Evie waited for the coffee to brew, then took a cup for herself and a cup for Bryce and joined them in the living room. She put his cup on the coffee table and sat in the chair while he and the kids, still close to him, sat on the couch with every picture book and coloring book piled next to them. Kendall's bin of Legos was on the floor near Bryce's feet. Janey's baby dolls, Barbie dolls, and Barbie boathouse had at some point landed in the middle of the floor.

Other than the quick glance Bryce gave her as she came in, her presence seemed to go unnoticed. She wrapped her emotions up tight while still in the kitchen and was happy to sit curled up on the chair and just watch the scene.

What she wouldn't have given to see this a year ago, or even six months ago. Why? Why could he have not done this when she needed it? When they all needed it? What could be worth more than them? She knew the hearts of husbands and wives often grew apart over time. She had come to terms with that, but how do you walk away from these two?

All the questions women ask themselves, even while knowing there wasn't going to be a satisfying answer, went through her mind as she watched the moments unfold.

Although she was just an observer, a watcher, each of them occasionally glanced her way with a smile on their face, and she'd smile back. She saw the play progress to the floor as Bryce helped Kendall build his Lego castle. "Funny, it would be a castle," she thought to herself. "I've been holding Camelot for some time now."

The Barbie Dreamboat was on the opposite side of Bryce. He successfully managed to aid Kendall in the castle development, but it seemed putting the shoes on the pointy toed Barbies required skills he didn't possess.

"No, Daddy! Those shoes don't go. Here, do these," Janey said as she pulled one tiny pair out of his hands and dropped in another.

Evie almost felt sorry for him as he looked up at her with a perplexed expression.

"Her foot doesn't bend," he said flatly.

"Toe first, then heel," Evie informed.

Watching Bryce sit on the floor in a pile of brightly colored Legos and the pastels of a pile of Barbie clothes, Evie felt her heart stir. It wasn't fear this time, or sadness, it was something much stronger.

They say there isn't anything much more attractive to a woman than seeing a man playing with her children. At that moment, Evie knew it to be true. But she didn't want to be attracted to him. She wanted to be mature. And responsible. "But dang it," she thought. "I think he has a shoe stuck on his shirt." She reminded herself he wasn't here for her. He left her. He was here for his kids. And whatever that was going to mean, they were going to responsibly deal with that so that these kids could grow up loved and safe.

"Safe," she thought. Were they safe? She knew she'd been battling for the answer to that question. "I don't know what or where that answer is, but I'm not going to stop until I have it."

Time somehow moved quickly, and Evie noticed Janey yawning. She looked at the clock on the wall and it read ten o'clock. She planned their meeting for seven because she knew the kids usually went to bed between eight and eight-thirty. The first visit would be easy and quick. Admittedly, it had been easy. At least for the children. But it had not been quick.

"I think it's time we're going to have to put things away and get ready for bed," she announced.

"No!" both kids cried.

Bryce looked at them like he was going to chime in with them, but then looked at Evie. She could see him struggling. She had figured she'd be the bad guy here, so was surprised when he said, "She's right, you know. I'm tired, and I think I'm going to need a nap soon."

Janey's eyes filled with tears and her lip tremble when she asked, "Are you going to go away again?"

This time, Evie felt like her heart had actually been stabbed. Hurt and anger battled as she fought the urge to sweep her baby up and hold her.

She saw Kendall look at Bryce and say nothing. He just studied him as Bryce swallowed the lump in his own throat.

He looked at Janey, then Kendall, and said, "No. I'm not going away again."

"You will come back?" she softly asked.

He looked back to Janey, "Yes. I promise. I will come back."

Kendall said nothing as he began to pick up his toys. Janey moved to Bryce's lap, and the sadness seemed to disappear from her face as she gave up her cuddles to the strength of his chest.

Evie didn't feel like she could breathe while her heart was doing battle. The things she wanted to say she knew were better left unsaid, for now.

"Okay! Say goodnight and I'll help get you into bed!" she finally managed.

Toys were picked up, and hugs were given.

As she stood to lead them from the room, Bryce stood, too. "Can I hang out here till you get back?" he asked.

Evie hesitated. She'd assumed he would just leave, but she also knew that they probably needed to talk, define boundaries, and make the plans that were necessary.

"Sure, give me a bit," she replied, and turned to follow the children.

It didn't take long to settle Janey in, since she was falling asleep as Evie was pulling the blankets up. She kissed her sweet cheeks and neck goodnight. "Thank you, Lord, for this child, and please protect her while she sleeps," prayed Evie as she watched Janey sigh and close her eyes.

When she got to Kendall's room, he was still awake and waiting for her. She smiled at him and sat down, smoothing his hair. "Are you ok, sweetheart?" she asked him.

"Yes, I am. Janey didn't pick up all her toys," he informed her.

Evie smiled, "I know. I'll have her help extra tomorrow. Will that work?"

"If I pick them up, can I have extra allowance?"

"Extra allowance? What would you do with extra allowance?!"

"I'm saving so I can get a scooter like Troy and David," he began. He rolled off all the coolest things he could do with a scooter. He'd apparently put some thought into it.

Finally, Evie was able to respond, "How about if I find ways to give you extra chores so you can save more money and then you help your sister just because she's your sister?"

There was a long pause as Kendall considered this option. "I suppose that's probably okay," he agreed.

Evie laughed as she hugged him. "I love you, Kendall."

"Is Dad going to live with us now?" he asked.

Evie was caught off guard with the sudden turn of subjects, but she instinctively knew if Kendall was asking, she needed to answer as honestly as she could. "I don't know right now, Kendall. Right now, we are just trying to work out a way that he can see you more. Are you ok with that?"

He paused again. "Is he going to come over again?"

"Do you want him to?"

"Yes," he said while he glanced away, "unless you don't want him to."

She knew that this sweet boy was trying to help his mom. Although she'd protected him from the situation as much as she could, his little, valiant heart wanted to protect her, even when he didn't know from what.

"Kendall," she began, "I've been praying for your dad for many, many months. And I'm praying every day that I will know the right thing to do. I promise you that I will keep looking for the answer and I also promise that whatever God wants for us, I will do. Until I know for sure,

I'm good with your dad coming over to see you when he can. Is that okay?" She watched as he studied her.

"Will you tell me when you find the answer?" he asked.

"Yes," she said softly. "I'm going to find it, and when I do, I will tell you."

"Ok, Mom. I love you."

"I love you too, Kendall."

They finished their goodnights. She closed his door, breathed another quick prayer, and stepped back into the living room.

Bryce was sitting on the couch, head down, comfortable and looking like he'd planned on waiting all night if needed. "Of course, he used to belong here. Why shouldn't he be here? Oh wait. Because he left... for six months," she reminded herself.

She felt his eyes on her as she chose the chair and not the couch. Most definitely not the couch. She sat and looked at him, grinning again. She thought to herself, "Does he ever stop grinning? Seriously? What does he have to grin about?"

"You sure you wouldn't be more comfortable on the couch?" he asked.

"Is he teasing me? Is he insane? I could punch him in the face right now and he'd never see it coming!" her thoughts went wild but aloud she said, "I'm comfortable right here. Thanks." He still grinned. Evie sighed, "Listen Bryce, I think it went well tonight..."

"Do you think so, too? It seemed like it did to me," he began to rattle. She hadn't been expecting chatty, so it took her a second to catch up with what he was saying.

"I can't believe how big they are. She's so beautiful. She's always been adorable, but she's beautiful, isn't she? I think Kendall grew six inches. How do they grow in five months?"

"Six," Evie corrected.

He stared at her before saying, "Five."

"Did you not have a calendar where you were? It's been six months."

Bryce paused a moment, looking like he was doing mental calculations in his mind, "Five-ish."

"It was six."

"Okay. I'll let you have this one. Six months," he conceded.

"You'll let me have this one? You can't let me have one when I'm right! It was six months!" she felt herself getting angry but couldn't stop for the life of her. "You let someone go first in line. You let someone have the first piece of cake!"

"You don't even like cake." "What the heck, Evie?" went her thoughts. "Why did you bring up cake?"

"Not the point," she continued without skipping a beat. "You can't let someone be right if they're right. That's not lettable."

He was grinning again. She stared at him.

"You're so beautiful," he said, his voice tinged with pride and wonder.

"Good grief," she thought. "What is wrong with him? He doesn't just get to say things like that!" Evie took a deep breath, "How I look really isn't the issue here, Bryce.

We need to talk about how we are going to work this out with the kids. I think it went fine tonight, and I'd like to be able to do this like two adults. But I don't really know what you want here, so I think you're going to have to fill me in so we can do what is best for them."

Bryce's playfulness was gone as he leaned forward, bringing his eyes to her level. Evie hoped things were about to get real, and the time had come to get some answers.

"What I want," he started, "Is to be their dad. I want to see them, touch them and be here for them."

"Define here."

"Here, as in here in this town, here in their life, here being their dad."

Evie waited for the relief. "Nope. No relief. Shouldn't I feel relived?" she thought.

"Here's the thing, Bryce," she said quietly, "You left. For a long time. I don't want them to go through that again. You can't just come and go whenever you feel like it without seriously hurting them."

"I'm not going to leave again."

"How can you say that? To me? I never thought you'd do that to us in first place and yet you did! I had no idea where you were! I still don't! How can I trust you aren't going to do the same thing all over again?"

"I'm not ever going to leave again. Ever."

He said it with so much conviction, like he really believed his own words. But she needed more than words.

"Where were you?" she finally asked.

He didn't answer, didn't move. She could see the muscle moving in his cheek.

"Why is this so hard to answer, Bryce? You want me to just throw a welcome home party and say here, take the kids for the weekend while you're at it? Were you at rehab? For drugs?"

"You know me better than that, Evie."

"No! No, I don't! I don't know you better than that! I thought I did, but I was so obviously wrong! Everything I thought about you was wrong." Evie felt herself getting choked up with every emotion she had been boxing up for so long. She did not want to cry. Not now, here, in front of him.

"Evie," he said, and stopped. "Evie, I messed up. I never meant for it to go as far as it did, and to end so badly. I see now that my hope for just easing back into this life was wishful thinking."

Evie's heart was beating so hard she could feel her pulse. Was this was going to be the moment she'd learn it all? She no longer knew if she wanted to hear it.

Bryce took a deep breath, staring at the floor, unable to meet her eyes he began. "It started so small." His words started again and there was no stopping them this time. "I wanted to move to another house after Janey was born. But I quickly realized I couldn't afford a better house," he snorted, sat up and leaned back on the couch and continued. "I tried to get more hours at work, but things there were slow, and I thought I was going to get laid off instead. I was so angry. Not at you. Angry at the house, stupid I know," he glanced at her. "Angry at the cars. Nothing felt...good enough. I thought if I could just make more money, I would be able to give you and the kids what you deserved."

"What we deserved was a present husband and father. We never cared about the house or the cars or stuff. I told you that, so many times," said softly.

"I know you did. I know, now, that you even meant it. I just got so... blinded. I couldn't focus on anything else. I started asking people at work if they knew of any side jobs, and some temp said he could help me."

Evie heard the story unfolding as the words were coming easier and faster. He began to look at her as he was speaking, as if he were trying to free himself with his words. "He said," he continued, "I could ride along with him as he did some pickups out of town if I didn't mind be out late for a few nights a week. I started with him, and then it grew to where I was needed overnight. All we were doing was moving a van full of boxes from one warehouse to another. After a while, they gave me my own van and route and I had to move stuff from county to county. I told myself it was no big deal. I didn't know anything more than I got paid in cash and I could make as much as I was willing to work for. They just said I couldn't talk about it. Not to you, not to anyone."

"I'm sorry," Evie interrupted with a look of disbelief. "I'm having a hard time thinking you could be so stupid and still blame us for it."

"I'm not blaming you! I felt like I was, I don't know... poisoned? Like I had to get money so I could take better care of you. I don't know how to describe it. I never thought it was a legit business. I just had it stuck in my mind that it was the only way I could do what I thought I needed to do. It was easy. So, I didn't ask, and they didn't tell. I couldn't tell you. I couldn't. Then the more runs I did, the more they wanted. And it was so easy. Just drive. I thought if I could just get enough money for a bigger house and put some extra away for if I got laid off, then I could just quit.

"I'd see some of the stuff I was moving when I'd deliver, and it wasn't TVs or stereos. It was art, and boxes of house stuff. I told myself it couldn't be all bad." He finally paused, and the room was silent as Evie sat stunned, putting the pieces of the past few years together.

"I just kept saying, it can't be all bad and when I have what I need, I'll quit. I knew it was bad here at home. I knew I couldn't keep doing this, with you not knowing, and me gone longer and longer. So, I showed up at the job one night, thinking I'd give my notice," he laughed bitterly. "As if they would take an actual notice. I figured I'd load up and do one more run. I was two counties over when I saw the lights. I pulled over and was surrounded by police cars. The officers got out of their cars, guns loaded and calling for backup. Turns out, we'd been watched at all the warehouses I'd been to, and I'd been stopped there with a van full of stolen property and money." He stopped abruptly.

"You never told me anything. Nothing. Not a word." She couldn't keep the accusatory tone out of her voice.

"I know. I know that, and I'm sorry. I know it sounds lame, and inadequate. But I am so sorry. I got in over my head and by the time I wanted out, it was too late."

"Were you arrested?" she asked.

He snorted. "Yeah. I was arrested. Turns out I wasn't just working for a small side business of stolen goods.

That would have been too easy. I was working for a big laundering ring. And I was the guy who had been transporting money and goods. When I was arrested, before I could call anyone, I was told I could either spend a long time in prison or I could tell them everything I knew in trade for just doing county jail time. So, I thought about it for all of thirty seconds, told them everything I knew, which wasn't much, and in turn I spent six months in their county jail." Bryce lowered his voice, "So when I say I am never ever leaving again, I know exactly what I'm saying."

The silence felt oppressive. Bryce stared at her while she looked anywhere but at him. On the outside Evie looked still and thoughtful, but inside she struggled with the chaos of conflicting thoughts and emotions. But his story fit, perfectly. Maybe too perfectly.

She broke the silence, finally looking at him, "So what you're telling me is that you've been in county jail. You've been in county jail for six months?"

"Did you hear me at all? I wasn't just in county jail. I was caught in a money laundering sting after a year of working for them. That's where I was. That's what I was doing, and that's why I never told you."

"Jail. You've been in...jail. And it never once occurred to you to tell your wife?

"Yes, it occurred to me! But I needed to know the job was over and that it was safe for you. I'm not going to pretend I was being a great husband..." Evie snorted, but he continued, "...I messed up. I sat in jail for six months and thought about every single thing I'd done wrong. When money first became more important than you and the kids. And I prayed. I prayed and said if I got another chance when I got out, I was never going to make the same mistakes. I couldn't call you. I just couldn't. Maybe it was pride, or shame...So I waited, biding my time, emailed once a week, and contacted you when I got out.

"I'm sorry, Evie. If I could go back, I would. If I could fix everything, I would. I don't know if there's anything left between us, but if you can help me with the kids, I will never leave them again."

Evie's head was spinning. She needed space, a moment to think and pray. She needed her friends. But Bryce needed an answer, and she didn't have one. Not yet.

Bryce was driving his truck home when he realized he needed gas. His thoughts were all over the place, with the kids, and Evie. She was so beautiful it made his heart ache. When he saw her in her sweater, he had to put his hands in his pockets to keep from reaching out to her. He'd expected, and been prepared for, more questions. He'd not been prepared for no questioning. No yelling, no confusion, no denial, nothing. She got up, said she needed to think and ended their conversation. She asked him to leave and said she would call him later. He had no experience here. None. But he did know Evie. He knew her as well as she knew herself. She needed time to process. She needed to examine everything.

He pulled into a gas station, pumping his gas like he'd done hundreds of times. His mind felt overstretched and overworked, with too many emotions to process. He decided to get a drink and a snack. As he entered the station's double doors, a man walking by bumped into him. Startled out of his own thoughts, he glanced at the man and felt his blood run cold. The man, looking back at him, walked on to his own car. The look of recognition was brief but powerful.

Bryce stood frozen in place as the glass doors swung shut between, his heart racing.

"He's not supposed to be here," Bryce thought to himself. "Not here, not now."

Bryce changed his mind about the late snack, walked back to his truck, and picked up his phone.

CHAPTER FIVE

*T*he oasis could no longer be called beautiful and tranquil, with mounds of dead and mutilated demons piled around the water. The Ventar scouts had sent messages back to their leader Storek, giving the details both about the destruction and about the enemies that were here just moments ago. Eventually, a scout would cease to exist. He became literally undone. Messages could be sent through the sand by putting any body part to their lips and speaking the message into it, then removing the body part and sinking it down into the sand. Jangis and Balid had removed so many parts and sent so many messages that they were simply wasting away.

The scouts impatiently waited for orders, observing the maggots that had poured out of the dead Corgs' bodies. They feasted on their hosts that had before contained them for centuries. It was an indulgent and frothy mess. Jangis' eyes were bright with desire and his remaining fingers rubbed the thick brown drool dripping from his mouth all over his lips. His normal high-pitched battle squeals became shallow breaths as his excitement and lust built. When he could no longer control his desire, he began chewing on the ends of fingers from Corg hands he had found, sucking the maggots that were consuming the ends of each fingertip. Jangis knew just how to hold the maggot on its end and pull in and out, swelling up the maggot until it was ready to explode. Then he popped the white, slimy creature into his mouth. Balid, lusty, sweating, and panting over the sounds and smells of the maggots, turned away from his need to chew and devour when he heard the crunching of Jangis' bones.

"A message." He bumped Jangis' arm. A clump of three fingers emerged and held the message saying that all remains were to be burned, and the scouts were to return to Oridon's cave for further questioning. The two demons summoned the small but evil power within them to harness the sun's heat and began to build fires with the piles of remains.

There was no feeling of loss for their fellow demons, as there was little unity outside of battle in this world of darkness, but the loss of the chance to feast on the slaughter was felt by Jangis and Styren. The flames grew, and their job here finished, they must leave for the cave. They didn't care who caused the carnage at this point. They would even like to thank them for making the oasis some place they didn't mind staying, for once.

Oridon's cave was dimly lit. No light would even be needed if Ventars weren't present. Ventar skin darkens when fighting and if violence broke out in the cave, they would become black as night, impossible to see. It was Loden, the ranking Jader, who had called the meeting, so it was he who sat at the head of a fused slab of bones serving as a table.

Demons weren't known for hygiene and the air was pungent enough to sting Loden's eyes. But Jaders were the cleanliest of all demons, so his disgust for these lower ranked demons was apparent. How he hated the stupid, expendable Corgs and Ventars. If he could conduct this meeting without them, he would have, but their expandability and rapid breeding rate made them important to this mission.

Loden's face held a tight smile that didn't fool any of his companions. He only had to call a summit meeting once before, and his irritation at having to be here, in this desert arena, was unmistakable to everyone at the table.

"Storek," whispered the grimacing Loden. The room became eerily silent. All that could be heard was the soft grunts of the breathy Corgs.

"Ssss, yessss."

"I've been summoned here because your scouts panicked. You know better than to call for a Swastik or enter their territory before you talk to me or Fairen. Did you forget protocol, or did you think to rewrite the written law of the demons?"

"Ssss, we forget nothing. My scouts had evidence of a serious threat to our campaign against the target, and I decided to deal with someone who could handle a problem correctly."

The clan of Jaders standing behind Loden had the faintest hue of red start creeping up their necks. The slight movement of their hands on their swords was noted by all as well as their agitated humming. As long as they were not red, blood would not be shed, the saying went.

Loden's control is what made him the leaders of the Jaders. No maggot sucking Ventar was going to cause him to fully change color right now. But if another opportunity presented itself, he was going to dismember these two Ventars in the most painful way possible. Idiots.

Loden's careful tone brought not peace, but unrest to the cave. "You smell of maggots, smoke, and..." he paused, inhaling as he leaned over the table to the Corg, "something else?"

Loden spoke to Jangis and Balid, evoking the memory of their oasis desires. He intended to give them a distracting thought. It worked. The eyes of the two quickly glazed over long enough for Loden to appear directly in front of them and put his sword to their throats. He leaned in so close the Ventars were able to smell him and his horrid breath in their nostrils. It was all they could do to not vomit on the Jader's boots.

"You disgusting, mewling meatbags. I'm going to let you walk out of this meeting and live another day for the simple reason that I have a mission for you. If you don't succeed, I guarantee you will never again have the delight you've just experienced with the maggots. Are you able to understand what I am saying?"

Loden's nostrils flared as he felt his blood pulsing. How he wanted to rip them apart now, but his vengeance was greater than his rage now. Choose your evil, he thought to himself.

"This is a planning meeting," he spoke loudly so every demon in Oridon's cave could hear. "The mission with the target has had some resistance. We are not unfamiliar with these humans and their futile attempts to delay the inevitable." Loden walked slowly back to the head of the conference table. He turned to face his team of Jaders, the loser Corgs and the waste of death Ventars. "Balid, tell us about this target."

"Sssss, yes. Her name is Evie. She's been abandoned and forsaken by her mate."

"Is she pretty?" asked Loden.

"Ha, no!" Balid made gagging movements and sounds.

"By human standards, Balid. Is she pretty by human standards?" Loden managed to ask through his clenched teeth.

"Oh! Yes. The males seem to think so, but not so much that females seemed threatened. She's...adequate." Loden filed away

the new lesson to never ask a Ventar about beauty. Anything that finds Corg maggots attractive is messed up. But he continued.

"What does she do?"

"She works in a diner."

"So, we have abandonment and exhaustion issues. Why is this a problem? Why is she still standing? Tell me it was not she who just wiped out a colony of Corgs!"

Jangis stood next to the favored Balid, his fury being fed as his companion got to answer one question after another. "Who does he think he is?" Jangis thought. "Mister big stuff now. So full of maggot juice, he thinks he's a leader. Just you wait, Balid. Just you wait." His hateful eyes glared at Balid, his demon brother.

Balid answered, "Sssir, we don't know who did that. We came upon it after the battle was done."

"Why is she even here, and why should I care? Is she tired of being poor? Did she find a wrinkle on her stupid face? Did she crack the screen on her phone?" His annoyance at humans was easily triggered these days. They came here for the stupidest reasons. They never lasted long and were a mockery to all things evil. He was too important to be bothered yet again with their pettiness. And these Ventars need to be reminded of his importance.

Balid answered, "She's been praying about her marriage, Sssir." There was a collective gasp throughout Oridon's cold and dark cave.

"We have an abandoned and exhausted wife coming here to pray for her marriage," Loden responded. "We are finding whole colonies of Corgs wiped out. I want to find her simply

for the sake of thanking her. I can only assume the Ventars will be next on her hit list," he smirked. "Now that we're here, let's come up with a simple plan to scare her or bore her away. We all know this won't last long."

Dripping water could be heard in the quiet of the thinking demons. Loden needed to draw them to the idea that was forming in his own head. He'd speak it out himself if he needed to, but it would be so much more satisfying if another suggested it. He would lead the horses to the water.

"We must capitalize on her needs, her desires. She's lonely. She's afraid or she wouldn't be here. This 'forsaker' of hers," Loden felt a very human moment as he used air quotes, "has he shown up?"

"No," answered Balid.

"Good, good. Then she still feels alone here. What if we satisfied her longing while she was here? Made her think she wants something else, something more attainable? Someone more...present?"

He looked around the room, making eye contact with a few Corgs and Ventars, but their eyes were still blank. He moved on to the Jaders who had a look of appreciation on their faces. They knew where he was headed. There is something to be said for breeding and intelligence, after all.

It was Fairen who stepped out of the darkness behind Loden. Until now, he had been so still, no one had even noticed him. Fairen knew vanity and he also recognized an opportunity to get rid of Loden once and for all. "Want to play who is the fairest in the land, Loden?" thought Fairen. "I can play that game."

"Perhaps if she saw someone here who was in the image of what she wanted as a mate, unlike the one she has now, it would stop her from coming here. She is looking for someone

or something. Let's give it to her." Fairen spoke smoothly. All were listening and when Fairen looked at Loden, he was sure he saw pride burning in his cold, dead eyes. "Humans often just need a desire to lead them away from here. Give her what she wants, what she thinks she needs. A potential mate is what she thinks she lost. She's here looking for an answer, is she not? Give her one."

"Who do you suggest, Fairen? You show immense wisdom. Tell us! Who is this 'answer to prayer'?" Loden made air quotes again. His excitement at what he hoped was coming next was just too much.

"There is only one who can do this," Fairen began, his voice wheedling. "It is you, Loden! Your beauty is unparalleled and your transformation to an angel of light has been perfected for centuries. There could be no one else worth considering, my fellow Jader."

Loden did his best to act surprised and shocked. But it was nearly impossible. He lived for these missions, this angel of light transformation. He was the best demon for this task. He knew it, but it was flattering to hear others agree.

"Very well then," Loden said, accepting the mission. "It shall be done. I will extend my help to you Ventars and Corgs and finish this target."

Jangis stood next to Balid, left out and resentful after not even being noticed. It was he who had cut off a finger and two toes to get the message to these filthy Jaders in the first place. It was he who alerted them to the presence of danger, therefore saving all these demon lives, and quite possibly all of hell itself. But no one even looked at him. He spoke up, attempting to get some of the attention he deserved.

"Aren't you forgetting something, Loden?" spoke the Ventar. All eyes were finally on him. This was his chance to show Balid

that he wasn't the only Ventar in the cave. "You need to get close enough to touch her, scratch her, anything. Spit on her for all I care. But you must infect her. Simply observing your so-called beauty won't cut it. And she's praying for her marriage. If she is not prevented from coming here again, we all know Who else will come.

"Remember Beth and Troy? Because I sure do. So just in case you thought standing and glowing was going to be effective, it won't be. You still need us, to get close to her. Don't forget these things, Jader." Jangis couldn't believe that he managed to say all that and was still alive and standing. He could certainly feel the tension, hatred, and the lust for power in the room.

Loden stood at the end of the table while the Ventar spoke. He calmly and slowly walked back around the table and stood in front of the loosed tongued demon.

He bent down to look him in the eye. "Never," he whispered, "Never!" he roared so loud the walls of the cave shook. Dirt and dust fell from the ceiling. "Never, ever refer to Him in my presence again or you will be dead! Do you understand me?" His voice blasted the space.

At his roar, every single demon fell to his knees and bowed his head. The reference to the One, here in Oridon's cave, was bouncing off the walls, echoing in their ears and rolling down the tunnels. It would be hours before they could hear anything above the horrible echoes of His name. That most hated, disgusting, and vile One.

"Meeting adjourned!" Loden motioned as stood up, now in his normal voice, trying to hide the pain inside his head. The One. "I hate you" was all he would be thinking for the next five hours.

He should have killed those Ventars at first sight.

The diner was busy with the breakfast rush hour. Vicki and Sam sat across from each other in the friend booth. They've each managed to get a cup of coffee as Evie walked back and forth, being everywhere and everything for customers getting started on their day. Beyond that, their communication was minimal. They waited for a chance to talk, as the caffeine kicked in.

Finally, Evie came for their order. "Okay, sorry about that! What would you like?"

"Egg white omelette and cheese," mumbled Sam.

"Easy," replied Evie, not even bothering to write it down. "Vick?"

"Bacon, toast, butter," came her quiet response. "In that order."

"Got it." Evie dropped off the carafe and headed back to the kitchen.

"You're not normal, you know," said Sam as she stared Vicki. "No one who looks like you should be able to eat like that. Do you know what bacon is?! It's fried fat. Fried. Fat."

"Haters gonna hate," was the nonchalant response. "And you don't exactly look like the egg white type, Sam."

"Whatever the egg white type is. Speaking of haters, you want to know what I hate?" Sam asked as she recalled their battle. "I hate not knowing whether we are the hunter or the hunted. What the crap was that mess in there??"

"You mean the piles of dead, rotting bodies that looked like a slaughter? That mess?! I have absolutely no idea."

"Yeah, well, I think we'd better be praying for some answers here soon. Looks like things are ramping up. I don't know if whatever did that is on our side or not!"

"Well, let's think about this for a minute. Whatever did that is stronger than all of us. And if they're on our side, they were either invited by one of us, which didn't happen, or they were called there by someone else," said Vicki.

"So, who do we know that is stronger than us?!" asked Sam. "I mean, not that I'm trying to brag, but really? We are da' bomb out there! Half the Christians we know have spent their whole life not even knowing about the battlefield. I mean, a year ago, did you?"

"Yeah, but I wasn't strong. In and out. Quick battles. I learned quickly. But I don't know. It's just so...weird!" Vicki said.

Sam sat thinking, fingers tapping out the rhythm to some tune in her head. Her eyes turned to Vicki. "And if it's not on our side?"

"I don't even know. Did you hear about Bryce meeting the kids?" she answered.

"I heard," Sam said as her melody still tapped out on the table.

"And? What do you think?!" asked Vicki.

"I think it's all too coincidental, is what I think! I mean, seriously. Has anyone considered that he might be, oh I don't know, lying?!"

Evie dropped the food on the table, startling Vicki and Sam. "Who's lying?" she asked.

The girls nearly jumped out of their seat. "Good grief, Evie!! Do you do that to all your customers? It's seven-thirty in the morning! Ever think that sneaking up and dropping plates on the tables might give someone a heart attack?!" Vicki was holding her heart with one hand and rubbing her temple with the other.

Evie and Sam stared at Vicki, amused. "You want to know what's going to give you a heart attack? Fried fat. If life were fair, it would also give you round hips. But apparently life isn't fair!" rattled off Sam.

"Who's lying?" persisted Evie, hands on hips, looking back and forth between her friends.

Just then, the doorbell jingled. Sam, thankful for a distraction, looked up. Vicki, in turn, twisted in her booth seat to see who Sam was now staring at and smiled. Evie stared at them both a second longer before turning to look.

"Really? You guys aren't off the hook. Lying is a big word. I'd like to discuss it!" She looked back at them both, gave them a warning smile and turned to greet the newcomer.

It was a tall guy with dark hair, perfectly unshaven, and he stood inside the door and looked around. Wearing a black flight jacket, black jeans, and aviator glasses, he glanced around and chose a seat at the bar. Evie walked to the kitchen bar and got him a glass of water.

"Good morning!" she said brightly as she handed it to him.

"Good mahrnin. Coffee?" he replied as he took his glasses off and put them on the counter.

"Of course!" She turned to get a fresh pot and smiled as she poured his coffee. "It's a small town, we pretty much know everyone. Are you new around here?"

"Naht new, really. Just back for work," he answered.

Evie sat the pot of coffee down. "Well, I'm horrible with remembering faces, but I'm pretty sure I'd remember an accent. Did you have that with you last time?" Evie teased.

"This accent? Girls love it. I take it wit' me everywhere I go. Admittedly, it gets stronger at different times. I usually try to keep it subdued." he responded in his Irish brogue.

Evie laughed. "Oh, okay! So, under what circumstances does it get stronger?!"

"Hmm. Let me think. Mahrnin before coffee." He smiled and raised his mug. "Then when I'm verry tired. And when there is a pretty girl interested in my accent." He smiled, winked, and took a sip of coffee.

"Ah. I see." laughed Evie. "Well, let's top you off and you can tell me what you'd like for breakfast."

"Easy 'nough. Two eggs, o'er easy, bacon, toast and a slice of tomato."

"Got it. I'll be right back."

Vicki and Sam watched with interest as Evie took the order back to the kitchen. It wasn't that unusual to see Evie laughing or people talking with her. Everyone loved Evie. She had a gift with people. That was part of her charm as a server, and the diner loved her. Not just the people who worked there or came there. The very building liked her. The booths and cups and walls and windows. It was just right when Evie walked in.

The man sitting at the counter had positioned himself so that his back was not facing the door. The girls watched him, and he watched everything else. He didn't seem interested in the people in the diner as much as the things in the diner. He seemed to be studying the very doors and walls. His eyes travelled around the room until he paused to make eye contact with Vicki and Sam. For a moment, they just stared at each other.

"You know who he is?" asked Vicki, staring.

"Nope," answered Sam, also staring.

"What do you suppose he's here for?"

"No idea."

"I think you should go and ask him."

"What? Are you nuts? Why?" Sam asked, refusing to be the first one to break eye contact.

"I don't know. Just gotta feeling we should know who he is. And I want to know who he is. So?" Vicki said, still watching the man.

On cue, Evie walked in with a plate of food and set it before him. Without blinking, he looked away from them, back around the room, and finally at Evie, smiling. "Thank you, I appreciate it," he said. "What's your name?"

"Evie. You're welcome. And what's yours?" she asked.

"Cody. Cody Bartrug. Interesting place you have here. Are you the owner?" he questioned.

The diner door opened suddenly, hitting the wall, and smashing the bell. Sam was in a good spot to see it happen and nearly choked on her coffee as she kicked Vicki under the table.

"What?!" Vicki jumped. She turned and got a good look at an angry Bryce. He stood in the doorway, arms to his side, hands flexing, feet planted wide, staring toward the counter with a dangerous look on his face. All the fun seemed to be sucked out of the room. The door was still open, and Bryce seemed frozen in the doorway.

Evie looked up, her smile fading, feeling the tension flooding into the room from him.

Sam's habit of anxiously humming tunes when nervous, or excited, or anxious was right on time as Vicki heard the chorus of Taylor Swift's I Knew You Were Trouble.

Vicki couldn't help but stare at her. "Really?"

"Sorry," whispered Sam.

Cody seemed to sit up taller, taking up more space than he did moments before. Bryce stepped into the room and Vicki and Sam could see he was seething. He looked like he hadn't slept at all, and his hands were closed into fists.

Cody warily sat his mug down as he watched Bryce walk towards him. Each was on their guard. Evie looked at Bryce, then to Cody, then back to Bryce. This felt wrong. She moved away from the counter. Without looking at her, Bryce walked up to Cody, who stood up, rather than allow Bryce to tower over him.

"Bartrug." Bryce said, hatefully.

"Bryce. How's it going?" Cody responded. They stood face to face, equal in height, and the mood in the room had gone from friendly to explosive.

"Bryce?" Evie's voice was soft. If anyone had been listening, they'd have heard a thousand questions in that one word.

Without acknowledging Evie, Bryce continued, "What are you doing here?"

"Getting breakfast. You look like you could use some coffee. On me." Even though Cody's words were friendly, they were clipped and guarded. He sounded like he was offering his own challenge to Bryce. Eye to eye, chest to chest. The rest of the diner was still, waiting expectantly, like the pause before the clock strikes twelve.

"Get out," Bryce said, growled, between clenched teeth.

Evie's initial surprise was wearing off, and while she didn't understand what was happening, Bryce running off a customer wasn't going to happen.

"Bryce! What are you doing?!" Her own voice rose while the two men stood, unmoving and unable to hear her.

Cody's finally spoke, "Where is it, Bryce?"

Bryce avoided the question, only said, "This is the last time I tell you. Get. Out."

Cody looked at Bryce and took a half step back, reached for his wallet and opened it for some cash. "Fine. Just paying for my breakfast."

Bryce's hand shot out and grabbed Cody's wrist. "You're not leaving a dime here for her."

Cody looked at Bryce's hand, and back to Bryce. Bryce let go of the hand, and Cody leaned in, making sure he spoke loudly enough for everyone to hear who was listening.

"You win this one, Bryce baby. But you got it, I know it, and I'm not leaving town till I know where it is."

He quickly stepped around Bryce and went out the door.

Vicki and Sam saw Bryce turn and watch Cody leave. He watched until the door closed behind him. His focus turned to Evie, and the diner resumed its normal morning commotion.

"Happy Hour's over," quipped Vicki as she and Sam both stood up from the booth.

"Right behind you," Sam replied as she fell into step behind Vicki on their way to Evie.

"What were you doing, Evie?" said Bryce as he took slow steps to where Evie had moved from behind the corner of the counter. Evie, never before fearing Bryce, hesitated. Something wasn't right. He wasn't acting right.

"What am I doing? Bryce?! What in the world was that about?"

"How long have you known him?" Bryce's voice was clipped and seething.

"Known him? I don't know him! I've never met him before. He came in for coffee! That's what I do. Serve coffee!" Evie's voice was escalating again and now the girls were standing there, completing a triangle, Evie at one point, Bryce facing her at another, and the girls offset between them.

They didn't understand what was happening. But they weren't going to let Bryce take another step towards Evie. Not the way anger was rolling off him right now.

"What was he saying to you?" Bryce looked like he was barely holding it together.

"He was saying his name! And thank you for the food! And that the diner was interesting! What all people say! What is wrong with you?"

The muscles in Bryce's face were tight, as he seemed to be processing what she was saying.

She paused and then continued, "What was he saying to you? What do you have?"

"I have no idea what he was talking about!" Bryce's voice rose to match Evie's, while Vicki and Sam inched closer.

"It sure sounded like it was something you knew about!"

"He was lying!" shouted Bryce.

Vicki and Sam were now in front of Evie, even before he finished the sentence.

Bryce reached up and ran his hand through his already tussled hair. "Listen, I don't know what he was talking about. But you're not to talk to him. Don't even let him in here. And call me if you see him again."

"Are you nuts, Bryce? Now you're telling me who I can or cannot talk to? Since when? I don't own this diner, remember? I'm an employee! And you probably just ruined that! What on earth, Bryce?"

He looked like he was calculating his words. Then he looked directly at Vicki and Sam. "If you love her, you will keep him away from her. Call me if you see him again. Please." He looked at Evie and, without another word, turned and walked out.

CHAPTER SIX

*E*vie was the first one to access the portal to the battlefield. The desert heat blasted her the moment she stood on the burning sand. She came early to be alone before the battle waged. She just wanted a moment to breathe the dry air and to see the red sky. The desert, this desert, was a beautiful place, and she only had moments before her presence would be made known. The beauty would remain, but the battle with the hordes of hell, resisting her prayer and trying to fill her with doubt and fear, would come upon her and she would no longer have the chance to admire this place. Her sword was still sheathed, but she was ready and waiting.

The quiet moment was lost when Sam entered the portal. Sam arrived, squinting with her sword drawn as if she would appear right in the middle of an attack. She squatted down and her eyes scanned the entire area around herself and Evie before she spoke a word. Only when she was satisfied that they were safe now did she put her sword in its sheath, but her hand remained on its hilt.

"Thank you, Sam," Evie whispered.

That her friends would come to such a hard and dangerous place, over and over, on her behalf was overwhelming to her. While she didn't mind being alone, she only truly needed a moment of quiet. Coming here alone to fight a spiritual battle would have been a lonely and dangerous, and who knows how long this fight for answered prayer would take without help from her faithful and godly friends. How would she ever make this up to them or even begin to express her love and thanks? She didn't hope to ever return the favor because that would mean some terrible horror or difficulty would happen to them. She could never wish a battlefield on them.

"I'd say this was no problem, but I'd be lying. I'm sweating already. A desert. Why did you get a desert?" Sam's complaining was good natured. "And while I know I look hot in my leathers, I would wear a cotton moo-moo right now if I could."

"I was surprised to see a desert. I wish we could choose. I'd choose someplace tropical," replied Evie.

"But what would tropical demons look like?" shuddered Sam.

The shimmering of the portal on the other side of Evie delivered Vicki to the desert arena. Not a hair out of place and still looking like a model. The tall, bronzed blonde looked like she belonged here.

"She's glistening. Good grief," said Sam. "Don't you ever just sweat?"

"Not if I can help it," Vicki replied as she scanned the horizon through her aviators. "We've been spotted. They're coming."

The three women stood shoulder to shoulder. Evie pulled her sword out. She noticed her sword was changing into stronger, higher-grade steel. She could tell every time she came here to the desert just how much better her weapon was performing, how it was forming to her hand and how swiftly it could now slice a demon in half. And by the looks of the size of the approaching horde, she would need it to work even faster.

The air shimmered with heat as silhouettes of the demons came into view.

Sam spoke, "See how the dust and sand are swirling around them? That means they are huffing it. Super aggressive, I'd say. Wonder what spooked them?"

"I think it means they are ticked off," said Evie. "That's good news for us, right? Means they aren't winning. But, holy moly, there's a lot of them."

Gently rocking back and forth, side to side, each woman held her sword with both hands, ready for the onslaught.

"Corgs!" shouted Sam. These were the most expendable demons, therefore there were millions of them being bred somewhere in the depths of the earth. They were not hard to kill, but after hours and hours of swinging their swords, weariness can set in, allowing even the smallest and weakest demon to get in a good swipe and do damage. While the Corgs weren't the fiercest, they were still demons. Anything birthed in the halls of hell is an enemy. The women knew this, knew their need for encouragement, the need to pay attention and not be distracted.

The Corgs sounded their high-pitched screams as they moved closer and within fighting distance. Sam, Evie, and Vicki took turns, one by one slicing through the Corgs, releasing the maggots from where their heads once sat. The Corgs only came one at a time. It was as if they were testing the women, methodically moving, gauging strength and swiftness. Sam noticed this first.

"They're hitting us in a pattern," she said as she nonchalantly lopped the head off the incoming Corg. "Watch. After me, it's always Evie, then Vicki, then back to me."

Evie didn't have time to watch as the next Corg came screaming her way. With a slice of the wrist, she easily beheaded the little creature. But Vicki could see that the Corgs were as good as lining up, waiting for their turn to die. The problem was that the lines were so long their ends blended into the horizon. They'd be here all day.

"This is ridiculous!" shouted Vicki, as she took her turn in the assault. "It's too predictable, too easy. This is going to get boring."

"Do you think this is planned?" asked Evie.

"Well, it would be a stupid plan, right?" said Sam.

"Not if we get worn out with these unending small fights," said Vicki, realizing the truth of her words as she said them.

Small yet constant, hit after hit. Nothing to bring you to your knees in a desperate cry for God. It would be a defeat by little hits, a nonstop barrage of a horde of demons. You knew you could fight with little effort. But how many women have fallen right here on a battlefield fighting the Corgs? It had to be quite a number for this to even be a tactic. The Corgs seemed confident in their mission.

Hit, die, repeat. Repeat all day everyday if needed. Eventually the warrior slips up, looks the other way, or just gets weary. Was anything worth this tedious fight? Wouldn't it be a better use of time to just absorb the pain and small cord of bondage than to come to the battlefield to pray? Any burden, once heavy enough to battle in prayer over, soon seemed insignificant.

Evie understood this. She'd experienced this a billion times before. Pray over a hurt feeling? Suck it up, Buttercup. Kneel because she got a new bill for a late toll fee she forgot to pay? It was her own fault. Little by little, these relentless hits to the heart, the burden and stress, takes a toll. Corgs definitely had an effective strategy.

But not today. This battle needed to be over. And it wouldn't be if they didn't step it up. They needed to start using the Sword of God, as was within their rights as the daughters of God. Using big guns on the little linemen from hell? You bet.

Evie stepped forward as another Corg dropped to Sam's feet. The change was obvious to her battlefield sisters and to the Corgs. Did she notice a look of fear in the next one's eyes before she thrust her sword into his belly? Why, yes, she did. Now they were afraid.

The desert pulsed with heat and the sound of the girl's grunts, as the falling bodies, the demons, started to sound louder than the thrumming from the portal. Sam was covered with sweat and slime, but her razored hair and tattooed body looked like it was just getting warmed up. Vicki was a tanned weapon, an unexpected killing machine. Evie looked at her sisters, here in a desert doing battle for her. Coming to prayer on her behalf, doing the hard, deliberate work of battlefield prayer bound them in a covenant of friendship she would never forget. It was in this loving pause that a demon lunged at her, out of the order of the steady pattern they had observed for the last half hour. Breaking rank, the Corg squealed his high-pitched scream, sending a chill down the humans' spines. It was a wicked cry from the belly of a demon.

The Corg lunged forward and grabbed Evie by the arm, holding a tight grip yet not breaking the skin. She looked at it and could see the drool dripping out of the corner of the mouth, the pulsing at the temple of its mottled gray and brown leathery skin. It was obviously hungry with lustful desire. The smell and the sight of the maggots were filling the Corgs with horrible desires, and Evie knew this was time to pray like she hadn't in a long time. Her cry went out and the scream from her own gut startled and repulsed the Corg, who released her. Sam and Vicki both looked at her and saw her fear and panic.

"You okay, Ev?" asked Sam.

"I am now, but we need to finish this up. Have either of you heard from Yahweh yet? Any clue as to what we are supposed to do or find?"

It was Vicki's turn to behead the next Corg. She did it with smoothness and finesse. "No, but it's not here. We need to get moving."

Sam looked beyond the immediate line of Corgs and could see the end in sight. There weren't any more coming from their own portal from the belly of the earth, so as soon as they can slice and chop these bad boys up, maybe they could find a clue. Maybe it would be an oasis again, or perhaps a map or even buried treasure. What else could there possibly be in a desert place such as this?

It wasn't long before the last demon finally died, unhappy and unfulfilled. It wasn't bad enough that headless bodies of demons lay strewn about with maggots slithering and feasting on their own hosts, but the awareness that these evil beings were also sexually aware reminded them that this was no game. Not that they needed reminding, but it's not like the subject ever came up in ladies' Bible studies. No one really wants to know or talk about these things. And Evie sometimes wished she was still ignorant of such evil.

Each warrior picked their way through the bodies, grabbing for each other when they started to slip and slide as if on ice. They finally moved onto dry sand that no longer was stained with blood or the stench of Corg. Looking back at what they had just defeated, the numerous piles of Corgs, the women knew that the victory only came from Yahweh.

Where is He? Where is the answer to this prayer?

The wind began blowing, and the sand began bearing ripples on its skin. Now that there was a moment for the women to walk and talk, Evie knew there were going to be questions about Bryce, questions she still didn't have answers to. Sam and Vicki had a right to ask and to be answered after their time and fight on this battlefield-her battlefield. This was all happening because of the turmoil in her life. And the answer to this turmoil was to be found here in the desert. Where Corgs are aroused, with maggots eating their hosts, a Ventar could be lurking under the sand at the same time, spying on them or waiting to thrust its angry head through the sand and take a chunk out of their legs. Evie remembered this, and started stabbing the sand with her sword, Sam and Vicki quickly following suit.

"Anyone remember the last time we were here?" asked Sam. "Anyone want to take bets on what lies just over the knoll before us?"

"That was the creepiest thing I've ever seen in my life," said Vicki. "But the demon with a large...member...might be a close second. I need vinegar poured into my eyes."

Evie remembered that there was still the mystery of someone else coming to the battlefield. Someone very strong. "So still, no one's told anyone about my burden, right?"

"No," said Vicki as she pulled her sword out of the sand.

"Nope," answered Sam as she stabbed her sword into the sand.

The sun set behind the girls as they walked. It could be a good thing if this was a normal desert, but this was a spiritual one. You didn't want to be caught out here with the Corgs, Ventars and Snappers when the sun went down, and the ground got cold.

They needed to find a portal. They'd been here in prayer for a long time with nothing much to show for it. If they dwelled on the fact that they'd come to pray over and over, exhausting themselves without getting an answer, they'd be tempted to just lay down and stop fighting or never step through a portal again. What would be the point?

But Evie had children that would be affected by what happened here. She needed an answer from Yahweh. She needed His help and His answer to her need. Where would they find it in this desert? It obviously wasn't at the oasis.

How did women pray for years over the same issue? How did they battle every day, several times a day, for decades before they found their answers? Evie's respect for the aged and faithful women in her church was beginning to grow. And so was an idea. Maybe there was someone who'd done this before, been here before, to a desert battlefield.

Yahweh, as always, never let her leave without a gift or offering of some sort being granted to her. She held the wisdom and the idea in her heart and spoke to her faithful girlfriends.

"Find a portal. I know what I need to do."

Climbing up the knoll of sand that had seemed like a football field away one moment ago, the prayer warriors stood on top. The portal they wanted and needed was just over there, behind the mounds of dismembered demons.

Someone else was here.

Again.

After he left the diner, Bryce walked to his truck, knowing Cody wouldn't have gone far. He wasn't disappointed when he saw Cody's car parked along the street, a few spaces away, with him leaning on it. Waiting. The "talk" with the girls in the diner had diffused some of the instant panic and rage Bryce had felt when he had opened the door and saw Cody talking with Evie. Bryce figured Cody would show himself again once he had seen him at the gas station the night before, but never had he thought it would be here or to Evie.

In all the time he had spent transporting for these guys, not once had his family been brought up. But it wasn't an accident that Cody was at the gas station and there was no way coming into the diner was a coincidence. Bryce may have been uninformed on all the details of the ring he'd been working for, and he may have been stupid in many ways regarding his involvement, but he knew a threat when he saw it. This guy leaning on his car with his arms crossed staring at him was exactly that.

As he approached, Cody didn't even bother to stand up. Just his posture angered Bryce, but he knew acting on that feeling wasn't going to get him what he needed. He needed answers. They'd faced each other, Cody looking as nonchalant as he had inside the diner, Bryce alert, braced for whatever was going to be needed.

"I see you're back," observed Cody.

"What do you want?" replied Bryce.

"I thought I made that obvious inside. I want what you took, and I want it now. That's it. Turn it over, give it back, and I'm gone."

"I don't know what you're talking about. So how about you skip to you being gone?"

"See, here's the problem," said Cody. "I don't believe you. No one believes you. I think you're a liar. I think you played this all off pretty well, to your own advantage. I think you played dumb. I don't know, maybe you weren't playing that part, but you convinced certain people that you were just a sad little man who didn't know what he was involved with. They bought it. You did a few months in a county jail, and voila! You're back! Funny, isn't it? Really? Most guys wouldn't have been quite so gutsy to try to come back here. Did you try to play that same line off to your wife? How'd that go, by the way? Did she actually believe you?" Cody finally stood as he continued. "So, did you tell her? Tell her what you'd managed to hide away for yourself? Where is it, Bryce?"

Bryce had been listening, even while his thoughts were shooting off in all other directions. But when Cody mentioned Evie, everything stopped. His focus narrowed. Slowly, he stepped towards Cody, his body tense and wary. They stood face to face, the air full of tension.

Bryce answered, "I don't care what you think. I don't care what you do or do not know. But just in case you have an issue with your ability to hear and understand, let me clarify. I do not know what you are talking about. As for my wife, she's off limits. This place, off limits. You want to talk to me, you let me know when and where. If you show yourself here, again, I'll have no problem going to the cops. They might find it very interesting that you're here. In fact, I find it very interesting myself. Why aren't you holed up in a cell with the rest of your group? What lies did you tell?

"Here's the thing," Bryce continued, "I know you. I know who you are and what your role was. Whatever it is you're looking for, I don't have it. And unless you want this to get very personal and very, let's just call it involved, keep moving and leave me out of it."

The two stood squared off, each assessing the other. Cody moved first, away and towards his car. Opening his door and settling in the seat, he turned to Bryce.

"It almost sounds convincing. Almost. You do what you have to do, and I'll do what I have to." With a flashy smile that set Bryce's teeth on edge, he finished. "I'll be in touch. Don't worry, I got your number." He pulled out of the space, flipped him a little wave, and roared off down the street.

Bryce had originally planned to drop in on Evie at the diner and have an easy, light, conversation, enjoying breakfast and coffee together. It was supposed to have been a chance for her to see him relaxed, approachable and hopefully cracking the door between him and her open a little further.

Instead, he'd ended up having her protective friends feel the need to surround and isolate him, as if he were the threat. He wasn't exactly sure what the little pixie and the blonde thought they were going to do if he actually had been the threat. And did Evie even seem concerned about Cody? No. No, she did not. She was more concerned with him. And it was obvious to him that it didn't matter what he said now. She and her friends were not going to believe it. He didn't even know her friends. They seemed to care about Evie, but they also seemed to have tunnel vision where he was concerned. Not that anyone had said that, but his own intuition picked up on their disapproval.

That might have mattered to him yesterday. But not today. Whatever they thought of him now ranked right up there with caring about the agenda of the town council meeting. He didn't care about what they thought, but he did care about protecting Evie from Cody, and he was prepared to tell them that when he went back at lunch time.

But when he arrived, Evie wasn't standing behind the counter. Instead, it was Doris, the owner of the diner herself.

When he asked about Evie, Doris looked him over and replied with, "Glad to see you too, Bryce. If I didn't know you better, I'd think you've been causing some trouble for Evie."

"I'm not trying to, Doris. I'm trying to fix things. Do you know when she'll be back?"

"Yes, darling, I do. But I'm thinking if she wanted you to fix things, she'd call you and ask you herself."

"Yeah, that thought did cross my mind," he replied, trying to hide the sarcasm, "but I was going for the casual, pop in, see how she's doing type thing."

"Oh, I see. From what I heard that plan didn't go so well this morning," she said as she moved a coffee cup toward him and started to fill it.

"Okay, no, it didn't," he admitted. "I just want to talk to her about that. I'm pretty sure she and her friends didn't see it the way I saw it, at all. In fact, I know they didn't. And they need to. Every time I feel like there is some progress, some possible path back for us, something else moves in. Now I can't even see that path anymore."

Setting down the coffee pot, Doris softened her tone, "Maybe something else is moving in. Have you considered it might not be flesh and blood?"

Bryce took a sip of his coffee, left a dollar on the counter, turned to leave, and said, "Yeah, I considered it. Then I saw it standing here at the counter chit chatting with my wife. Thanks, Doris. I'll see you later."

As he turned to go, Doris grabbed his hand. "I'm praying for you."

Bryce tried to smile but couldn't. He squeezed her hand instead. "I appreciate that. But along with that, please keep that guy out."

Doris watched him walk out the door and whispered a prayer. "Lord, there are a few people around here who need some answers. Now might be good."

After getting off work, Evie had an hour to herself before the babysitter brought the kids home from the park and her evening would be taken over with dinner and laundry. She'd left the diner earlier than usual, after Doris came in, and she, Sam and Vicki had spent some of that time in prayer.

What she'd seen, what she'd felt, on the battlefield, was still fresh in her mind and she'd planned to spend a few minutes visiting with the one who'd introduced her to this work of prayer, Mrs. Taylor.

She knocked on the door to the little house that looked like it belonged in the 1950s, complete with a narrow cement walkway to a doorstep with metal railings. She saw the heavy drape move in the window, and the door opened.

"Evie! Won't you come on in?"

Evie smiled, opened the screen door, and stepped into the cozy house. "Thank you so much, Mrs. Taylor. How are you feeling today?"

"Oh, you know, in my head I'm a young girl, but my body moves like it has forgotten that, deciding to be an arthritic old woman instead."

"Are you hurting today?"

"Not enough for you to worry about. I've just set the tea, so how about we sit, and you tell me what's on your mind?"

While Evie poured the tea for each of them, she asked what she'd been thinking about. "Well, I just have some questions about the battlefield."

"Oh, I imagine you do. You've been called in a few times now, haven't you?"

"Yes, I have. How do you know that?"

Chuckling a little, she answered, "Some things become obvious when you've been there awhile yourself."

"Really, well, that's kind of what I wanted to talk to you about. The last couple of times we've been there, we've come across something that is kind of freaky."

"Who is 'we'?"

"Me, Sam and Vicki. I've been there for some personal matters, and they joined me. Both by my invitation and since then also by the call."

"I love it when the shofar blows."

"Yes, me too," Evie smiled warmly. "But every time I've been there, there's been evidence that we were not alone."

"Of course, you're not alone! The enemy is also there."

"Right, we've been in a few fierce battles, and some that were more annoying than anything. We've found rest as well as strength there. But I think there's something, or someone, else there. Whoever it is, they are strong. Stronger than the three of us. How do we know who or what it is? Or if it's even on our side?"

Setting down her teacup, the old lady sat back in her chair, hands folded. She was considering her words, taking her time.

Finally, she spoke. She spoke as one who was recounting her own experiences. "On the battlefield," she quietly began, "things are not like here. Our bodies are not what give us strength there. You may see it that way, but it is not that way. It is different. Alternate would be the word your age knows. The spirit, whether good or evil, valiant or cowardly, is not bound by these earthly bodies."

"So, you think it was someone from here, someone human?" asked Evie.

"I didn't say that. It may be. Have you told anyone about your battle besides your two friends?

"No. I haven't. And they haven't shared it either. Like I said, it is a...personal matter. I have only shared with them because, well, I don't want anyone to know yet."

Mrs. Taylor smiled warmly. "Some battles are meant to be private. Some require great numbers."

"The scenes look as if it's someone on our side."

"Do not be deceived by the way it appears. There is no loyalty among the evil ranks. None. They will turn on each other if it serves their purpose. Perhaps it was a trap, or a moment of great passion, such as rage."

"Uh, speaking of passion. Um, you never, no one ever, I didn't know that the enemy could um, you know…"

"How in the world do I ask this old lady this," Evie thought to herself. "Just spit it out, Ev."

"When we were battling, one of the demons seemed to be, well, aroused," she spat out.

The old lady just looked at her, the silence in the room accentuated by an old clock ticking on the wall behind them.

"So…" Evie continued. "They can do that?"

"Yes. They can. All that is good, beautiful, pure, lovely, they pervert, twist and use for their own evil purposes. They use this perverted good to terrorize any human who gets close, paralyzing them in fear if they can. Amongst the enemy, all that God intended for pleasure they distort and make grotesque. They serve themselves and only themselves, becoming their own idol and master."

Evie felt that more was being said here than she understood. But, for the moment, she was still stuck on the thought that what she experienced was to be expected. "So, it's not enough that they have weapons…"

"Don't go there, don't go there, Evie," her thoughts warned. But she pushed on, "It's not enough that they can fight. They can also…assault… us?"

"Harm can come to the body, but it can come to the mind and the spirit in many ways."

"Great, now the Oracle is becoming all cryptic," Evie thought.

"How do we defend against that?!" Evie asked.

The old lady smiled. "Who is your defense?"

"Yahweh."

"Who is your shield?" "Yahweh."

"Who is your strong tower?"

"Yahweh."

"Remember that." She paused. "Now, let me ask you a question. What are you fighting for?"

Evie looked at the old lady before her, knowing she was a veteran in these wars. She knew that she could tell countless stories of victories won in battle, and maybe some lost. Perhaps her own battle was trivial. It seemed likely that it was not, in the big picture, of much importance to anyone but her. She felt like the lack of an answer or direction from Yahweh meant that she was wasting time and energy where it wasn't needed.

She replied softly, "I don't know anymore. I thought I was fighting for my family. But now it just feels endless. It feels like I am fighting just to fight. I was looking for an answer, but nothing is happening."

Picking up her cup of tea again, the old lady responded, "Oh, yes. I know that feeling. Did you feel the call to pray?"

"Yes... I did. I do."

"Then don't stop. When you wake in the night, step on the field. There is a reason. Whatever it is you are fighting for, don't stop until it's over. Not for anything or anyone. Fight. And one more thing, dear."

"What's that?"

"I've seen your young man. I may be old, but I'm not dead. Something tells me he's worth fighting for."

With that, she stirred in another teaspoon of sugar and smiled that sweet old lady smile.

CHAPTER SEVEN

*L*oden followed Jangis, Balid and a small pack of Corgs and Ventars. They were on a mission to stage a battle in front of the woman so the one could get a good look at Loden, an angel of light. It had been a while since Loden had performed his most favorite trick and his excitement was hard to control. But demon rule number one, never let another demon know you want something, or they will take it for themselves. There is no honor among demons.

While he'd been to a desert battlefield many times, Loden hadn't been here with this target and didn't know where her portals were. Along with his excitement, he also felt resentment. He resented having to follow and not lead. If he was honest, he was burning with anger. It felt like rocket fuel was in his veins. The only thing that could soothe him was imagining how much better he must look next to these ugly, inferior demons. His transformation was completed in private, the ritual known only to himself. If the target came upon them suddenly, she would think he was a captive, in no way thinking he was the leader. He would have to be patient and finish the job. A promotion was the motivation for this teamwork.

The sand, thick and deep, made keeping on course difficult work. Slowly, the pack advanced through the mounds and arrived at a portal the Corgs had promised was used by the target. Evie, he must start referring to her as Evie. Remembering her name would be easy. Almost like Eve, the hated and dreaded mother of the living. The one who was hated above all women.

The Covenant of the Serpent and the Seed had not gone unbroken in eight millennia. If anything, the hatred had grown between their master and women. Her seed had been weakened many times and over many centuries, but it was not at a weakening stage this decade. The war on women sometimes had negative outcomes, and they were enduring one this season. Women were producing stronger seed, a higher quality offspring that were proving quite difficult for some other hordes and on some other battlefields.

Loden would never, could never, forget about the Covenant of the Serpent and the Seed and was so looking forward to taking out one of Eve's offspring. They just needed to find her. She had been coming to this battlefield long enough to win her own assassination team. She would be back, and he was ready. He flipped one of his long braids over his strong, muscular, tanned shoulder. Yes, he knew how that move looked, having perfected it in the looking glass after hours and hours of AOL (angel of light) training.

"Here!" shouted a Corg, as he pointed to a portal. The cluster of demons stopped and stared at the passageway to the realm that was forbidden them. They've heard tales of what was on the other side, but no one they knew had ever made the crossing. No one had even tried. It was the topic around many fires, but that's all it was, talk and superstition.

Loden spoke, broke the quiet and interrupted the portal staring. "Let's move over the hill and out of sight. When we hear her come through, you three Corgs engage her," he pointed to the demons nearest him. "I'll move into view and do my thing. The rest of you come to assault me. She will see me, and she will be hooked."

Jangis had traveled with the AOL agent all day without saying a word. Styren was acting like the Jader, Loden, was someone from the halls of heroes. And he wasn't. Unless it was a Swastik, Jangis wasn't going to give it honor or respect. Jaders looked down their unclogged noses at everyone. And look at how hideous the disguise! He couldn't stop looking at him. But the vanity of a Jader always assumed that you stared at him because of his beauty. The Jader couldn't have been more wrong.

"Pardon me, agent Loden, but the orders were to get you near enough to touch the target," Jangis said.

"Evie," corrected Loden. "Call her Evie."

"Right, Evie," he said her name carefully. "You are to get close enough to...Evie... to make contact. Not eye contact, but, like, real contact. Get your DNA on her. It doesn't work just by looking."

Loden could swear he heard mocking in that Ventar's voice. He was looking at the Ventar to see if eyes rolled or even if they moved because they could stage that fight right here, right now. Oh, he couldn't wait to see the look in their eyes when they realized it was not a practice fight but a real one. He would leave the Ventars for last before finally killing these two idiots.

But before Loden could act on his Ventar hatred, the thrumming of the portal began and the target, Evie, was coming through. The three expendable Corgs left to meet and assail her, acting on his orders. She came through the portal ready, and without much struggle, took their heads off. With quick thought and action, Loden began making scuffling noises and grunts.

He clanged his sword with some of the Ventars' swords standing nearby. It took a minute, but they finally caught on to his plan to draw her over this mound of sand by the sound of a battle.

Loden waited until just the right moment to change this faux battle into a real one. The Ventars that would be lost today would be martyrs for the kingdom. They should be thanking him. The grunting and sword tapping continued, each demon looking at the crest of the sand hill. They were not disappointed when she topped the sand pile and her silhouette stood against the clear blue sky.

Evie heard a skirmish just after she came through the portal and finished off the first Corgs. She had assumed she would meet Sam or Vicki here, but when she topped the drift where the sound was coming from, nothing could have surprised her more than what she saw. A man. A real man, surrounded by the squealing Corgs and a mass of short, teethy Ventars. The Ventars had not turned black yet, so the battle must have just started.

She scanned the area to see if more demons were on the horizon, but thankfully there weren't. She gazed back at the tall and striking man, here on her battlefield fighting demons. He looked like Thor, and he fought like Thor. She could only stare as she watched him swing his sword and cut off the head of the nearest Corg. He swung in a complete circle and then impaled his sword right into the heart of the Ventar that still had his sword sheathed. Ah, now the Ventars began changing color. They were mad. And what seemed a little skirmish now seemed hostile and fierce. Whoever this person, this man-Thor was, he could use her help.

Evie ran down the sand drift and joined the fray, working from the back side of the horde. The Corgs and Ventars realized she was there and besting them as fast as the man-Thor, they began to focus their attention on her. She was strong, and the blackened Ventars small heads were not too brawny for her. Seeing an ally on the battlefield gave Evie a strength she didn't know she had. She thought about the piles of defeated demons she and her friends encountered and assumed this man was the one responsible for the carnage. He must be fighting for her! Who was he, and why did she matter to him?

Loden couldn't have been happier. Killing Corgs and Ventars in the bright light of day with the blessing of Oridon was a dream come true. When he spotted his human target, he burned with hatred. The Corg standing next to him received the full slice of the sword and was split from the top of the head down to his hip joints, dropping in halves. Even the maggots did not survive.

Oh, yes, she noticed him and if he was not mistaken, she was admiring him. He made sure to flex with every swing of the blade. He'd had to squat to avoid his own head being taken off by a Ventar that had taken offense at being used for the greater good. He was happy for the opportunity to show off his muscular and tanned thighs. His braided hair looked good. He had no doubt whatsoever that he appeared as the angel of light that he was trained to be. She moved closer, apparently coming to his aid. The real test of his strength would be to not kill her, while hiding the loathing and disgust he felt from the very sight of her face.

While the Ventars were momentarily shaken and infuriated at Loden's very real attack on them, it was the Corgs who remained focused on the mission. Good old Corgs. Task oriented grunts are what they were. Machines. They kept backing away *from Loden, allowing him to advance on them, leading them closer and closer to Evie. Soon, the two would be close enough for contact.*

Loden followed the Corgs into the battle and as Evie became surrounded, he saw his opportunity. With his deceptive smile, Loden moved within sword distance of the human target. His posture was strong, and his breath remained easy. He exaggerated each and every movement he made.

Evie couldn't believe it. For once, she came here to battle without all the weight of it resting on her and her strength alone, forgetting that it never did. She didn't know who her new ally was, but right now, it didn't really matter. She continued to drop enemies with very little effort, and if she had stopped to think about it, she might have realized that the Corgs were all but impaling themselves on her sword. The Ventars were angry, but their anger seemed projected at Thor and not her. Huh. Eventually, Evie and Thor found themselves back-to-back with only a few Corgs and Ventars remaining. Gripping their swords, swaying to the same rhythm, eyes focused on the last remaining targets, Evie and Thor knew the battle was all but over. And so did the demons.

With looks of hostility and hatred from Jangis and Balid, Loden watched them turn and trot away. Evie started to pursue, but Loden reached out and grabbed her by the arm. "Mission accomplished," he thought.

"Hey, let them go. We've more than done enough here," Loden spoke in his smoothest, most attractive voice.

Evie looked at the hand on her arm, then looked over her shoulder at her ally. "Who are you, and why are you here on my battlefield?"

"I'm your friend. You know how this works. A friend of mine asks for prayer for a friend of his and eventually we hook up-I mean, meet up-here. Glad I could help. You seemed to be in trouble. They attacked me just as I showed up. Quite a hostile bunch. I'm surprised someone so little and charming could have so many enemies. Forgive me," Loden bowing in a dramatic way, "My name is Jim."

Jim. She hadn't expected that. Not Rambo or Thor.

"Thank you for what you've done. For coming to help me, a stranger. I don't even know what to think or how to thank you properly." She moved out of his grasp.

Loden had already put his scent and touch on her. But his vanity was not yet satisfied, and he moved in closer to her. He reached up to touch her hair and move it off her shoulder.

"You are not alone, Evie," he gagged out her name. "You don't have to be alone or afraid anymore." Knowing when to leave a stage was key. Loden dropped his hand and put a look of desire on his face. He stepped back ever so slowly. One, two, three steps. Then he turned and ran away. Into the sunset.

Evie touched her strand of hair and the place on her arm that Jim had touched. She was no longer alone, or afraid. It was all she ever wanted.

These twenty-four hours seemed to last longer than even possible for Bryce. He'd left the diner, went to work his afternoon shift, and having just clocked out, sat in his truck in the parking spot outside the small factory. He watched everyone else leaving, while he sat just outside the reach of the building's security light.

He'd called her three times. He tried to tell himself she was probably busy with the kids, but the feeling in the pit of his stomach reminded him that she'd been noticing his calls for a few weeks now and it wasn't likely that she was suddenly too busy.

As he sat in the truck, he couldn't stop his mind from running through every possible scenario. He imagined everything from one of the kids falling and being taken to the ER, to Bartrug sitting in the living room having coffee with his wife and kids. Whatever it was, she wasn't picking up the phone. "It really didn't matter, did it?" he thought. Bartrug knows who Evie is, and whether she knows it or not, she's not safe.

Putting the truck in gear, he pulled out of the parking lot and turned in the direction of the house. It wasn't a long drive as the small town was deserted at this time of night. Brick store fronts, the diner on the corner, lamp posts lining the streets. It seemed hard to imagine that anything bad could ever come to this sleepy town. Bryce tried not to think the bad had arrived at his own invitation.

Parking in front of her house might be a bit obvious, he thought, even if every person on the street was asleep. Choosing a spot a few houses down made it easy to see the house and give him a little peace of mind that they hadn't been invaded by the creep from his past. He turned off his lights as he rolled up and shut the engine off, all while not looking away from the little house that held his wife and children.

He almost smiled when he saw the kitchen lights on through the window over the sink. He would have smiled if it hadn't ticked him off so much. There were no other cars besides hers in the drive, so she was alone. She wasn't in the hospital. She wouldn't be there if one of the kids were in the hospital. So that meant she was sitting in the kitchen.

Ignoring his calls.

Bryce picked up his cell and hit the number he'd last dialed and waited. As he heard the pickup of the voicemail, "Hello! This is Evie, please..." he ended the call before it finished, the sound of her voice not helping his anger at all.

"Maybe I should just go knock on the door," he thought. "That's a stupid idea," he argued with himself. "If she wanted to talk to you, she'd have answered the phone."

As the inner debate continued, he saw her shadow pass by in the window. His first thought was that she needed better window protection. His second thought was just a feeling, a feeling of loss, and hopelessness.

He was an idiot to think he could come back. He was an idiot to think that she'd listen to him, even if he was right about anything. It wouldn't matter what he said about Bartrug. He'd left her and now it didn't matter what he meant or what he'd wanted before or wanted now. There was no way she would hear anything he said.

He stared at the window, waiting for her shadow to pass by again, feeling completely lost. After a while, he felt that despair shift into something else. Anger.

Evie had seen her phone ring. She'd wanted to pick up. Her nurturing nature wanted to see if Bryce was okay. The fear she'd felt earlier in the diner had begun to fade, and she chalked that up to her inability to hold a grudge.

The truth was, she really didn't want to talk to him. Not now. Everything was off. She'd come home and spent a relatively quiet evening with the kids, cooking dinner, getting baths done. Both kids had asked if Daddy was coming over, but it wasn't that hard to deflect the question, even with Kendall looking at her with his perceptive eyes. What did they think, anyway? That he'd be over every day now?

They probably did think that, and maybe she had made it way too easy for them to hope, but one thing was evident; she needed to slow this train down.

She'd been looking, praying, battling for an answer, and she needed to examine whether today was in fact, the answer she'd been searching for.

Trying to figure out if Bryce was lying or not made her head hurt. And today had made her heart hurt as well. One thing was obvious; the two men had known each other. There was history there, history Evie didn't know anything about. She'd been sitting at the table, praying and thinking, when she figured it was time to talk to the girls. She knew they'd be waiting, and it was completely possible if she didn't call them, she'd be getting a text right about the time she was falling asleep.

She dialed Sam's number.

"About time," came the greeting. "Want me to add Vick in?"

"It would probably be easier than doing this twice."

"K, hang on." After a few seconds, she heard her other friend join in.

"You're aging me, Ev, aging me."

Evie couldn't help but laugh. "Right, please let me age like you!"

"Okay, this meeting has been called to order. I move we skip the reading of the last meeting's notes and move right onto new business. So. What's the scoop, Evie?" started Sam.

"I second that move and call you on the business," added Vicki.

"What? This isn't poker, Vicki! This is business. You don't call in business meetings. You make motions and notes," Sam continued.

"Stop!" Evie butted in, then sighed, "This would be so much easier in person."

"Want us to come over?" Vicki quickly offered.

"No. This is fine. I'm just exhausted. And tired. Can I be exhausted and tired?"

"I know all this chit chat is exhausting me, and I personally am tired of it. So, yes, it's possible," said Sam.

"Nice, Sam," Vicki responded. "Go ahead, Evie, fill us in."

After a pause where you could hear each girl take a deep breath, Evie got started. "Okay, to start with, I don't know who the guy is. I know his name is Cody Bartrug. I know he has an accent that rolls his r's. I assume he's not local."

"Ooooo, sexy! You should have talked to him, Sam!" piped in Vicki.

"No, I should not have talked to him. For one, I don't like rolling r's. Two, there was no time to talk to him before Evie's guy stormed in, and third, I didn't want to."

Getting them to stay on track was grating on Evie's nerves. "Anywho," she continued, "I also know that he and Bryce know each other, but I don't know him. He asked Bryce where something was and…"

"Where what was?" interrupted Sam.

"I don't know what. I was getting to that. He just asked where it is?"

"What is it?" asked Vicki.

"Like I said. I. Don't. Know. He wanted to know where something was. Bryce said he didn't know what he was talking about, and you guys heard the rest."

"Well, Bryce seemed pretty intent that Leather Guy was lying. So, I guess with our unparalleled deductive reasoning skills, we can deduce and settle on the fact that one of them is lying," reasoned Sam.

"Wow. You're amazing. I can't even. How do you do that, and so fast?!" laughed Vicki.

"Herding elephants," thought Evie.

"Yes, Sam, I think it's safe to say one of them is lying. I think it's also safe to say that unless it directly affects me, I don't think it actually affects me." The line was silent long enough for Evie to look at her phone and see they were, in fact, still connected. "Guys?" she asked.

"Sorry," Sam said. "I just thought you said this didn't affect you. As in, the possibility of Bryce lying not affecting you. I thought that's what you said. Then I realized that you would not possibly say that. So, repeat what you said."

"Sam, be serious," said Evie quietly.

"I am being serious. Forget for a moment whether Bryce or Leather Guy is lying and tell me why you think it doesn't matter to you."

"I'm joining Sam on this, Ev. If you're considering your life back with Bryce, then it matters. It matters a lot," Vicki added, gently.

Evie sighed. "I don't know. I don't know if I am considering my life back with him."

Evie could feel the lightness of the conversation change into more of a heart to heart and she suddenly felt tired. And maybe even a little angry. "Isn't that what you both wanted to hear anyway?!" she asked.

She heard Sam blow out a breath while Vicki spoke. "Evie, where is this coming from? Honestly, we can't say we've been supportive of Bryce." Evie snorted. "But..." Vicki continued, "we have been supportive of you. We've been supportive of you exploring and searching for answers about your marriage. I know that today seems to have just caused more questions, but are you saying now that you don't even want answers? You don't want to know for sure what is happening?"

"This is what I'm saying right now. I'm tired. I'm tired of my emotions going all over the place with him. I'm tired of feeling hope and then feeling confusion. I'm tired of hoping we are on the same page to realize we probably aren't even in the same book. I don't want to do this again. I don't want to start over to find myself standing alone. Again." She knew she was starting to ramble, but the words kept coming.

"I got to this place because Bryce left me. He made decisions for this family alone. Bad decisions. And whatever his motives then, it doesn't matter now. They just don't! Because right now, today, all I see is a man who left me once, and who still hasn't told me the whole truth. What's stopping him from leaving me again? I don't want to fight alone!" she finished, exhausted.

Sam quietly responded, "Ev, you haven't been alone. We've been there. We are here. And you, of all people, know God has not left you to do this alone."

"Right." Evie said with some finality. "You've been there. But you know who hasn't been there? Bryce. You know who has been fighting, looking for direction? Me. And yes, you two have had my back, and front, and side. But who should have been there? Bryce. And frankly, maybe that is my answer. Maybe I'm supposed to look at that field, and ask, why is he not here?? So that's what I did. I went back tonight, and I asked that. And you know what I saw? Not him. I remembered how it felt to be alone. I remembered that he had made choices that hurt us. I remembered that he's still keeping something from me. And I might be somewhat new to the battle, but I do know that the answers aren't always given by a pillar of fire and smoke. Sometimes we have to see what's in front of our face and accept it for what it is!"

"Do you still feel bonded to him?" asked Vicki.

Evie knew what that meant. The bond between a husband and wife is not easily broken. It can be damaged, frayed, but broken is not done easily. The weight of this question landed on Evie's chest like an elephant. "I don't know. I don't know if what I have been feeling is based on history, or hormones, or just a desire for something I want but don't have. All I know is I'm not sure anymore."

Sam asked, "You went in alone tonight?"

"Yes, I did," Evie answered.

"Okay," Sam continued, "I know that a lot of times we battle on our own. But I feel the need to remind you that something else has been there. Something or someone else. We've seen the results of it, we've felt it. And I'm a little worried that it's not as simple as you are making it seem. It might not be as easy as saying 'you're tired, so it's over'. Have you thought of that?"

"Of course, I've thought of that!" Evie said. "But I also have to ask myself why? Why is this of consequence? Why would anyone, for or against us, spend time there besides us? Have you thought that maybe we are wasting time? Maybe we are supposed to be directing our energy for something a little more important? I've been fine for six months. I was fine before that even. Our failed marriage is actually old news. And I can swing my sword around in the desert all I want, but that doesn't make Bryce someone he isn't, right?"

Evie pictured both of the girls sitting in their rooms with their mouths open. But as much as she'd like to be able to assure them everything was okay and say all the nice things they hoped to hear, she was done. Over done. Burnt, in fact. Crispy. "Girls, I think I need to be done for tonight. I'm all right. Everything is all right. For now, I'm going to bed. I love you both, and I'll check in with you tomorrow. Okay?"

"Check!" Sam's reply was brief.

"Yep!" was Vicki's attempt at a happy reply.

They saw Evie disconnect and knew it was just the two of them.

"So," said Vicki, "that weird to you?"

"Oh yeah, that was weird. Now what do we do?"

"I say we go in and look around for ourselves."

"Right behind you."

Evie walked back to her sink to rinse her last dishes. "Lord, is this your answer?" she thought to herself. She thought of all the nights she'd spent praying for Bryce, but all she felt now was sadness.

She finished the dishes, shutting off the light over the sink. Just as she turned to go to bed, she saw lights go by the house, and a cold tingle up her spine as she realized whose truck they belonged to.

CHAPTER EIGHT

*T*he view from the top of a sand dune in the late hours could be breathtaking. The reds and yellows contrasted gloriously with the purple highlights. If he hadn't already been on his knees, he was sure he would have fallen to them in awe. The evenings were his favorite times to arrive on the battlefield of prayer. Well, favorite was a strong word for anything about this place. He'd been coming here for weeks, kneeling in solitude, hearing nothing but the sand blowing around him. He'd come through his portal every day only to go back, feeling alone and like he'd wasted time.

He'd started coming back to prayer when he was locked up. All those years he said he never had time to pray? Yahweh granted him a period with nothing but time. And he had prayed his guts out, for repentance, for restoration, pleading for one more chance.

Finding promises in the Scripture had revived his hope, not in himself, knowing now just what he was capable of but hope in Yahweh. That's when prayer seemed to change. When Bryce took the promises with him to his prayer time, he closed his eyes and awoke in a desert. But months here alone in this place had made it feel like a Yahweh-forsaken desert. His faith said it wasn't, but his feelings told him he was alone.

All he did was come here and sweat and feel alone. Feeling alone wasn't something he had expected when coming to pray. He had expected answers and for those answers to be given in a glorious display and vision. He had the idea of using prayer to tell Yahweh his wants and needs, and then those wants and needs would be promptly provided. Bryce knew that sounded horrible, but he was finally able to admit the truth to himself. Instead, he's been standing in a sand pile waiting for something that wasn't coming, and which he clearly didn't deserve.

"Unworthy," the wind seemed to howl around him. What was there to howl back? It was the truth.

Bryce picked up his sword and began swinging at the wind. He slashed at it over his head and then twirled and thrust into the air. He bent down on one knee as he stabbed his sword into the ground and for one moment, he thought he heard something other than the wind, like a grunt and a cry even. He stood, sweaty from endeavor rather than from heat. If anyone had been watching, they would not be able to distinguish tears from sweat rolling down his face. Cry to Yahweh. It was a literal thing.

Not being heard, not receiving an answer had only fed his fear that he was not worth saving. But he could not give up the hope that his family was worth this effort and whatever feelings he must endure, he would not give up on the kids or Evie. They were the only reason he was still coming through that portal several times a day.

"What was that?" he thought. There was a sound coming from the east, cries and high-pitched squealing. He wasn't alone after all? He took off running as fast as he could in the sand toward the direction of the noise.

He came to the top of the sand dune and saw something he hadn't before. There were piles of something unknown. His feet moved before his mind could and he ran down the sand, nearly falling headfirst down the dune. He managed to keep upright and reached the first pile. He was near enough now to not only see what it was, but to smell it. The maggots that came out of the heads of three creatures were gorging on the bodies of their hosts. They were getting bigger and bigger every second he watched. Finding such vileness was the alternative to feeling alone? He wasn't sure this was a better deal.

But he wasn't alone.

There were creatures here. Demons, it appeared, and someone else who was a threat to the demons. And someone had chopped off their heads. Another believer? Here on his battlefield? What?

Bryce knew that he was praying for the restoration of his family. Not just forgiveness and peace, but for him and Evie to be united in faith and body and for the kids to have a stable home. Was someone else praying for the same thing, and fighting for his family?

Why did this tick him off so much? He had been coming here for months, seemingly fighting the air, feeling his unworthiness and wretchedness. He sweat his weight out here in this place, crying to Yahweh for the honor to lead his family once again. And here was someone in the same place, but someone who got to fight and kill something.

No more of this. He was going to come through that portal as often as he could, and he wasn't going to camp around the opening. He was going to hunt down the enemies of his home. So help anyone who stood in his way.

"Not sure that qualified as sleep," Bryce thought to himself as he rolled out of bed. His apartment, despite the opened windows and cool evenings, felt hot and humid. He snorted to himself. "Think I'd be used to that by now, right?"

Nothing in the past year and a half had been what he'd expected. This little apartment on the opposite side of town, complete with peeling plaster and thrift store furniture, was right up there on the Not Planned For list. Bryce knew who to blame for that, but that didn't really help his frustration.

Buttoning up his jeans, he reached for the coffee pot a mere two feet from his futon. This is getting old, he thought. As he went through the motions of adding the coffee and filling the pot, he began to prioritize what needed to be done. Talk to Evie. See kids. Convince Evie that they were okay. Kill Bartrug.

He watched the coffee slowly drip into the glass pot and thought his list might need adjusting. Kill Bartrug first, then talk to Evie. Filling his mug with one hand, he pushed his futon up into a sofa with his other. He looked through his blinds and knew that no matter what he had hoped to be doing this weekend, it all depended on one thing: Cody Bartrug.

Later Bryce sat outside a seedy little hotel, allowing himself to take pleasure in the fact that Bartrug was living in more of a dive than he was. Just outside of town, the hotel looked like it could pass for a place that offers an hourly rate as well a nightly rate.

"Who knows," Bryce thought smugly to himself. "Maybe it does." The fact that he himself was sleeping on a futon in a one-room apartment was not going to rob him of the joy in seeing Bartrug sleeping at Bed Bugs Inn.

From his truck, Bryce could see Cody's car and he wasn't about to fool himself into thinking that he'd found Cody, but rather that Cody had deliberately placed himself where Bryce could easily reach him. He replayed all that Cody had said a thousand times in his head since yesterday. As he got out of his truck at the back of the parking lot, he knew no matter how many times he went over it in his head, his answers were with the one guy he knew to be a threat to everything he'd dared to hope for over the last few months.

He'd felt Evie warming to him, in their brief interactions. He knew it wasn't wishful thinking or imagination that the pieces of their lives had a chance to resettle into their right places. Even though she wasn't sure it was the right thing, she wanted him back in their lives. She was still attracted to him too, almost as much as he longed for her. He felt the check in his spirit to pull back on the reins where that was concerned. His playful nature wanted to remind her what their intimacy had been like. He could still make her happy, of that he was certain. But he'd kept his hands in his pockets, trying to listen to that quiet voice telling him to hold back. He knew he needed to win her heart back first, and he wanted to do things in the right order.

He was tired of sleeping alone. His body longed to be touched as much as his hands ached to touch back. But it was more than that. He ached for his family to be whole. He'd learned from a jail cell all he had lost. He entered the battle, thinking he was doing this for his family. The truth was, he had become ungrateful for all he had, and he had lost himself and his family as a result.

They had never needed a bigger house. They had never needed the things he had convinced himself he had to get. Evie had needed her husband. The kids needed their dad. The other things would be great, but not at what it had cost him to get them. From here, he traditionally would settle into a mental room where everything he'd had and everything he had personally sabotaged would hang like pictures on the wall. He'd look at it all, unable to reach or change any of them, just knowing he was an idiot. He was an idiot for losing his good life to begin with, and an idiot for thinking he could get it back.

He wasn't the first man to ruin his own family. There was nothing new under the sun. And he knew he wasn't the first to want to fix the wrongs, but he didn't know how. He didn't know where to start and didn't know when to end trying. What he did know was that he was done standing in a room staring at the pictures of people he loved on the walls, waiting for an answer. He'd made one mistake after another but standing around while his family slipped away wasn't going to be the next one.

"I've got everything to fight for and nothing to lose," he thought as he walked toward the lineup of dingy doors.

The door opened to a shirtless, scruffy Cody.

"Expecting someone else?" Bryce mockingly asked with raised brows.

"Things to do, people to see, Bryce. Unless you're here for business, leave." Cody voice was cold.

"Business? Not really planning on doing 'business' with you this morning, Bartrug. But since you're awake and all dressed up, we might as well talk."

"Ah," Cody looked amused. "Finally found your voice, did you?" He let Bryce in.

Cody stood with his back to the door, leaving Bryce in the center of the room. "Go ahead and block the door," Bryce thought. "If you think I can't get past you, you underestimate me."

"Nice place you got here. Love what you've done with the place. Did they hand you the sheets when you checked in or did you find them all fluffed and ready for you, just so?"

Other than the twitch in Cody's cheek, he remained still, feet apart, arms crossed. "Do you have information or do you really want to talk about linens?"

"I'm here to get information. Information that you seem to have," Bryce squared off.

"Really. That's interesting," Cody paused. "I'm not here to give you anything. I'm here to get something from you. Unless you have information on that, I think we're done here." Cody remained still.

The two stood facing each other, tense, Cody with his arms crossed and Bryce with his hands still in his pockets. Bryce knew he was missing critical information, but he also didn't want to admit that. He hated knowing that Bartrug knew something he didn't. After a brief stare down, Bryce yielded.

"You mentioned that I had something you wanted. I don't know what that is, or more importantly, why you want it."

"Here's the thing," Cody bit back. "I have no reason to believe you. I have every reason to believe you're lying. How about you start by telling me what you did with the list?"

Bryce felt like he'd fallen through a bizarre rabbit hole. "You worked with the same people I was, Bartrug. You saw what I did. I drove a van. In fact, I drove a van where you told me to. I don't know anything about a list. I told everything I did know to the cops. That allowed me to sit in a jail cell instead of prison. Funny thing, I don't remember seeing you in the same jail. Why is that?"

"Because I'm better than you," Cody deflected. "So, about that list?"

"What list?" Bryce bellowed.

Cody didn't flinch but did pause. The room was quiet enough to hear people moving on the other side of the wall. "Tis a good act, Bryce," he finally responded. "Almost convincing. The problem is, there are people out there who think you have other information. Yeah, you drove the van. You moved the goods. Part of those goods was a list of information. It was handed to you, yet it never reached the destination. So, it stands to reason, whether you have it or not, you know where it is. And I need it. You don't need to be involved; you don't have to do anything that would jeopardize your budding relationship with what's her name? Evie?"

At the mention of his wife's name, the protective beast in him rose up in Bryce. He stalked towards Cody, stopping only when his face was within inches of Cody's. He snarled, "My wife is nothing to you. You don't talk to her or about her. Ever again. You don't say her name."

Cody came alive. He grabbed Bryce by his jacket, pushing him backwards until he hit the wall with a force that knocked the dated picture off the wall. His arms had blocked Bryce's from coming up and his weight was pushed onto him. "Do I need to remind ya," he breathed into Bryce's ear, "that you have no options here? You don't get to make any demands. You understand that? None. All you get to do is give up and I'll be gone. But until then, you will have to get used to seeing me. And if that means I get more acquainted with Evie," he taunted, "then I'll suffer through that, I suppose."

Bryce shoved Cody off, grabbed him and pulled him close while bringing his head back and forward for a head punch. As Cody's head snapped back, Bryce barreled into him and took him to the ground. Bryce reached back to hit him in the face, and felt the gun touch his chest.

"Check mate, Brycie" Cody said coldly. "Now, let's do this my way." Bryce leaned back and let Cody up. Cody motioned him with his gun to step back. Bryce gritted his teeth and moved back. "You're going to stand here and I'm going to make sure you don't have any more surprises for me. Nice head butt, by the way," he said and wiped the blood off the bridge of his nose.

Cody opened Bryce's coat with his free hand, patting him down, before moving on to check the inside pocket of Bryce's jacket.

"Hmm? Got a little something in here, do we?" Cody asked.

Before Cody could search further, Bryce knocked Cody's gun hand wide and planted a right-hook on Cody's jaw. Cody quickly managed to get regain control before Bryce could capitalize on the hit.

Gun back up, Cody said, "Little punchy about the pocket, are we?"

"Nothing in there is any of your business." Bryce said through clenched teeth.

"How about you let me decide that?"

He reached back into the jacket, jerked the pocket zipper open, and pulled out the book with his eyes still on Bryce. He stepped back and motioned for Bryce to take a seat at the little table.

Cody looked down, staring in disbelief at the pocket-sized orange book with faded gold letters. He looked back at Bryce, who stared at the floor.

Cody flipped the small book open with one hand. He saw the marked pages, and the underlined places. He took it all in, then slowly looked back at Bryce, whose face was blank and devoid of emotion. "Is this a joke?" asked Cody.

"It's nothing to you. Nothing!" Bryce regained his voice.

"A Bible?! You're telling me you're carrying a Bible?" Cody asked incredulously.

"Now you have a problem with a Bible?! It's none of your business!" He started to rise from his seat.

Cody motioned him back down. After a moment of flipping through the pages, he walked over to the opposite side of the table and sat down. Bryce looked completely defeated. Cody laid his gun on the table. With his other hand, he slid the worn Bible across the table to Bryce, who snatched it up and shoved angrily back into his pocket.

"Where did you get it?" asked Cody.

"Did I get it from the job, you mean?" Bryce replied sarcastically.

"Sure. Did you get this on the job?"

Bryce snorted, "I got it because of the job, complete with jumpsuit and a two-inch-thick cot mattress."

"I'm going to put this away," motioning to his gun, "for now. If I do that, I'm trusting that you are able to have a reasonable discussion. But I'm not going to let you get in another head butt or punch."

Bryce gave a curt nod of agreement. Cody tucked the gun into the front of his jeans and leaned back in his chair.

"This is what I know," Cody began. "You were transporting stolen goods. Part of the stolen goods was a list. I don't know what it looked like," he added quickly at the look Bryce gave him. "Maybe a book, maybe a paper, I don't know. But you had it, whether you knew it or not."

"I didn't," Bryce cut in quickly.

"Okay. Maybe you didn't. But you were supposed to have it. And it didn't get handed off with the other things."

"I gave up all the people I knew who were involved. I didn't hold anything back."

"I know."

Each was measuring the other.

"How do you know?" asked Bryce.

Cody let out a resigned sigh. "I'm part of a task force. I was planted on that team running merchandise. We are looking for the information, the list, that you had."

Bryce's poker face was in top form as he weighed Cody's words. "What information were you looking for? Or what did the list contain?"

"Next question."

"Who else is looking for it?"

"Can't say."

"Is there anything you can say?!" Bryce snapped.

Sighing, Cody answered, "I can say that the list is a list of names. Names of people who wish to be anonymous. I can say that the quicker we get it, the safer a lot of people will be."

"Is my family in danger?" Bryce asked.

"I don't know."

Bryce's poker face broke as a wave of fear washed over him. Cody continued, "As far as I know, no one outside our task force knows of your involvement."

"I wasn't involved!" shouted Bryce.

"Call it what you want!" shot back Cody. "I'm just saying that as far as I know, no one else knows that it was supposedly transported by you. We would like to secure the information, as quickly as possible, and make sure it stays secure." Here he paused, before asking, "Did you ever see anything that didn't look like the normal stuff you moved? Did you ever take anything on the side, off the books?"

"No!" Bryce said, desperately. "No, I just loaded up what I was told to, drove where I was told to, and started it all over again when I was told to." After a moment, he continued, "How do I know you're not lying?"

Cody slowly reached into his back pocket, pulled out his badge, and laid it on the table.

"So." Bryce let out a breath. "You're telling me you're one of the good guys?"

Cody snorted, "Mostly."

"What now? I need to keep my family safe. I want nothing more to do with this. I made my last run the night I was arrested. I did everything I was told to do. But now I'm trying to put my family back together. I need to know they're safe," he finished, quietly.

Cody heard his sincerity. "Okay. The best thing you can do is think back on everything you handled. Maybe with an idea of what you're looking for, you'll remember something. I don't think you're in any immediate danger, but for now, I'm not going anywhere."

"Are you working on your own?" Bryce asked.

Cody just smiled and stood to show the conversation was finished.

"Right," Bryce said. As he opened the door to leave, he turned and added, "This doesn't mean I trust you."

"That's ok, it doesn't mean I trust you either."

With that, Bryce closed the door, walked to his truck, got in, and bowed his head.

CHAPTER NINE

She came through the portal with tears streaming down her face. Her heart threatened to shrivel and dehydrate from all the tears shed in the last few months. She couldn't, scratch that, she wouldn't go to her own battlefield, so she came here.

Vicki was the best intercessor there was in her circle of friends. She could always be counted on arriving and fighting for someone else. She had a battlefield of her own, but she never invited anyone to it and rarely ever went there herself. Not anymore. She wasn't going back. She'd believed the lies that she wasn't worth an answer to her own prayers. She believed the lies that God had not heard her. She believed so many things about herself, things she would fight to the death to protect her friends from believing.

Her strength was fragile, but she kept that knowledge firmly to herself. She stood on the sand, closed her eyes for a moment and felt the hot wind blow in her face. Yeah, this was nothing like her battlefield. This was glorious sunshine and heat and sand. All that was missing was the ocean.

She drew her sword purely for comfort and not for battle. She held the blade so she could read the inscriptions melded into the steel, words moving and fading in and out as if it was living and pulsing. Words she had forgotten from long ago. She read them out loud in a soft, whispering voice. The words that were spoken increased in size and glowed white. Vicki loved this about the Sword of the Spirit. Despite the lies that she believed about herself, this Sword had never failed her and always seemed to know just the words she needed to hear.

The tears still came quite easily for Vicki, but now they were being made from a tender heart, not a brittle one, flowing for a friend in her time of need. Evie, Janey, and Kendall were a family, a package deal. But no one knew yet if that family still included Bryce or not. Should it? Does it have to? Vicki knew what she wanted the answer to be, but was it Yahweh's answer?

Vicki's quiet time of prayer and meditation on the Word ended when Sam came rolling out of the portal. She couldn't just step through and arrive. She always came through as if she would enter the battlefield immediately surrounded by a legion of demons. What experience could have taught her that? For all the closeness of their friendship, there was still a lot that wasn't shared between the girls. One day, they would figure out why Sam's portal entries were so bizarre. But for now, she laughed at Sam, who rolled and jumped up, twirling around looking for her enemies. She was ready to fight. Always ready for a fight. That's our Sam, thought Vicki.

The girls looked at each other, clanging their swords together to begin this battlefield prayer meeting. 'Clink, clink!' Vicki pointed her sword to her right, and they both began to jog over the dune with confidence and strength. They were beautiful to behold, daughters of God, armed with His Word, arriving to pray for someone else.

The glory of Yahweh shone on them and hovered around them as they moved through the desolate place. In faith, they looked for an answer for Evie. They prayed for Evie. This was her battlefield. She would one day face an epic battle here if she wanted to ever conquer it. She would need to be strong, stay diligent and for this, they prayed. And wouldn't it just be great if they also stumbled upon the answer to her prayer and could safeguard it until she got here?

Vicki figured Evie would arrive soon. She'd find them and the three friends would have another battle day under their belt.

"Hear that?" Sam grabbed Vicki by the arm and stopped her as they were running up the dune. Vicki closed her eyes and listened. Beyond the wind there was a small sound, a clinking of metal that sounded like chimes. Only a few swords and was that...laughter?

Vicki and Sam fell to their bellies and army crawled up to the top of the dune. They slowly dug, displacing some sand so their whole heads didn't just pop up over the knoll. Demons loved a good game of whack a mole.

The sand filled in quickly, but there was enough time for Vicki to see where the clinking sound and laughter came from. There was a small oasis just beyond this dune, about one hundred yards away. But what she saw was unbelievable. Un-freaking believable!

Evie. She was already here. It wasn't odd to find her on her own battlefield. They had found her here many times, after she'd been here for a night, fighting by herself. But that never made the hair stand up on the back of Vicki's neck like it did now. Sam watched Vicki quickly flip over to her back, holding her sword tighter to her chest. She could see Vicki controlling her breath, breathing like she was in labor. Sam started flinging sand as quickly as she could without drawing attention to their spot. She needed to see for herself what spooked the unspookable Vicki.

Sam's reaction wasn't the same as Vicki's. After her quick look, she laid her head down on her arm. She stayed belly down and while Vicki's breathing pattern had increased, Sam stopped breathing altogether. They looked at each other, both trying to gauge the other's reaction. Sam was furious. Vicki could tell by the way Sam was punching the sand with her fist and pretty sure those were some four-letter words she just mouthed.

"Who the heck is that?" Sam demanded to know.

"I have no clue." Vicki rolled back over to her stomach so she could do the scoop and scope technique once again. There they were, still at it. Evie and a tall, Jader demon were fighting side by side with a natural rhythm and flair. Like they were partners. It was only a small band of Corgs they were killing, but still? Evie and a demon? What the ...?

Sam made the first move to get up and was obviously going towards the endearing little scene to take on the Jader and save Evie. She'd do it without a game plan, instinctually, without thinking. Vicki grabbed her by the arm and pulled her down before she was seen.

"What are you doing? You can't go down there until we know what's going on. You don't know if Evie is up to something or if Yahweh told her some freak battle plan. You just can't run down there, Sam. Not without thinking."

"You're kidding me, right? You have got to be kidding me!" Now Sam breathed hard, her lungs struggling so much that she couldn't seem to catch the next breath. She had to make herself lay still for a moment to slow her heart and catch her breath. Even she knew she had better not get caught by a roving band of demons in this condition. Her thoughts focused on her own breath. "Breathe in, good... out a little...good." And there it was. Sam had almost lost all focus, almost risen in anger, not based on justice and righteousness but just an impulsive, emotional reaction.

"Thank you, Yahweh," she whispered.

Sam turned back to look at Vicki. "Freak battle plan? You think she's down there being all tactical and running a mission on point with a Jader? A Jader, Vicki. Those things don't just pop up like Corgs. They're like, level four demons. They use charm to worm their way close to you. They touch you and you believe the lies they tell and fall for any disguise they are wearing. They speak and you swear you hear every promise made to you that you thought you wanted. Did you see him?" Sam kept talking. "Yeah, you saw him from the back! But you didn't see him from the front. He's gonna be all gorgeous and beautiful and look like everything you ever wanted in a man, and he will say the right words and be your dream, but in a demon body. You saw a Jader, Vicki. And you saw Evie playing with him."

"I was not aware you knew so much about Jaders, Sam." Vicki looked her right in the eyes. Sam was the first to look away, but not before Vicki saw a wave of shame in her eyes.

Well, this tanked fast. "Some prayer meeting this turned out to be," Vicki thought. First, she found the person who owns this battlefield frolicking with a demon, and then one of the best prayer warriors she has ever known just bowed her head in shame on the same battlefield.

"Yes, I said freak battle plan." Vicki tried to sound confident. "Like Jericho wall stuff. I'm sure walking around a wall for seven days, then shouting seemed a little like a freak plan. Or how about put a candle in a pitcher and hide in the dark then break you pitcher and shout? You know, Gideon. Yahweh is full of weird plans. This could be one."

"No. It's not. I know in my gut that it's not." Sam slammed her fist into the sand, then pointed her finger at Vicki. "But you know what is in both of those plans you mentioned? A lot of shouting. I could get behind that plan, Vicki. You in?" she asked.

Vicki sighed. She preferred well thought out plans and strategies. Clear commands from Yahweh were good, too. This was not on a list. But it was her fault for giving Sam the idea. So yeah. She was in.

Vicki nodded her head and on the count of three, both women stood and ran screaming down the hill as if they had just arrived. They shouted as loud as they could, running with their swords in the air. They knew they didn't look like warriors at all, but like silly girls. But they didn't care. A sister was in need and all vanity was gone.

"Yay! They're here!" Evie was so excited, not that they needed back up but that her friends would meet Jim, the man who had been praying with and for Evie.

Loden started running away when he saw Vicki and Sam running down the hill towards them. When he looked back, all he saw were two wild women running full speed down the sand dune coming right at him. All he heard was the blasted name of Yahweh screaming into his head and echoing so loudly that the pain nearly brought him to his knees. He had to get out of the battlefield before they got here. As if his master knew his need, two Snappers popped up out of the ground between the banshees and Evie.

Evie screamed in surprise at the sudden rising of the Snappers and ran towards them, assuming Jim would be by her side. She never saw him disappearing over the horizon. The women met the Snappers at the same time. The long-necked Snappers had an owl-like ability to twist and turn their necks and saw Evie coming from behind. They fought with little swords, having no need for big ones, as their arms were long enough to reach the ground.

The Snappers weren't prepared for the fury of Sam or the precision of Vicki. They were rescuing and safeguarding their friend, who didn't even know she was in danger.

Sam never slowed but brought down her sleek, heavy sword with all of her might as she jumped in the air. Her sword split the gray monster in two. Sam quivered with rage, releasing her emotions as she fought. When she looked at Evie, she wanted the rage to be gone and to look at her friend with love. But she also wanted an explanation.

Vicki was more fluid in her fighting style. Vicki's sword gleamed and twinkled before she brought it up from beneath the Snapper's body and plunged it into its guts. She did so with a smile on her face and didn't need a moment to gather herself before looking at Evie.

Evie looked a bit startled at the fierceness of her friends. "Wow, you could have saved some for me! Look at you two! Just wow! I'm so glad to see you!"

"You are?" asked Sam. This was unexpected. No shame from Evie. No reproach. No sorrow and not a tear, just happy to see them, when she had been playing with a demon.

"Yes, of course! I've been fighting the little Corgs and wasn't expecting the Snappers. They kind of caught me off guard. Hey, I want you to meet Jim. Jim, this is..." Evie turned to her right to motion Jim to come forward. He wasn't there. Evie looked all around the small oasis. "He was just here. We were just fighting the Corgs together. He must have been called away. He does that. He works the battlefields. I really wanted you to meet him!"

Sam and Vicki looked at each other. Vicki's head tilted to the side and her lower lip stuck out, eyes squinting. Sam stuck her neck forward while her eyebrow shot up in exasperation.

Vicki followed that with a look of warning. Sam understood. This wasn't her first rodeo on the battlefield... she could give be subtle when she wanted to. But she didn't want to.

"Oh, you mean the Jader demon you were practically making out with? He ran that way when he saw us coming." Sam used her sword to point over the horizon where Loden had run.

"Nice," whispered Vicki.

"Well, she needs to know!" Sam loudly whispered back.

"No," corrected Evie. "Those were Corgs and Snappers. It was Jim with me. Tall guy with a sword. Like ours. He was just here. I'm sorry you missed him. I was telling him about you guys."

Vicki laid a gentle and soothing hand on Sam's arm. It was a small miracle when Sam responded to Vicki's leading. Vicki stepped forward and reached out to touch the loose, flowing hair from Evie's braid. She gave it a playful tug.

"We've been looking for your answer, Ev. Do you have any more clues or has Yahweh told you anything yet?"

"Well, I'm pretty sure I'm done here. I don't have to come back anymore. I see now that I have options. There are other ways. Other people. After talking to Jim, I realize that what I want is out there. Maybe I've just been looking in the wrong place." Evie turned and started walking back up the sand dune the women had just come running down from. She was heading towards the portal, calling an end to the prayer session.

But Sam and Vicki knew a battlefield simply didn't end without an epic battle. Either way, ground is gained or lost for the Kingdom of God, but it was never just shrugged away or ceded. It's battlefield prayer and there has yet to be the arrival of the host of heaven or Yahweh Himself. No way was this ended simply because Evie said so.

Sam and Vicki followed their beloved friend to the portal and let Evie climb through first so they could stand there and have a moment together before rejoining her on the other side.

"No way is it gonna end like this!" shouted Sam, not caring if every demon in the desert heard her and rushed to the portal. She was torn between being ticked and panicked. "What happens when the one who owns the battlefield doesn't come back? Are the other warriors stuck here forever, like in limbo?" she asked Vicki.

Vicki knew the answer to that question. "No. We won't be stuck here. But Evie will seal off her heart to this issue until she comes and wins this battle by the hand of Yahweh. You just don't walk away from a battlefield. It waits for you. But you'll need all the help you can get when you return because by then, it's become a camp to nothing less than level fours just waiting for you to step through the portal. You may not know you're coming back, but they do."

Sam asked Vicki, "Why didn't she know that was a demon and why didn't you let me convince her?"

"Because it's too late. She's not going to believe us."

Those words hung coolly in the air as Vicki stepped through the portal, followed by Sam with one last look around the desert battlefield. No way would she leave this place unprotected, only to return later to a camp filled with level fours and higher. She'd come every day for Evie. She owed her that. Sam thrust her sword into the ground one last time with all her might before stepping through the shimmering vapor suspended in *the hot desert air. She couldn't help but smile when a demon travelling through the sand screamed out in a death cry.*

Yeah, she wasn't quitting this place.

Evie was enjoying this quiet Saturday morning. Since she worked the morning shift during the week, she typically had the weekend mornings off. This particular morning felt peaceful. She'd made the kids pancakes and bacon, candied bacon, in fact, and they were busy eating as if they had been deprived of food for an extended period beforehand.

With syrup dribbling on her chin and a mouthful of bacon, Janey sighed and said, "I love candy. I love it so much."

"It's not candy, Janey, it's meat," Kendall quickly corrected.

"I think it's candy, right Mommy?" she asked.

"Actually," confirmed Evie, "you're both right. It is meat that is dressed up to be candy."

"You can't dress up meat," Kendall said, looking exasperated.

"Well, it's called dressing up, meaning you make it fancy. It's more like fancy bacon."

"Can you dress up broccoli?" asked Janey, with a hint of humor.

Kendall, boring quickly of the conversation, asked, "Do we get to see Dad today?"

"Well," Evie started, "I think the plan is that he comes and picks you up and takes you to the park this afternoon."

"I want to play here today, with my Barbie boat," Janey scowled.

Kendall, who had stopped shoveling in his pancakes, looked at Janey, then looked at his mom, and added, "Me, too."

Evie was quickly losing that peaceful feeling. She'd made some decisions, and she had planned to have this conversation a different way. But apparently big revelations are the perfect side dish to pancakes and bacon.

"I think we will stick to the plan today and let you two have your playtime with your dad at the park," Evie responded firmly. Jayne crossed her arms across her chest, tipped her chin down and muttered a "humph" while Kendall studied his mom.

"Are you going to come with us?" he asked.

Evie avoided eye contact and said, "I think you three will have so much fun today and I will do our grocery shopping. Is there anything you would like me to pick up?" she diverted.

"Fruit snacks," Janey said around her mouthful of pancakes.

Evie could feel Kendall's eyes still on her and she silently cursed the seriousness of her man-child. "Why in the world can't he be like a normal little boy who is clueless and just wants to play ball?" she thought. Evie looked into his brown eyes and said softly, "It's going to all be okay, Kendall. I promise."

To Evie's surprise, Kendall smiled, "I know, Mom. Can I go to my room?"

"Can I have the rest of his candy?" Janey asked while reaching for the half piece of bacon still sitting on his plate.

Evie laughed. "I think you should ask Kendall that!"

"Sure," he said as he got up from the table and set off for his room.

With the serious mood elevated, Evie began her clean up quietly. Ignoring the needling feeling of doubt, she chose to focus on the rightness of her decision to move forward without Bryce. She ticked off all the pros and the myriad of reasons that made it right. She saw Sam's car pull up and wasn't sure what her emotions were — relief, apprehension, excitement? No, probably not excitement. Finality. Yes, finality. She'd wasted so much time, tears, energy the last few months, it felt good to see an obvious ending to it.

She smiled at Sam's impatient knock. Opening the door, she saw Vicki was with Sam and she welcomed them into the kitchen. "Good morning, Sunshine," she chirped as Sam stormed by on her way to the coffee station.

"Don't mind her. Beth let someone else sit at our friend booth this morning. We had to have a table in the middle." Vicki said middle like it was a tainted word.

"Oh, how terrible." Evie responded, in a matching tone. "Those weekend waitresses are hideous. I think we should hate her."

"Already there," Sam muttered as she filled her coffee mug. "Why can't you be there when I'm there?"

"Well, think the better question is," Evie said, "Why aren't you making your own breakfast on a Saturday morning? How do you two never have to cook?"

"Jack spent the night at his friend's house," Sam replied, referring to her teenage son, "and since when does Vicki have to cook?"

Vicki leveled a glare at Sam. "As you know," she said curtly, "Steve is out of town on business." She nodded her head as if to say, So?

Evie knew that life held so many uncertainties. But at this moment in time, she was as certain about her love for these two women as she was for her children. Her heart swelled as she looked at them. Both were beautiful on the outside, light and dark, tall and tiny, but inside they were even more so. Strong, loyal, ferocious. She whispered a prayer of gratitude for their presence in her life.

"So," Sam looked up with determination, "Is Bryce coming over today?"

Evie sat down and looked from Sam to Vicki, who was now busying herself looking at something unseen on the table. After a moment of hesitation, Evie said, "Actually, he's only coming here to pick up the kids and take them to the park."

Vicki, with her head still tilted down at the unseen speck, lifted her eyes to share a look with Sam.

"Is that ok with you two?" Evie questioned.

"Well, that sounds fun! And cute! You two pushing the kids on the swing, playing football, playing..." Sam said, sounding oddly happy.

"Oh, I'm not going," Evie interrupted.

"Why not?" Sam asked while Vicki scrubbed at the non-existent spot that was starting to annoy Evie.

"Because I have stuff to do! And why are you making that sound bad? Since when do you want me to go hang out at the park with Bryce?" Evie asked.

"Hey." Sam held her hands up. "I'm not saying it's bad. I'm just confused by the sudden change, that's all."

"I haven't changed!" Evie retorted.

Vicki stopped scrubbing and lifted her eyes at Evie.

"I haven't changed! I just have stuff to do," Evie insisted.

"And you don't want to go to the park with your hottie husband and play with the kids together?" Sam asked in disbelief.

"He's not my hottie husband," Evie responded, now really annoyed.

Vicki sat up and said quietly, "Actually, he is your husband. And you're on drugs if you don't think he's hot."

Evie sat back in her chair and folded her arms and glared at each of them. "What is the matter with you two? First, you want me to avoid him, now you want me to play in the park with him?"

"Actually, I'd play with him anywhere if he were my husband," Sam nodded to Vicki, who nodded back.

"Ok, I guess it's time for me to state the obvious," Evie said. "I thought we were all on the same page, but apparently not. I've decided that the right thing to do is move on with Bryce as the kids' parents, and not as my husband."

Except for hearing Janey in her room making Barbie conversations between her dolls, the room went quiet. Evie threw her arms in the air and then held her face with her hands. "I don't get you two! Isn't that a good thing? Isn't that what you wanted?"

While Sam seemed to dissect Evie by looking at her, Vicki asked quietly, "Are you saying you found your answer? You went to the battlefield looking for it. You asked God for it. Are you saying He answered?"

"Call it an answer or call it a revelation. Either way, the conclusion is the same! You two were there, you saw what I saw. I think I can say I devoted enough time for something to change. And you know what? Something did change! I looked around! I woke up! And I don't want to do this anymore. I don't want to fight anymore. So yes, that's my answer!" Evie finished, flushed.

"How much of this has to do with what's his name, Jim?" Sam looked to Vicki for confirmation.

"Jim." Vicki confirmed.

"It doesn't have anything to do with him!" Evie denied. Both Vicki's and Sam's eyebrows shot up at this. "It doesn't!" Evie continued, "But you know who Jim is? Jim is willing to pray for me! He fights with me, not against me! Somewhere, right now, Jim is battling on my behalf! And even if I don't know who he is yet, I know there is someone like that out there for me. And that is answer enough. Don't settle. Don't you get it? That's a good thing!"

"Did it ever occur to you it could be a trick?" Sam asked.

Evie snorted, "Really? A man praying for me is a trick? What in the world, Sam??"

Vicki let out a breath, "Okay, we hear you," she looked at Sam, "we both hear you. We're going to take off and let you have the rest of your morning with the kids. We love you. Call us if you need us. Okay?"

Evie, feeling annoyed, replied, "Yeah sure. Thanks."

With brief hugs for the kids and Evie, Sam and Vicki walked out and got in the car.

"So, what do we do now?" asked Sam.

With both girls staring out the windshield, Vicki answered, "We go to the top."

At Mrs. Taylor's home, she invited them in and was just ready to pour the tea.

"Sugar?" she asked Sam.

"Sugar, yes, please." She couldn't resist.

Mrs. Taylor hadn't looked up while pouring the tea. But now she set the pot down and moved the sugar in front of Sam. "Need some sweetness in your life, do you?" she asked innocently.

Sam and Vicki's heads snapped up at the reply. They looked at each other and grinned.

"What can I help you two with today?" Mrs. Taylor asked.

Vicki started, "We think something happened, or is happening, to Evie on the battlefield."

"Oh? Well dear, as you are learning, the battlefield is filled with things happening, even when it seems like nothing at all- sometimes good, sometimes bad. But all for our good."

Sam jumped in, "This isn't for her good. And it's definitely bad."

Mrs. Taylor studied Sam. "Okay. Why don't you tell me what you saw, and I'll see if anything sounds familiar?"

Vicki took over. "We found Evie battling with a demon. But she doesn't seem to know it's a demon."

"Are you positive you saw what you think you did?" Mrs. Taylor asked.

"It's a demon," Sam shot back.

"How do you know?"

"We know because we saw it. What we don't know is why Evie didn't. She actually thinks its name is Jim. They were fighting demons together and when we ran up to them yelling, he took off."

"You ran up to them yelling?" asked Mrs. Taylor. "That's an interesting strategy. What happened then?"

"It was the only thing I could think of at the time to get her away from it." Sam defended. "Evie didn't bat an eye. She even tried to introduce us to it. But he had already left."

"She's been acting weird ever since," Vicki added.

"How has she acted weird?"

"Suddenly, she decided the battle is over. Just like that. She said she got her answer when she didn't get anything! She said she's done on the battlefield. She walked out. Nothing about that sounds final or like Evie."

"Did he touch her?" asked Mrs. Taylor.

"Touch her? What do you mean, touch her?" Vicki asked.

"Did he brush up against her or touch her in any way?" she clarified.

"We don't know," said Sam. "But they acted like they'd been there together for a while. They were comfortable with their stance. What does it mean if it did?"

"If he touched her, even casually," Mrs. Taylor began, "then he could have infected her." At the girls confused look she continued, "Infected her mind. Like a virus. It plants an outside element like a thought that she thinks is hers. From there it reproduces, usually quickly, sometimes fermenting, before it attaches itself to her own ideas and thoughts. Have you noticed a change in the way she thinks since then?"

"Yes!" they both answered.

Vicki continued, "Yes. Almost overnight, she has become fixated with the idea that Bryce is not and is never going to be what she needs. She talks as if Jim, or someone like Jim, is out there somewhere, for her, and that her answer is to end her relationship with Bryce and find that guy."

"You disagree?" Mrs. Taylor asked.

After a pause, Sam answered, "We didn't, at first. But now it's all wrong. If she's been infected, and it looks like she has, then it is most definitely to move her away from Bryce."

"And if it's causing her to leave her battlefield before the right time, then it's obvious she's supposed to still be there fighting. Which means Bryce is not the bad guy we thought he was," Vicki continued.

"Things are rarely what they seem," smiled Mrs. Taylor.

"Yeah, don't know what that means, but more importantly, how do we stop the infection?" asked Sam.

"Infections of the mind are difficult. They take the things we long for, and for Evie it is to be loved, loved enough to be worth fighting for, and loved enough to want to battle alongside her. The infection then twists those desires, infuses them with evil intent, and deflects the goals to another place, or in her case, another person. Even an imaginary person can take on hero status with this type of infection. For what human can love perfectly? Who can love enough to always make it to the battle on time? Who can love enough to never become wounded? The infection of a demon, and I suspect this was a powerful one to infect so quickly one such as Evie, distorts all of our views, our perspectives and penetrates our thoughts even through our very bones."

Sam and Vicki looked at each other. Sam mouthed the words, "The Oracle has spoken."

Vicki mouthed back, "Cahhhreeeeepppy."

Out loud, Sam said, "So how do we get it out?"

"You must cut it out."

"Cut it out, as in stop that, or cut it out like, literally cut it out?" Vicki asked incredulously.

"If it has penetrated her bones, there is only one thing that will slice into the marrow," giving them a knowing look.

Sam blinked. "I got nothing."

"Yeah, me either," Vicki echoed.

Mrs. Taylor sighed, "I forget you are both still learning. Only the word of the King is sharp and powerful enough to cut into the marrow."

It was Vicki's turn to blink. "Oh! Ha. Right. My bad. Okay, word of the King. And how do we do that?"

Mrs. Taylor reached for the tea pot, "My dears, have you never looked at your swords?" She smiled and poured another cup.

Sam first broke the thoughtful silence as they drove across town. "Do you ever feel like weird organ music should be playing as we talk with her?"

"You're the only person I know who thinks every conversation is a music score. But I definitely thought she was going to say, 'Run to the light!'"

They spent the few minutes driving across town quoting every creepy music, film, and literature line they could think of until they pulled into the park. Sitting in their car, they could see Bryce standing at the bottom of the slide waiting for Janey to take her turn down. Kendall was tossing the football in the air as high as he could waiting to play catch.

The girls enjoyed the view for a few minutes until Sam spoke. "Evie's nuts."

Vicki sighed, "Bat cray-cray."

Sam turned to look at Vicki, "So how do we do this? Do we invite Bryce to the battlefield? How do we say that?"

"I think you should just ask him," said Vicki.

"Me? Why me?"

"'Because he already thinks you're crazy. If he doesn't know anything about it, just remind him that love is a battlefield, and that he is strong..." Vicki hummed a few lines of the Pat Benatar hit.

Sam stared at Vicki. "That's a stupid plan. I love it. Let's go."

Bryce saw them as they walked toward him. It would be hard not to notice these two beautiful women walking his way. He instinctively took a step back, but then held his ground.

"Don't know what you two want, but whatever it is, not here and not today," he said defensively.

"Simma down, we come as friends," Sam smiled.

He looked from one to the other. "Friends?" he snorted. "Think I missed that part of our relationship."

Vicki responded, "Consider it a...fluid relationship. Ever changing. Ever evolving."

"Right," said Bryce, "Changing and evolving. What is it today?"

"Allies," stated Sam promptly. With a questioning look from Bryce she continued, "I'm going to go out on a limb here and ask if you are familiar with the battlefield?"

The look on Bryce's face gave the girls the confirmation they needed. "I'm going to take that as a yes," said Sam.

"Here's the deal," continued Vicki. "Evie has been infected while on the field and now she believes that there is no long-term happiness, yada yada yada, for the two of you."

"There's a guy on the battlefield," Sam blurted out. At the look on Bryce's face she hurried, "Not a guy, a demon, named Jim."

"This is not helping..." growled Bryce.

"Well, if you're familiar with the field you know there are demons, right?" she asked impatiently.

Bryce didn't feel like this was the right time to reveal how little he knew, and that he hadn't actually fought anything yet, but just hung out in the battlefield swinging his sword, getting used to it, hoping for a day when he could use it. "Sure," was his reply.

"Well, it's not the conversation she likes, I see." Vicki whispered in an exaggerated tone to Sam who quipped back, "You think there's something else? Look at him. He's nothing but blonde hair, tan skin, scruff, t-shirt and perfect...."

"Stop!" Bryce interrupted before the list went any further. Vicki and Sam fixed him with their innocent looks. Bryce calmed himself, took a breath, "You mentioned a demon and an infection?"

Vicki smiled. "Okay, well, this demon has infected her, and the only way we can rid her of it is to go into battle and cut it out of her."

"Cut it out of her?" Bryce asked incredulously. He looked shocked as his voice rose and his eyes squeezed shut, "Are you two on drugs?"

Both girls stared back at him until Vicki looked at Sam, "Newbie."

"No kidding," she answered. "Here's the deal, we are going in. If you want to fight for Evie, this is the time to do it. Let us know and we'll arrange the time."

There was a determined look on his face as he put his hands in his pockets, grinned his perfectly dimpled grin and said, "Try and stop me."

CHAPTER TEN

*B*ryce stepped through the portal and into the desert battlefield. He came well before the planned time of eleven at night, wanting to be the first one here. Maybe that was a bit territorial, but he really didn't care. This was his family, his wife and children. He was going to be the one boss of this place. He was beginning to be glad that these women were Evie's friends. At first, he had been a bit jealous of their relationship with his wife, but now that he was more spiritually aware, or at least trying to be, he hoped that he could experience this companionship with Evie as well. He longed to be able to satisfy this part of her heart. But for right now, he would endure Sam and Vicki until he learned what they knew about this place.

But when his eyes adjusted to the bright light from the high sun, he saw Sam and Vicki were already waiting for him. Standing with their swords out and placed into the ground in front of them with both hands on the hilt, they looked bothered and had that man-eater look about them. What could he possibly have done wrong already? He's only been here for two seconds!

"If we were demons, you'd be dead right now," said Sam.

"Wait, you can die here?" asked Bryce with a raised voice.

"What, you afraid and want to go back now?" Sam spoke with a slightly condescending tone.

"No!" yelled Bryce. He walked towards them, angry, and both Sam and Vicki picked up their swords and scooted back a few steps from him. "Are you telling me my wife has been coming here to pray for our family and she could have died here? Is this some kind of sick game for you two? Why would you allow her to risk her life like that? You could have told me that she could die, and I would have left, no questions asked. I would have walked away from her and the kids, just to keep her safe. I don't know what she sees in either of you." He kept walking towards them, so they kept walking backwards.

He was transforming right before their eyes, getting bigger and obviously stronger by the sight of the bulging muscles in his arms and chest. Were his shirt buttons going to pop? How did his sword get into his hands? Gee-whiz, was he going to attack them? Sam and Vicki finally listened to what he was saying, not just how he was looking. He seemed angry and afraid. A dangerous combination, especially here on the battlefield.

"No, no, Bryce," Vicki talked in her soothing voice. Her voice was calming him. She moved towards him and fought the urge to keep stepping back. Perhaps this beast can be soothed. "No, you can't die on the battlefield. Evie has always been safe. Yahweh has never once left her. She was never physically in peril when praying. Sam didn't mean to frighten you, did you, Sam?"

Vicki looked at Sam who was not in the best mood for prayer now. Sam set aside her anger at Bryce's aggression and responded calmly.

"I honestly did not think that would frighten you, Bryce. But for the record, you come through a portal lackadaisical like that, and there might be a demon ready to slice you up or a horde ready to attack you and feast on your flesh. Metaphorically speaking, of course," she nodded and slightly bowed to him. Bryce was calming down and about to put his sword back in its scabbard. "Wait on that, Bryce. Don't put that away. I feel we're going to need that real soon," said Sam.

Bryce swiveled his neck, looking around him in every direction. He squatted and put his hands up like there was a demon right in front of him, facing off.

"Um, Bryce, you seeing something we aren't?" Sam asked him. Vicki looked at him quizzically, wondering what on earth this strange man of Evie's was doing? He went from raging warrior to panicked nerd in a split second.

"Well, no, but I just wanted to be ready. When will they come?" he asked.

"When will who come?" Vicki asked in her still soothing voice. He was going to notice soon that she was talking to him like a child.

"The demons. Do they just appear?"

"Oh. My. Word! You've never seen a demon on the battle-field? How long have you been coming here? What have you been doing all this time?" Sam was about to start laughing out loud. She could not believe this development. Bryce, this big bad warrior, acted like he knew all about the battlefield, but he didn't know squat! Good grief. No wonder they've been stuck in a desert forever. Only Sam and Vicki were coming to do the hard work. Well, that wasn't fair, Sam thought. Evie was doing well until she got infected.

"No, I haven't seen a demon. Don't they try to hide from us? I thought things were getting better because they were all *gone. That my coming had stopped them from hurting us. I thought the battle was almost over." As soon as Bryce spoke these thoughts out loud, he realized how naïve they sounded.*

"Just the opposite, brother," said Vicki. She laid a hand on his shoulder. "Quite the opposite. As a matter of fact, you're gonna see a lot of action tonight. Listen, Sam! Do you hear that?" Sam tilted her head slightly and closed her eyes. She was obviously listening, but Bryce didn't know what she was listening for. He closed his eyes, hoping to hear it too.

"I don't hear it," he said.

"Listen for the sound of pounding on the sand. You can feel it, too. The weight of the earth moving beneath us. Anything?" Vicki asked.

Bryce kept his eyes closed. He focused on sound and feeling. It was kind of like standing in the woods when hunting. When you closed your eyes, your ears got better. There! Sound and feeling. Just like Vicki said. It sounded like a herd of deer running closer and closer.

"I hear it. What is it?" Bryce asked.

"Demons. About a hundred of them, maybe a bit less. We just don't know which kind yet," said Sam.

Sam and Vicki turned their bodies and held their swords high, ready for battle.

"What do you mean by 'which kind'? There's more than one kind? Are they coming?" Bryce heard the panic in his own voice, but he didn't really care, anymore. It was obvious he was not the leader here on the battlefield. He was willing to learn from these women. To save Evie and his family, he would submit to whatever was needed. At least he was going to finally get to kill something. "So, we just wait for them? How long before they get here?"

Sam and Vicki looked at him, their impatience and scorn gone, feeling compassion for this man that they hadn't before. He was here. He'd shown up to the battlefield prayer. Nobody can fake their way into this prayer field. Whether he knew he was doing or not, he showed up to pray. But they couldn't help but chuckle at him, either. He had grabbed his sword and was constantly turning and waiting for something to suddenly appear in the air and attack them.

"Brother, this is our battlefield, the place where Yahweh comes to deliver us. We don't wait for anyone to attack us. We charge the enemy. We hunt them down. We are the children of God. We have not invaded their place; they have tried to make strongholds in ours. Hang on to your sword. Don't trip whatever you do. And try to keep up." Vicki spoke with an affection in her voice. She was growing fonder of the man every minute. She was good at forgiveness. Whatever he did to Evie, God could use for good. And they could certainly use his presence here on the desert battlefield.

Vicki took off running up the sand dune. Bryce ran after her with a fierceness born of a rekindled love for Yahweh and love for his family. He was miraculously adept at running in sand uphill even though he'd never run or moved away from his portal in all the trips he'd made here. Sam took the back of the train and found it an effort to keep up with Bryce. Bryce caught up to Vicki and passed her, the first to reach the top of the dune. He stopped suddenly and looked at something he had never seen before.

It was a horde of demons. He wasn't sure what kind they were, either. But if they came here, to his family's battlefield, then they were going to die. No one had to teach Bryce what to do next. It is innate in every child of Yahweh fighting on their own battlefield.

Bryce raised his head and closed his eyes. Sword down to his side, he dropped down on one knee and then both together and worshiped Yahweh.

Vicki and Sam arrived next to Bryce and raised their swords to tap together. Then they turned to Bryce and offered him the same. 'Clink, clink!' All three swords chimed in unity and love.

Then all three warriors ran down the dune.

The believers fell upon the Corgs with their swords. Bryce had no trouble matching each Corg swing for swing, despite Corgs being some of the fastest demons the women encountered. In a matter of moments, the horde had lost a large portion of their group. When the Corgs spilled maggots rather than blood, it was all Bryce could do to not fall in the slop of writhing worms.

"Noticing this, Sam?" Vicki asked.

"Yep."

Vicki decapitated a Corg with a smooth swipe of her sword. The head fell to the ground with enough force to bounce twice before landing in front of Bryce. The motion of the head caught his attention, and he looked down to see what he nearly stepped on. Within seconds, the maggots had crawled out of the neck stump and onto the face of the Corg, consuming the eyes, crawling up the nose and into the mouth. The maggots were already bloated and getting bigger by the second.

Sam noticed the lack of movement coming from her left side, where Bryce was supposed to be fighting. She gave a quick glance and saw that he was certainly not fighting. He was green and looked like he was going to pass out. He didn't notice the Corg that had moved into position behind him, ready to pierce him through with its filthy sword. She lunged and put her own sword through the gut of the Corg and ripping up as high as she could, then yanked it out and jumped out of the way as the Corg fell forward and maggots again poured out.

"Move it, Bryce!" she yelled, shoving him as she went back to her spot. She didn't want to lose any ground to the Corgs and if they kept it up just a little longer, they would have this entire horde down on the ground rotting.

Bryce jumped and came out of his daze at Sam's shove. He couldn't believe the horrors of this place and felt ridiculous that he had been coming here standing around the portals thinking everything was getting better while the women fought these things, these demons, face to face. And this was only one 'kind'? And what were Sam and Vicki noticing that he wasn't? "Better pay attention and learn fast, Bryce," he told himself.

He began looking at the Corgs in between swings, stabs, and swirling around. Most were already covered in wounds, even before they became engaged with the believers. Some wounds were significant, and the Corgs were not only struggling to move themselves through the dunes but were having to haul the engorged and huge maggots attached to them and growing out of them. He also noticed that the Corgs looked panicked or alarmed, and if he didn't know better, they also looked afraid.

The battle was fought in relative quiet for the next fifteen minutes. The only sounds were the grunts and heaves of the warriors and the squeals, squishes, and cries from the Corgs. Finally, the last demon dropped at Bryce's feet. And boy, did he feel this first victory on the battlefield of prayer.

Sam really thought she was going to have to kick the backs of Bryce's knees to make him drop to the ground. She assumed he would do the whole machismo guy thing, a "you want a piece of me?" routine, maybe along with some chest thumping and crotch grabbing. But he didn't.

This man truly loved his family, and loved Yahweh, and he willingly knelt in the sand, dropping his sword and raising his hands high to the heavens. It had been a long time since the women had a man lead them in anything, let alone praise to Yahweh after a battle. It brought tears to Sam's eyes and surprisingly, she found herself kneeling next to him, having dropped her own sword, lifting her hands as high as she could.

Vicki was moved by the Spirit of God to worship as well, giving praise to the One who had given them their swords, their strength, and their faith to fight those that would make strongholds. This was always one of Vicki's favorite moments, the sound of quiet after the battle, after dropping her sword that had grown heavier and deadlier by the moment.

All three gave tear-filled adoration and honor to Yahweh. When they were done, they again heard the feasting maggots and it brought them back to the mission.

"So, these are Corgs?" Bryce asked. "Do I even dare to imagine what the other kinds of demons are going to be like?"

"Corgs are the only one with the maggots. You did better than the first time I saw them. I threw up all over the ice." As soon as Vicki said "ice", she realized her mistake. She had, until now, kept her own battlefield private. Sam's head swiveled towards her, her sharp eyes looking right at her. She missed nothing, but Vicki shook her head to say, 'not now'. Sam honored that request and stood to her feet.

"So, something about this was different?" Bryce persisted. "You asked Sam if she was noticing. Has something changed?" Bryce wanted to know as many details as he could, hoping that the sooner they got this battle over, the sooner Evie and the kids were going to be safe.

"These Corgs were already hurt," Sam started to explain. "They weren't running to attack us. They were running away

from an attack. They were afraid. I've never seen them afraid before, nor have seen enough survivors to make up a horde. How many were there to start with if a horde was what was left? And who scared them bad enough that they ran?"

Vicki spoke up. "Sam, remember all the piles of carnage we've been coming across?" Sam nodded. "I think whoever or whatever was doing that is here right now. What do we do?"

"Follow the trail."

Sam and Vicki returned their swords to their scabbards while Bryce clung to his, not yet letting it go. They started running single file, but this time Bryce was in no hurry to be first. The horde had not covered their tracks, and their path was as plain as day. The sand, displaced by the feet of at least seventy-five Corgs and the weight of the heavy, feasting maggots, was hard with the congealed and drying body fluids and guts.

"So, someone has been coming here and killing these things and you don't know who it is?" Bryce asked with more irritation and fear in his tone than he intended to reveal. But he couldn't believe what he was finding out about prayer in such a short time. Battlefield prayer, and portal entries he knew about. But types of demons, maggots, and now unknown visitors to his wife's battlefield? Who wants her so much?

"We thought it was a super demon, maybe level four or more. Did you know that demons have rankings and levels?" Sam spoke these words with such nonchalance that Bryce had to look back and see if she was serious. Dear heavens, she was.

When Bryce didn't answer right away, Sam kept on, "Level four is high. Like, super high." Level four demons... super demons?! He wanted to get back home and hug his wife. What had he done to her?

"*But now you're not sure?*" *he asked as they began ascending the dune where the trail of blood and footsteps led. He wiped sweat off his face, the salty drops stinging his eyes.*

"*No, we're not. I think it's a person, a prayer warrior, but whoever it is, they are powerful. They've done more damage and left more carnage than I've ever seen in all my years of battlefields.*" *Vicki didn't dare look back at Sam but felt her eyes boring through the back of her skull. Why was she giving away so much? She was normally much more guarded about her battlefield and her past.*

As soon as they crested the hill, a form could be seen down at the bottom of the dune. The desert sunset was dazzling with pinks and yellows, and the swirling cloud pattern was a stunning declaration to the beauty of Yahweh Himself. The form was kneeling, hands raised and in front of it was an unbelievably sized pile of demon parts. The group slowed down in disbelief at such a display of force and power. Who was this?

Even as they walked slowly closer to the form, it did not increase in size. The figure remained small, and eventually the shape took place.

"*Yahweh, no! Oh no... Sam! It's him!*" *The panic in Vicki's voice shook Bryce to the core. He had no idea who Vicki was talking about, but she looked like she was about to pass out. He looked to Sam, who had stopped dead in her tracks. She paled and her face seemed filled with anger. He felt fear deep inside himself, but he didn't know why. Vicki went on ahead, walking as softly as she could. She was careful not to startle the small creature.*

With a look of anguish on her face, Vicki held a hand up to Bryce, signaling him to stop. He did, and she moved in front of the figure, kneeling as tears poured out of her eyes. She held her arms out. The little thing went into her arms, and they embraced, hard and long. Vicki wiped away the tears with one hand and held tight with the other. Finally, she grabbed the person by the face and kissed it before she helped it to stand.

And in the deepest moment of horror Bryce ever thought he would endure, he saw who it was. Vicki turned the person towards him. Here it stood in front of untold thousands of demon parts, hacked and dismembered to death with a bloody sword by its side. All he could do was drop to the ground in agony. All he could do was whisper the name of his son.

"Kendall."

By 11 p.m. Evie had already put the kids to bed, taken a shower, and finished cleaning up the kitchen for the night. It had been a quiet day for her. She'd had the day off from work, enjoyed breakfast with the kids, and then Bryce had taken them for a few hours. As she finally sat down to relax, she began to think back through the details of the day.

It had been a strange feeling to have the house to herself. She'd thought back and couldn't remember a time when she'd ever been home, completely by herself. It had been quiet. At first it felt off. She had sat in the chair and just stared into space for twenty minutes before she'd made herself snap out of it. Lots of women did this, she'd told herself. They did it because they'd had to. Either the choice had been made for them, or they'd made it themselves because they thought it was the best, not the easiest, but the best. They'd watched their kids take off with their dads for the weekend and somehow, they managed to get used to it. She would too. It had only been for a few hours this time, but it would be just a matter of time before they'd have the weekends and holidays worked out for sharing. She'd poured her coffee and thought about whether she'd choose to work the weekends when they were with Bryce or maybe take those days off so she could do...girl...things. She didn't know what the girl things would be, but now she'd have the time to find out.

She smiled when she thought of her girlfriends. Even with each of them having their own families, they'd always managed to find time to hang out, get pedicures, see movies, and they did it all without sending their kids away for the weekend. That thought had been followed by a moment of panic and despair. Was she being selfish? Did she want time away from her kids and was looking for a way to get it by sending them off with Bryce? After another twenty minutes, she reached the conclusion that she was a horrible mother and a hideous person. Normally, when she was filled with self-doubt, she'd pick up the phone and call Sam or Vicki. She didn't this time.

Remembering their conversation from this morning, she had been more and more annoyed with their attitudes. Now she went back and forth between talking out loud to herself and talking to God.

"I don't know what they want! Seriously? They can't stand Bryce! How can they say they think I didn't try? Why are they against me? Why are they for him? Are they his friends now? Why am I being treated like this?" And on and on she had gone. This conversation had lasted another twenty minutes. That was when she realized she had wasted an entire hour on literally nothing, or nothing good anyway. Nothing that would make any of this hard stuff easier.

She had walked herself into her room, dug in her closet until she had found her old running shoes, changed clothes, and did something she hadn't done in a very long time. She emptied her mind and went for a run. It felt so good. After she had found her rhythm and got her breathing under control, it felt like her body remembered what to do. She looked at the trees as she steadily ran and soon felt like she could think clearly once again.

"Have I given all I have to give?" she asked herself. "Yes. I have. Before the Lord, I can say that I have done all I know to do. Then that's it, right? What more can anyone do? I have prayed. No, I battled. I gave it time. I avoided making decisions in the heat of the moment." She smiled through her breathing as she thought of Sam's love for the band Asia.

She had slowed her pace down, before finally stopping to stretch. With her hands on her hips, she had bowed her head and whispered, "Yahweh, I know sometimes You are silent for a reason, and I know you love me and that all things work for my good. I think I was looking for something that wasn't there, and I'm ready to accept that and move on. I'm sorry it took me so long but thank you for helping me get where I need to be."

She had lifted her head and waited. She had been expecting peace to flood her like it had always done before at the end of a battle. There was a feeling of peace that descends and wraps around and through you, and you know without any hesitation that it was a gift from God Himself.

But when she had turned to walk home, she felt unsettled, the opposite of the peace she was expecting. After some musing, she chalked it up to either being new emotional territory or a ploy from the enemy to drag her back onto the battlefield. "Nothing good comes from going back and revisiting old ground that had already been fought over," she reminded herself. It didn't feel like the other battlefields that had been fought and won, but this wasn't the same battle either. Of course, it would feel different. Of course, she might be tempted to not accept an obvious answer. And the answer was obvious to her, and eventually it would be to everyone else. God had spoken, or rather not spoken, which also had meant something, right? That was what she tried to convince herself of on that walk back home.

Evie continued to think back through the day, remembering how her heart had skipped when she had heard the truck pull up. She had reminded herself that she was a big girl, and her heart could skippity beat all it wanted, but she wasn't going to give in to it.

The door had burst open and two little blurs had run by her, "Hi, Mom!" "Hi Mommy!" then disappeared into Kendall's room. The house had suddenly filled with the sounds she hadn't heard all day.

The door had been left wide open, and she turned and saw Bryce leaning in the doorway, hands in pocket, looking at her. He studied her for a moment, until she said, "Oh hi!"

"Oh, hi?? Are we still doing lame greetings??" ran her thoughts.

Then had come his grin, slow and easy. She realized her heart hadn't jumped up and down that time. It had been just a little flutter. "Thank you, heart," her thoughts continued.

"Hi," he had answered. "Did you have a good afternoon?"

"Me? Oh, yeah! It was great. Well, not great, but good! I ran and then took a shower. Well, of course I showered, but that doesn't matter and it's not a big deal. Everyone showers after they run. So. Yeah. I did too."

Bryce hadn't seemed to notice her awkwardness, or if he had, he chose not to mention it. "Well, we missed you today. I missed you."

"Oh, don't go there. Not here, not now," she warned herself. Evie felt a little panicked and annoyed at her heart picking up a fluttering tempo.

"Yeah, about that, we need to talk, Bryce," she had finally said while mustering up a determined look, a look she had practiced that looked firm and settled.

Bryce had studied her for a moment, pushed off the door and said, "Sure, Ev. Whenever you want. I just can't tonight."

Evie felt the sudden rush of annoyance. "Oh? You got something more important to do tonight?"

"Why am I doing this?" she thought to herself, "You didn't want to do this right now, anyway!"

"Actually, I do have something important to do. But we'll talk soon. You okay with that?"

They had both watched each other for a moment before she had responded, "I guess I'll have to be, won't I?"

She let the annoyance eat at her all night. He didn't have to share every detail of his twenty-four hours with her, but this felt like secrets all over again. From a man who said he wanted to put his family back together again, she struggled to trust this unknown.

But now the house was quiet, a good quiet. She didn't need to go kneel by her bed and spend the next hour battling. She could just continue to sit here. Maybe even watch tv for a change. The sound of her cell phone startled her and when she saw Bryce's number, she stopped herself from reaching for it. He didn't want to talk earlier, but he does now, when she is finally chilling and trying not think about him?

"I don't think so!" She sent her phone to voicemail. Thirty seconds later, he called again. Anger flared this time as she took the call.

"Not now, Bryce. Call back tomorrow. I'm not interested in talking tonight and you should..."

"Evie! Listen to..."

"... have picked up on that when I didn't answer the first couple of times!"

"... me!"

She hung up the phone. Her hands were shaking, and she felt fearful, but couldn't quite tell why. It was then that she saw the headlights swing into the driveway and the two sisters of her heart rolled out and headed for her door.

She knew immediately something was wrong. Bryce's phone call, the girls running to the door. Fear of the unknown flooded her veins with a surge of adrenaline. She watched them through the window as they came to the door and let themselves in. She saw the worried looks on both of their faces, as they both took deep breaths and paused.

"What is it?" Evie yelled, voice shaking.

Vicki stepped forward. "It's okay, honey. It's okay." she soothed. Evie's eyes darted from her to Sam and back again.

Vicki continued softly, "You need to go check on Kendall."

Evie turned and ran towards Kendall's room.

She flung open his door and saw him peacefully sitting in his bed with the soft light from his bed stand, sending a glow around him. She frantically ran to the window and confirmed it was closed and locked and checked the closet. Nothing.

"What is it? What's wrong?" she asked desperately, looking at him.

"I'm fine, Mom," was his simple response.

She sat on the bed and took his face in her hands. "What happened?" She looked into his big brown eyes and saw them fill with tears, saw the quiver in his lip.

"Kendall, what is it?" she whispered.

"I'm sorry, Mom. I didn't know when I started what it would be like. I just wanted to help."

Evie could feel panic welling up inside her but didn't know whether to push it down or embrace it. "Kendall, there is nothing, absolutely nothing, you could have done that we can't fix. I love you and I promise it will be okay. But I need you to tell me because I don't know what you are talking about," she kept her voice a soft whisper.

"I started praying."

She stroked his hair and face, soothing him, but felt confusion replacing the rush of panic. "That's good, honey. God loves to hear our prayers. It's okay! Can you tell me what you were praying about?"

The tears swelled and began to spill over, breaking her heart for whatever was causing this pain. "You, Mom. I was praying for you. And then I started praying for Dad. And I didn't know it would be like that. I looked for your answer."

Cold fear, like a knife made of ice, began to inch its way up her spine as she felt the hair stand up on her arms and neck. Her mind was racing over his words. Bryce's call. The girls in the living room, here to check on Kendall. "No. Please God, no. He's just a baby."

She looked at him through the blur of tears in her own eyes. "Oh baby, were you praying differently than our normal prayers?" He looked like a small toddler when he nodded his head. "Did you go to a battlefield?"

He lunged forward and wrapped himself around her. "I had to, Mom, I had to. I woke up at night and knew I had to pray." His words tumbled out. She held him as he told her how he had begun to pray fighting words, for her, for Bryce, for each of them. He had heard her prayers one night and took the same words to his own room and began to repeat them. In his childlike way, he prayed for victory in battle, the destruction of the enemy, and for the power of Yahweh to be demonstrated through him.

His words had yielded power of a seasoned warrior. Now as Evie rocked him, comforted him, and bathed his soft head with her tears she knew who had stormed that battlefield, leaving the path of carnage, slaying more demons on his own than she and her team ever did. She knew who it was, and she knew why, and all she could feel was rage.

When she finally left his room, he was sleeping peacefully after falling asleep in her arms. Sleep hadn't taken long to come, as he was physically and emotionally exhausted.

Evie walked back into the living room where Vicki and Sam sat on the couch, waiting.

Sam started to say something, but Vicki touched her arm signaling her to wait. Evie sat down in the chair, staring at the floor.

Minutes passed. With her head still down, she asked, "So it was him all this time?"

She couldn't see them looking at her with love and compassion, but she heard Vicki's soft answer, "Yes."

Evie drew a deep, steadying breath, "Who found him?"

After a pause, Sam answered, "We did."

"You two?'"

Sam and Vicki exchanged tense looks. They knew she'd be upset by Kendall, but this seemed to be anger, not just concern. Sam looked at Vicki and gave a subtle shake of the head.

Vicki rolled her eyes and said "Well, me, Sam and Bryce."

They saw Evie flinch when Bryce's name was mentioned. The air was so thick it felt hard to breathe.

Evie looked at her two best friends with hard eyes, "You took Bryce to my battlefield? You didn't ask me? You didn't mention it to me?" Her voice was trembling as she continued. "You found my son there? In a place I told you we were done? Has it occurred to you that had you respected me and my wishes, Kendall would never have been there?"

Evie sat rigid and unyielding as she waited for their answer. Tension continued to fill the room. And for the second time tonight hair stood up on arms and necks, but this time it was Sam and Vicki's. This didn't feel right. They'd expected emotion, but this felt like something different. Evie's deep and powerful anger felt like bondage.

Before they could answer her, they all heard the truck pull in, followed quickly by a door slam shut and boots walking to the door. There was a swift rap on the door, but Evie didn't move, just staring at the girls, who stared at the door, then back at Evie.

Soundlessly, Evie stood and walked to the door, opened it, turned, and came back to her seat. Bryce watched her walk away and saw the girls signaling something to him with their eyes, but he had no idea what.

He followed her into the room, stopped at the hall and seemed as if he were going to turn down it when Evie said, "Don't. He's asleep."

He looked from the hall to Evie, before joining the girls on the couch. "Is he ok?" he asked, desperately.

The girls, still silent, both shook their head again, but Bryce just looked at them, before staring at Evie. "Is he ok?!" he repeated.

With a hardness in her voice she answered, "He will be."

Bryce opened his mouth to say something but was stopped by Evie. "Let me see if I understand this right. You three, and now my son, have been on the battlefield praying. Together. For me? So, you're all what, friends now?"

No one answered, so she continued, "Bryce? You've been on a battlefield? A battlefield?" Her short laugh contained a mix of hurt and anger. "I have to admit, I never saw this one coming. My two best friends, you, Kendall…" She winced. "All fighting, back-to-back, for me? So, I'm the one needing the prayer now? When did that happen? I guess I'm the last to know, right, Bryce? Again?"

"Ev, it wasn't like that at all. We just…"

"Don't," she said to all of them. "Just. Don't."

Bryce blew out the breath he had been holding, then tried again, "I didn't know Kendall was there. I didn't ask him to come, and I don't know how he learned about it. I just want to help. Please, let me help."

"You want to know how he learned? Let me tell you," she snapped. "He learned from overhearing me. From night after night after night of me praying for you, and for some stupid, ridiculous answer! And look what good that did!"

Sam started to interrupt but Evie stopped her. "How long did you know it was Kendall? How long have you been taking Bryce there without me knowing?"

Sam, usually the direct one, sensed the nudge in her spirit to be soft, replied, "We didn't know it was Kendall until tonight, and tonight was the first time we took Bryce."

Sam leaned forward in her seat moving to reach for Evie's hand. Evie jerked her arm away from her. Sam continued, "Something's not right, Evie. I know you can sense it!" she pleaded with Evie to understand. "This isn't you! This doesn't feel like it is coming from God! Your battlefield, your story, doesn't end like this. You know it doesn't!"

Evie seemed to stare right through them before she replied, "Let's get a couple of things cleared up before we call this a night. I will tell you what I feel. I feel done. Absolutely done." She looked at Bryce, "You wanted to talk later but I'm done with that too. It's over."

Bryce flinched like he had been hit.

Now Vicki reached out to touch Evie, but she jerked away again. "As for Kendall, he will be absolutely fine. I know this because he is never, ever, going in there again to battle for me," she pointed at herself, then each of them, "for you, or for us. If he needs to know that we found an answer, here it is. God said no. That's it. And if either of you ever step foot on that battlefield again," she looked to the girls, "we will be done too." Evie stood up, "I think each of you know how to find your way out."

She turned, walked into Kendall's room, and closed the door.

CHAPTER ELEVEN

*L*oden sat at the head of the table in the sulfuric cavern that belonged to Oridon, the greatest Swastik ever known to the Hall of Hades. Loden was sure Oridon wouldn't mind the use of his headquarters if it were for advancing the greater evil. The brimstone gave off a shadowy glow of orange and yellow that bounced off the wet, oozing walls. Moans could be heard coming from the far places of the cave. The table, made of bones and skulls, was worn with age. The count of battle plans made here was untold. Millions of campaigns had been thought up and designed right here in this spot. Some of the greatest attacks on saints were plotted in Oridon's cave, at Oridon's table.

Loden was a Jader. A level four demon. It was nothing to be ashamed of, but he was going to get his name on the Hall of Hades if he had to use every Snapper and Corg in hell. No Jader had ever had such an honor. No Jader had ever had such advanced angel of light training and ability like he had. He would not squander this gift on a low-level task. No, he was going to take down that Evie shrew and he was going to get recognized doing it.

Fairen, an equally powerful Jader, called the meeting to order. Fairen gained power with his skillful use of flattery, with which he had taken down many an enemy. His smile was deceptive, and his heart filled with fraud and lying. The warlords of Snappers, Ventars, and Corgs knew this and did not trust him. But they all sat submissively in their seats, waiting for the battle plans to be made before they could effectively go to war.

"The great and powerful Loden of the Jaders has called this meeting. Hear him!" spoke Fairen in a smooth voice. Fairen the Flatterer. Every demon had his gifts. Loden knew that Fairen had just spoken the truth. It was the only truth he believed in. He knew his own greatness and that he was becoming more powerful as this campaign against the female continued.

Loden stood at the end of the table, looking down the expanse of bones and skulls and into the black eyes of twenty of the greatest warlords in the region, all here under his authority and submission. "I have summoned you here to give an update on the mighty task that was given to me. I successfully infected the human named Evie, and she will return no more to the battlefield. My mission is nearly complete. I've only yet to post the banner into the sand and the victory is ours. I will return to the field after this meeting to complete that task. Let us give cheer and a shout to the Dark One."

Loden turned his head aside and spit on the hardened lava floor. He fully expected them all to spit with him and was surprised when they all stared at him, not one warlord moving or shouting. He sensed anger, maybe even rage? What was their problem? They were probably jealous. Corgs, Ventars and Snappers would never be as beautiful or as useful as a Jader. Their jealousy was deliciously satisfying.

"What? You lowlifes are so jealous that I, a Jader, could complete the mission so quickly and easily? You can't even spit to honor our wicked king? Just wait until I tell him. You'll be sorry for your disrespect, then."

Loden noticed the looks exchanged between the principalities. A margin of worry crept into the back of his evil mind. They knew something that he didn't. It was Nerod, the local head of the Snappers who spoke out after they all had turned their blackened eyes back to him.

"We mean no disrespect, Loden. We are just not sure it is wise to say the campaign has ended." He spoke with contempt in his voice, and Loden heard every bit of it.

"That shows what you know, Nerod. I was given the opportunity to infect the human, and I did it. No one comes back to the battlefield once infected. Mission accomplished, like I said." He raised his voice, his pitch getting higher. He wasn't turning red with heat yet and needed to avoid that. He still needed these servants to build his kingdom.

"Pardon me, if you'd please," continued Nerod, with his sickening tone. Apparently, he was the voice of the principalities now. "Watchers have been spotted."

The pungent air was sucked out of the cave, almost all sucked out by Loden himself when he gasped with shock. No one else seemed surprised at all, and the demons didn't even move. They sat perfectly still, looking directly at him. Apparently, the demons knew. Everyone knew but him. He was being set up. He recovered and held his panic tightly in his chest. He wanted to rip their faces off. Loden looked at Fairen. The other Jader still had that deceptive smile on his face, and Loden was unsure if he knew about this.

"Wa-aatchers?" He stuttered and swore under his breath. "Where were they spotted?" He should have pretended that he knew about the watchers, but this caught him completely off guard. Now the others knew that, and weakness spotted among the wicked was like blood to a shark. He may need to go red here, after all. That would teach them. Another look passed between the leaders. They were now aware that the great Loden wasn't in as much control as he seemed to think, which meant that someone, or something else, was.

"A couple of Ventars, Jangis and Balid, spotted them while you were with the human. We've awarded the demons for their surveillance and discovery. We thought you knew. But this appears far from over, Jader." Nerod said the name deliberately, openly disrespecting the top level of demonic power at the table.

But was it over? Who was the highest power here if it wasn't him? If there were Watchers, they were reporting to someone. Does that mean there are Briners and Lappes here? Was one here disguised? Who could they be reporting to? Oridon? No, Swastiks don't use Watchers. No way were Briners and Lappes interested in this. It was one stupid human woman, with a couple of friends, from the middle of Nowhere, Indiana. Calling upon his angel of light training, Loden masked his fear and agitation.

He slammed his fist down onto the table with all his might. A crack began at the skull embedded at the head of the table and splintered off the entire length. Powerful evil emanated from Loden. He looked white and angelic, but the breath of the surrounding demons was taken from them. His power bound their clawed and blackened hands to the splintered table, and they could not reach for their swords or move from their seats. They were unprepared for the power contained by this angel of *light. Loden may not have all the knowledge, but he did have power. Fear replaced breath, and the demons drank it in.*

"Listen to me, ferrets of the underworld. If you see another Watcher, catch it and bring it to me immediately. Do you understand? You all think this is a game? Playing hide the information while hordes and hordes of your demons are massacred? Did you not notice the carnage at the oasis, the piles of Corg maggots just yesterday? Nearly four thousand Corgs were destroyed while none of you were watching! Maybe the Watcher is reporting your own incompetency? Did you ever think of that? Someone is successfully slaughtering the Corgs and annihilating the Ventars! And Nerod," he said with derision, looking straight at the rebellious demon, "there has been no extermination of the Snappers. Only Corgs and Ventars. Perhaps the Watchers have noticed that as well."

Loden sat down, folding his hands together and holding them high to his face. He tried to suppress a smile as the demon's doubtful eyes now focused on Nerod. The demons thought over the past battles and the discovery of the massacres, recollecting that no Snappers had been found. There were no Jaders either, but no one was clever enough to think of this. Distrust, the drink of the underworld, grew towards Nerod. How the cracked tables had turned. Time to adjourn the meeting before any reconciliation was possible.

"Leave me." Loden gave the command quietly and with a flick of his hand. His own vanity made him believe they would obey, and their own distrust led them to do as they were commanded. Within seconds, the Corgs, Ventars, and Snappers had evaporated into the air which they ruled. All that remained were Fairen and Loden.

Fairen looked at the powerful Jader with appreciation. "Well done, Jader. They tried to emasculate you at your own meeting. The master will be proud when he hears how you have ruled today." He gave a slight bow of the head when he spoke the words.

"Watchers, Fairen? Why are the Watchers here? I've had much bigger and more important battles than this. I had thought at one time I was being tested or disciplined when I was given this mission. Now I find out there is something bigger going on than I knew. It doesn't make sense."

"Tell me about your human," said Fairen.

"She's a woman! What's there to tell? Wife, mom. Busy with work, kids, church, friends. Has a jerk husband who was missing, and now he's back. She can't decide whether she wants him or not and was coming to the battlefield a lot until I infected her. I haven't seen her since. Case closed, I thought."

"Hmm." Fairen nodded his head, acting sympathetic. "The Watchers never come unless it's big. Loden, this is your chance. You're gonna get your name known. All your training will be noticed, and the Hall of Hades will soon bear your name and image. Never doubt yourself or your power and authority."

Loden listened and believed every flattering word his Jader partner spoke. He would soon be known and be infamous, like he always dreamed. Who knew Fairen was a prophetic demon?

"The Evie woman has not been back. I have no doubts the infection has run deep into her marrow, where it will infect not only her brain but her heart. I've wasted stronger people than her before. She is done. I'd stake my fame on it. And I also would bet that this battlefield is now dormant and unoccupied. Perhaps it is time to notify Oridon that level fives can now come to dwell and breed."

But Fairen had other plans. He was going to find Jangis and Balid. He wanted to know exactly where the Watchers had been seen, where the nearest portal was, and finally figure out how to get to the other side. He heard it had been done by a level seven before. It was only a matter of time before Loden screwed his mission up and Fairen ruled the Jaders alone. Maybe that's what the Watchers were looking for, a real leader. No, he wasn't going to send for Oridon. Oridon would end up saving Loden's pungent backside. And he needed Loden to die for all eternity.

"No, don't send for Oridon just yet," suggested Fairen. "Let's capture a Watcher and see who sent it. There's no rush, right? The battle is over. The woman is not coming back. Let's wait until the carnage piles completely decompose and blow away with the desert wind. No sense in letting Oridon see your mistake in millions of bones." Fairen hoped the images of the carnage would feed the fear and doubt in Loden. And by the looks in Loden's eyes, he had hit the mark.

Loden and Fairen left Oridon's cave and parted ways. Besides the crack in the table, Oridon would never know it had been used. But Loden was sure Oridon would understand if he even noticed. Oridon rarely showed up. He acted like this whole area was beneath him, as if other places and regions were more important. But if Oridon found out the Watchers were here, Loden bet he would come back to the lowly Indiana station and want to act like he was the big shot. But Loden had this covered. He'd done well. Sure, they lost a lot of demons by someone on the battlefield, but he also infected a Christian. Just that thought made him elated at his accomplishment. It is never, ever a small thing to infect a spawn of Yahweh.

"Ahh!" he held his hands over his ears as he dropped to the ground in excruciating pain. Even thinking the name of the enemy was debilitating. This only fed Loden's hatred and swelled his blackened soul.

As soon as the pain stopped, he started planning. He was going to go back to the battlefield, not to battle but to scope out the spies and watch for the Watchers. He needed to figure out what they were looking for, because for all the darkness in him, he could not fathom what was so important about this stupid woman and her failing family and life. She was certainly expendable to the enemy, a no-name commoner. Was it those friends of hers? The tall leggy blonde or the fierce dark little one? He couldn't be losing his edge, but not once did he get the impression this was a high-ranking mission. But from now on, he was certainly going to act like it was. He was also going to kill that ferret Jangis as soon as he saw him.

It had been a long night lacking in things such as rest, comfort, peace, and sleep. Given the lack of sleep, Bryce didn't feel exactly friendly when he heard the knock on his door. He grabbed the shirt draped across his chair, put it on without bothering about the buttons, picked up his coffee and stalked to the door.

"What?" His voice was as grim as his unshaven face, as he opened his door.

He stared at Vicki and Sam, no expression, no movement, clearly annoyed with their presence at his door. The girls returned his look with glares of their own as they faced each other in silence.

The stare down lasted for a few seconds until Sam broke the silence with a hard blink, admitting, "I never win at the stare down game. Can we please come in?"

"I have no idea how you found my address. Don't ever come here again." Bryce swung the door shut and turned to walk away.

He heard the soft thud and whispered words as he turned to see Sam pulling her foot out of the door, pushing it open, and walking in with Vicki right behind her. They said nothing as they helped themselves to coffee pot and sat at his tiny table.

He stood there with his shirt hanging open, his mouth set in a tight line, and stared at them.

"Bryce, you won. You can blink," said Sam while reaching for a powdered creamer container. "Is this all you have? It's not really cream; you know that, right?"

Her flippant tone snapped him out of the stupor he was in and pushed him into full blown annoyance. "Get out. You weren't invited. I don't want you here." He took two steps towards the table before Sam looked at him.

"Good grief, Bryce! Can you put some clothes on?! It's not that you don't look all nice, you do, you really do, but we need to have a conversation and you can't stand there like that!"

He grabbed for the front of his shirt, then stopped. "Wait, you break in here, uninvited, steal my coffee, then tell me to change my clothes? You're delusional! I'm comfortable. I don't want to button my shirt! It's freaking seven in the morning! People don't have buttoned shirts at seven in the morning! What did you not understand? I don't want you here!" his voice getting louder with each point he made.

Vicki and Sam both stared at him as if he had grown horns, and for the life of him, Bryce couldn't figure out what they didn't understand. Did they really think he was the freak?

"I don't think it's a stretch to expect you to be buttoned." Sam responded as if she were talking to a small child.

"Get out," was all Bryce could manage with gritted teeth. He was pretty sure he filed another tooth completely flat every time he was around one of them.

Vicki, who had had enough of Sam and Bryce's exchange, slammed the creamer down onto the counter. "Okay! Sam, not helping! Bryce, I'm sorry we barged in, and I promise we will leave as soon as we finish our coffee. Can we just talk to you for a minute?"

Sam shrugged and looked at her coffee. Bryce, too exasperated to argue, refilled his own cup and joined them at the table.

Vicki gently nodded at his bare chest. With a sigh and a scowl at Sam, he buttoned his shirt.

Sam sweetly smiled at him, "There. Doesn't that feel better?"

He held his glare for a moment, then turned to Vicki, "Listen. I know you probably mean well, but neither of you are helping by being here. I think last night pretty much settled it that our trying to battle together is a bad idea. You guys being here is another bad idea. So whatever crazy idea you two have come up with is likely just another bad idea."

Sam started to speak up when Vicki stopped her. "I know—we know what you are saying." She looked back at Bryce. "And we know it looks like we made a mistake. But we didn't. Going to the battlefield together, that was right." Bryce started to interrupt her, but she quickly added, "It was! We were not just praying for Evie; we were praying for the answer that God already has for your family. That is not wrong, no matter how it has twisted itself to Evie."

"She's right though. I brought all of this on. Kendall," Bryce's head dropped, "I can't forget that, ever. He was there because of me. He never should have been there."

"Says who?" demanded Sam.

Bryce looked up at her. "What do you mean? You saw him. You think that is okay for a kid?"

"I'm not in charge of who gets entrance into the field. I'm not in charge of who gets weapons. And neither are you! If he was there, it was because the portal opened for him. I think you need to remember who mans that door—and it's not me, and it isn't you."

"Listen," Vicki said, "I have a lot of questions and I'm guessing you do, too. We asked Mrs. Taylor if she'd talk to us this morning and she said she would."

"Who the heck is Mrs. Taylor?" Bryce asked,

A slow grin came across Sam's face. "She's the Oracle."

With a sigh, Bryce set his cup down and stood. "An oracle. Of course, she's an oracle. What was I thinking?"

After more arguing they reached two conclusions: the first was the three of them were probably going to argue about everything before they actually did anything and two, Bryce had a hang up about who got to drive. The girls decided it was better to let him win this one. They all piled into the truck.

"Well, isn't this cozy!" quipped Sam as she slid into the middle seat next to Bryce, with Vicki folding up into the passenger seat.

"Don't talk to me," retorted Bryce.

"Vicki? Will you please tell Bryce that the country music coming out of his speakers is making me want to shove sticks into my ears?"

Bryce grinned, reached forward, and cranked the volume, "Great song."

She looked at him singing along, "You seriously think this is a great song?" She shut the radio off.

"Okay," Bryce said, ignoring her. "What's the story with the Oracle lady?"

"Well," said Sam, "Vicki's known her the longest, but she is the one who has taught us about the battlefield. We got to know her in a women's Bible study. We don't know much about her history, but she has some major experience and whenever we have a question or a situation we can't handle, we go to her."

"And does she already know about me and Evie?"

"Yes, Evie has talked to her before, and we went to her with our concerns about Evie. She's the one who told us Evie had probably been infected."

Bryce remained quiet for the rest of the ride. It wasn't long before he pulled into Mrs. Taylor's driveway.

"I'm guessing she's old?" Bryce asked as he took in the 1950s style house. The planter boxes under the window were filled with plastic flowers, and the mulched bed around the porch was complete with whirly gigs and wind catchers. The brick facing and mint green siding completed its dated look.

"You're only as old as you think, Brycie," said Vicki as she hopped out of the truck.

They were met at the door by a seemingly frail old woman. Bryce took in the grey hair, thin skin, and blue-veined hands as she opened the door to them. "Hello! Come in, come in!"

Their bickering left outside, Sam and Vicki led the way, both now filled with a gentleness Bryce didn't know they possessed.

They sat down on the matching couch and loveseat as Mrs. Taylor sat in her rocking chair. "You must be Bryce," she said softly.

He leaned forward and grasped her tiny hand. "Yes, I am, thank you for seeing us. I understand you have been a friend to Evie."

She studied him a moment before speaking. "I have prayed for you and am so glad to finally meet you."

Bryce felt a lump rise in his throat at her sincerity. "I'm sorry for that, and thank you," he said quietly.

She laughed softly and as she did, her face took on a lovely youthful transformation, "Don't be sorry! I am always happy to respond when the shofar blows!"

Bryce looked confused at the girls, who just smiled back at Mrs. Taylor. "Yeah, well, I'm not very familiar with what a shofar is, but thank you for the prayers, anyway. I'm sorry Evie had to tell you about me."

"Oh, Evie didn't tell me much about you. Let's just say we have some mutual friends. I've been praying for you for some time now. I'm happy to know why that battlefield has gone quiet!"

All three of their eyes got a little bigger with that one. They exchanged looks while Sam silently mouthed "Oracle" to Bryce.

"But enough of that," Mrs. Taylor continued, "What can I help you with today?"

No one wasted any time, all talking at once.

"I think it's over for Evie and me..." said Bryce.

"We're losing ground and it's going south..." said Sam.

"Evie is in trouble, and we need to know how to help," said Vicki.

They all stopped as quickly as they started. Mrs. Taylor looked from one to the other. "I see. Well then, let's start with Bryce."

"But..." Sam started to argue. Mrs. Taylor looked at her and Sam stopped.

"Of course. Bryce?" Sam said sweetly.

"Yes," Mrs. Taylor looking to Bryce continued, "So why do you think that it is over for you and Evie?"

"Because she said so."

"And?"

Bryce looked confused. "And what? We found Kendall, our son, on the battlefield, surrounded by dead demons. She found out and said it was over. And I don't disagree with her. Kendall learned about the battlefield," he paused to clear the catch in his throat, "from listening to her pray for me. I can't let him be hurt like that again."

"Has he?" she saw his confusion. "Has he been hurt?"

"What do you mean? He had piles of dead demons surrounding him. Of course, he's been hurt! No kid needs to see that!"

"Ah," she responded. "At what age is one ready to fight for the King?"

"I don't know!" he said, shaking his head. "Maybe when one is old enough for a real sword?"

Mrs. Taylor leaned back in her chair and studied Bryce. "I hear your concern and at one time, I shared it. But there are things you must know. First," she continued, "this is the most important. Do you trust Him?"

"Trust Kendall? He's six!"

"Do you trust Yahweh?"

Bryce sighed, "Yes. Yes, I trust him, but that is not the point. I think as a father it is also my job—,"

"No, it is the point. The whole point," she interrupted. "If you trust him as you say you do, then you would not be fearful of your child praying this way."

"Okay, I get what you're saying. But these are adult matters. I think as a parent, he should be protected from these things."

"I understand, but did you or Evie ask him to fight for your family?"

"No! Of course not!"

"So then, who invited him into the portal? It was not you, and it was not Evie. Who does that leave?" she looked at each of the girls who both shook their heads.

"Exactly," she continued. "Make no doubt he came by divine invitation. And God does not bring any of his children into the battlefield without His protection."

"All he had was a tiny knife! That's not protection!"

Mrs. Taylor smiled, "Such great faith children have, and such amazing power. On the field, they have vision that we do not. They see right and wrong clearly, as well as friend or enemy. They have speed because they have no doubts about their God. They have the strength of a giant! If you are blessed to see one on the field, it is the most amazing thing to watch." She spoke as if remembering, "Just like in this life, they have little fear, and the spaces that fear could take up are instead filled with courage. They have no weaknesses," she looked at them, "not one. Everything we see as weakness is in their favor on the battlefield. The smallest becomes the greatest, and the weakest becomes the strongest. They hold the favor of God, and nothing can stand against them. To have your Kendall invited onto the battlefield is the work of a gracious God who is for you."

The room was quiet as each absorbed her words.

"Can he be harmed?" asked Bryce.

"He cannot. Not there. His innocence is his shield of faith. It will not always be this way. He will grow older, and as this world distracts him and gains a grip on him, he will be as we are. He will become more fearful of what he has to lose, and more doubtful of what he can gain. But for now, he is safer on the battlefield than he is in his own home."

Bryce winced at that, but Mrs. Taylor continued, "Bryce, do not be afraid of how God uses him. Kendall is a gift in this fight. He has power that cannot be matched."

She sat back and looked at the girls. "Now. What are you two worried about?"

Sam and Vicki looked at each other. Vicki took the lead. "We don't know what to do. Evie has been poisoned. That seems obvious to us. She says she's done and won't go back."

"And you think she should?"

They each looked at each other, and Sam spoke, "We think so. It's not about her marriage anymore." She felt Bryce look at her and she turned to him, "Sorry. That probably sounds bad."

"Oh, of course not. How could that sound bad?" was Bryce's sarcastic reply.

"What I mean is, we want, we all want," she nodded at Bryce, "what God wants. We can accept whatever outcome He has planned. But we don't feel like it's ending the way it's supposed to. Something else is strongly affecting her decisions. Her decisions to quit seeking God's plan, interpreting His absence to mean that there is no reason to even be there, and to walk away from the battle and Bryce," she paused, "They don't feel right."

"Why in the world do you think He's been absent?!" asked Mrs. Taylor.

"Um, because there's been no sign of Him?" said Sam, who looked to Vicki for support. She nodded in agreement.

Mrs. Taylor laughed and lifted her face. "Oh Lord, they are blind to you and your ways!" She continued, "Have you not seen the activity?! Why do you think that is? Do you not understand the child was invited? How has the field not been overtaken by demons in Evie's recent absence? You must learn to look at the bigger picture, not just the landscape of the situation. Something there is worth fighting for, or there would be no fight, no desire of yours to continue." The room fell quiet again.

"So, what do we do?" asked Bryce.

"You get her to the field, and then you cut her open," came the even answer.

Bryce flinched, as Vicki jerked backwards, putting her hand over her mouth.

Sam lurched forward. "What the heck?"

"I think you're going to need to explain what that means," Bryce said coldly.

"Do you think the Sword only works on the enemy? What else can heal the invasive poison of the enemy but the Sword?"

Vicki spoke slowly, "You're saying we need to cut her open, with a sword. How will this help her?"

"Will it...hurt...her?" came Sam's voice, now small.

"Yes. It will. When we are poisoned by the enemy, this kind of healing hurts. But it is necessary. Do you three love her?"

"Yes," came each firm reply.

"Then you must."

"She refuses to go," said Bryce.

"Then we ask God to get her there." She looked to each of them, "Will you join me?" She held out her hands and they joined hers, making a circle as she began to pray.

"Most High God," she said, "We come to you believing all your ways are right. We believe you see Evie, and Bryce, and Vicki, and Sam, and young Kendall."

Bryce felt chills running up his spine as she prayed in power. "We believe you do not intend to leave these, your own, as they are. We believe Evie is yours and the enemy has no claim to her. We have no power left to persuade her to return to her fight and the place to claim victory in your name. So, we come now, to ask you like it says in Hosea 2, to 'allure her, to bring her into the wilderness, and speak comfortably to her, give her vineyards thence to her and make her (valley) a door of hope.' We pray she will respond as she did in the days of her youth and in the days she first came to you. Shatter the bow, sword, and weapons of war that have been used against her and make a place for her and her people to rest safely. Take her to be yours in righteousness, justice, love, and compassion. Say to her that she is your people and let her say that you are her God. Send one to lead her in. Amen."

A collective 'Amen' was given.

Sam smiled, "Gotta love Hosea."

"He's the man," said Vicki.

They each looked at Bryce as he moved a trembling hand down his face.

"I don't want to do this," he said quietly.

"But you will," said Mrs. Taylor.

"Yes, I will," he said, and he lifted his head.

"For the Most High God," said Sam.

"For the Most High God," came the unison reply.

It was late in the afternoon when Bryce knocked on Evie's door. He saw the stiffness in her expression when she opened the door. The warmth he had begun to feel from her was gone and replaced with a coldness he had never sensed before. He knew this was not the time or place to try to be charming. Instead, he silently prayed that he would appear as sincere as he felt.

"Hi," he said lightly as she stood looking at him.

"Look, Bryce," she started after a pause, "this isn't a great time. If you want to see the kids, then the right thing to do is call me and we can arrange a time to meet you."

"Actually," he said, "I'm here to talk to you."

"Yeah? Did it occur to you to call?"

"Yes, it did, but it seems as if my number keeps getting sent to voicemail somehow," he replied with a half-smile.

Evie didn't reply but just stood looking at him.

"I really just want to talk. Do you think we could do that?"

Evie glanced behind her to check that the kids hadn't come into the living room or kitchen, "I really think it's best if we don't do this when the kids are here. In fact, I know it's best."

"Okay," Bryce agreed. "How about you just come out and sit on the step with me? When you want me to leave, I'll leave. I just want to talk."

After a moment of hesitation, Evie stepped out, shutting the door behind her. She sat down on the top step and stared ahead. Bryce could feel all the walls up, doors closed and locked down. He took his hands out of his pockets and sat down next to her. He could feel her shoulder close to his.

"I don't even know where to start," he began. "But I need to tell you I'm sorry. Again. When I started really praying, back when I was in jail, I had no idea what was going to happen. The first time I entered the battlefield, I had just been praying like I always had before, you know, God help me with this, God help her with that, help me fix things, help her forgive me, let me start over. It was the same every time. One day though," he paused, "one day it was different. I couldn't think of what to say that hadn't been already said. So, I was just quiet." He could feel Evie look at him, and he continued. "I was quiet for a long time, and I could tell something was different. Like, I was praying, but I wasn't, does that make sense?"

He heard Evie's whisper. "Yes".

"I sat there in this silence, listening, waiting for something but I didn't know what. Then I remembered a Scripture from the Psalms that I knew as a kid, 'Blessed be the Lord my strength, [Who trains] my hands to war, and my fingers to fight'. And I don't know why, but I just said it out loud. Just like that. Then I asked God to train my hands to war and my fingers to fight. Let me fight."

It seemed like all other noises quieted as they sat together, lost in memories and thought.

"You probably know what happened next, right?" he looked at Evie. She searched his face then simply nodded.

Bryce resisted the desire to reach over and tuck a stray hair behind her ear and looked away instead. "The battlefield opened. I had no idea what had just happened. I thought I was dreaming. That was the moment I knew spiritual battle was not a metaphor." He smiled. "It was so vast. And empty. There was nothing there. Somehow, I had gained a sword, but I had no idea what I was supposed to do with it, so I just stupidly swung it around.

I figured I was just supposed to do exactly what I prayed, train and learn. Probably I should be listening too, but I'm not very good at that, yet."

Evie smiled and a comfortable silence began to grow between them. "When did it change?" she hesitantly asked.

He looked over to her then replied, "When the girls asked me to join them."

He waited a moment and heard her breathe out a sigh.

"I've been on that field so many times," Evie started. "Both by myself and with them. I think I even began to like it. But it's a horrible place. Somehow, I'd forgotten that. Knowing Kendall has been there," she caught herself before she started to cry and then continued, "knowing Kendall has been there made me remember. It's evil." She turned to look at him. "There is nothing good there."

"Evie," Bryce spoke slowly and gently, "I think I'm going to have to disagree with you. I get it. I saw it too. But I don't think that God brought us there and left us alone. I don't. I didn't see Him. But I felt Him. I felt my sword come to life. I saw the enemy taken down. Baby, I might be good, but I'm not that good!" he laughed, teasing.

She looked straight ahead and smirked, before turning to him.

"Thank you for telling me. It helps me more than you probably realize." She sat up straighter, determined. "But I'm not going back. I'm sorry. I just can't." She gave him a half smile, "Thanks for coming over." Bryce felt his heart sink, and a deep ache started in the pit of his stomach.

Evie stood up and walked into the house, closing the door behind her.

Later that night, Evie tucked Janey into bed and headed into Kendall's room.

"Look at you! It's like you're eight or something. Toys put away, pajamas on and already in your bed. Are you sure you're not eight? Or ten?" she teased as she sat on his bed.

"Mom, seriously. I'm six. But I also brushed my teeth without you telling me," he proudly informed her.

"What? No way! That's like, eleven!" She leaned forward and kissed first one cheek and then the other, tickled his neck as he responded with "Ew, Mom!"

"Ok buddy, it's been a great day. It's time for you to go to sleep."

Evie had intentionally kept Kendall busy all day in the hopes that he'd now be exhausted, falling asleep quickly.

"Okay. Will you still pray with me?" he sweetly asked.

"I will always pray with you, buddy. Ready?" He nodded, as she began praying, "Lord, thank you for Kendall and Janey. Thank you for the good day. Help Kendall to sleep well through the night, Amen."

As she busied herself with the tucking him in, she could feel his eyes on her.

"Mom?"

"Yes?"

"That isn't what I meant."

Evie looked at his serious face and sat down. "Kendall, I know you don't understand all of this, but I already told you, you are too young to pray like that, and to pray on the battlefield. You don't need to be worrying about things between me and your dad. Everything is going to be okay."

"I know! That's what Evan said-that it was going to be okay."

Fear coursed through Evie. "Who is Evan, Kendall?"

"He's my friend. He was with me on the battlefield."

Evie tried to keep the alarm out of her voice, "Yeah? How did you meet him?"

Kendall scrunched up his face as he relayed the details, "Um, I don't know. He was just there."

"Really? What was he doing?"

"I don't know! He was just standing there by my rock. I think he was waiting for me."

"Okay, what did he look like?"

"Mom!!!! I don't know! He looked like a grownup guy. And now he's my friend. I said I'd stay and help him, but I got too tired, so I left."

Evie's mind searched for clues and possibilities of who Evan might be and whether he was friend or enemy.

"Okay, honey. It's fine. I'll check it out, you go to sleep now!"

"Are you going to pray fight?" he asked her as he rubbed his eyes and snuggled deeper into his blankets.

"Don't worry about it, Kendall. I've told you that we don't need to do that anymore. Everything is good. Goodnight!"

She made her way into the kitchen and sat at the table. She thought about calling her friends. Then she thought of Bryce. But she kept coming back to the feeling she needed to fight alone. This was her battle, not theirs. Everything had gotten complicated when she invited them in to help her. She never should have done that. Now there was some stranger in 'prayer' with her son.

She pushed her phone away. "Aww, heck no. I am so done with this."

CHAPTER TWELVE

*T*he last time Evan had been at this oasis was when the child warrior slayed horde upon horde of demons. It was quite impressive. Level five demons were falling under the small but deadly sword of a little boy. Evan hadn't seen a fight like that in a long, long time. He was sent to supervise and assist if needed, but truth be told, the boy didn't need his help. Instead, he watched, making mental notes to take back and then report to his authority.

By now, the dry desert wind had blown away every last bit of carnage. The oasis again looked as it should, green and lush, and felt as it should, tranquil and peaceful. He wasn't sure when it was going to happen, but one day there would be a great meeting here at the oasis. Warriors, coming after battle in their weariness and glory, to be blessed with a meeting with their King Himself. But today wasn't that day. He was sure of it. One clue was the smell of demons nearby. Another was the movement of the sand around the edges of the oasis. Corgs. Man, how he hated Corgs.

Casually, Evan pulled out his broadsword and walked to the edge of the grass. He waited for the right moment, just the right ripple that revealed their presence. He stabbed and kabobbed the piece of Corg that was traveling through the sand.

This was the height of the Enemy's spy network. Evan never understood how the fallen ones could trade the glory of the heavenly hosts for such a base, dark, and even primitive kingdom doomed from the beginning. As he raised his sword back up, and the sand fell away, he could see this was a whole hand of a Corg, sliced off and sent to deliver a message of urgency to a principality. They wanted a message? He'd give them one.

He raised the sword with the skewered hand close to his mouth and whispered to it. The hand stopped moving, listening, but then started thrashing as if it was trying to escape.

"Are you gonna eat it?"

Evan was startled and jumped. He was caught unaware. That rarely happened to him. He looked and saw Kendall, the brave young warrior, looking at him with curiosity.

"Um, no, I am not. I have better taste than to eat this slop. But I am going to use it for Yahweh and His glory."

He flipped his sword down and pushed the hand back in to the sand. Then he put his foot on the hand and pulled out his sword. You could see the hand squirming and fleeing under the ripples as fast as it could to deliver the message.

"What brings you here, little one?" Evan asked.

"I just come here a lot. I like it here."

"Have you found any of the treasures Yahweh has left for you here?"

Kendall was sleepy and rubbed his eyes. It was clear this wasn't going to be a long conversation, and Evan was glad for that. It was about to get busy here and he would prefer Kendall to be gone before that. But it was not his job to send anyone away, or even to direct or guide anyone on the battle-field. That responsibility belonged to Yahweh alone, and any urge to do this work was avoided as temptation.

Kendall yawned, big and long. "Yeah." He scratched his nose and then his head.

Adorable, thought Evan. The children of humans, just adorable.

"I found that the rock over there is like a water fountain." Kendall pointed to the rock by the southern edge of the oasis, large enough to create shade and shelter from the afternoon sun. "I came here and got thirsty one time and got some water out of it, just like it said in the Bible."

Evan couldn't help but chuckle. This man child was going to be a giant of a man for God one day. But for now, he needed sleep. "Please, go, little boy," Evan thought to himself. It took discipline to not get him out of here before the demons responded to his message.

"I'm going now. You sure you wanna stay here alone? It gets kind of scary sometimes. I can stay with you if you want, so you aren't scared."

Evan bowed in honor to the child. "Thank you, Kendall. Yahweh watches over me too and I will be fine. I have some work to do for him. I hope to see you soon."

"Okay, 'night. Call Yahweh's name if you need help. That's what I do. I'll tell Mommy I saw you today. She knows I'm here now."

"No!" Evan reached to grab Kendall, but he vanished into the desert air. Maybe he will sleep and forget to tell Evie that he saw an angel. Mothers weren't people you wanted to scare about the safety of their children. Evan had heard that she was infected, and the last thing he wanted was her showing up here ready for a fight with him at the same time the hand of the Corg was delivering his message.

Evan stood still, expecting a portal to open with a bear of a mother charging out. But nothing happened. Kendall must have fallen asleep. Evan raised his eyes to the sky and whispered, "Thank you," to his Creator. Nothing was too small to give thanks for. But in his moment of thanksgiving and simple worship, the air began to ripple and a current of electricity could be felt.

They were coming. Game on.

Loden appeared on the north side of the oasis with a small entourage of his minions. He was in his angel of light disguise and looked very much like Evan. They could be mistaken for brothers. A flicker of recognition quickly flashed across Loden's face, and he made a show of dusting the sand from his chest and arms. Loden puffed up his chest, acting as if he was familiar with the oasis, as if he'd just welcomed an expected guest into his own home.

He contained his surprise extremely well, thought Evan. There's no way Loden was suspecting an angel of his rank.

"So, Evangelisto. I see you've been given the honor of looking out for me. Seems I've made a bit of a disturbance in the throne room, and you've received a promotion. You are most welcome." Loden squinted his eyes at Evan and smiled.

"Well, okay, I see you are still delusional. Must be the dry air has sucked all the moisture out of your fetid brain. I am here to tell you to tell your boss that judgment is coming. Our Creator is aware of your boss's plan, and you are to relay the message to him that heaven is notified and has been readied. We only await the command. Once again, tell your boss that he has already lost."

Evan's voice was relaxed, as if he'd spent the whole day at a spa, or rather an oasis. His calm and unbothered manner was going to drive Loden insane. The demon really believed he was all that. Pride always surprised Evan, who lived in the realm of the Creator. But it was flowing out of Loden. Evan could feel it coming in waves across the small distance of the oasis.

Loden rolled his eyes and looked at his fingernails. "I don't give messages. I am the one who receives messages. As you know, because you just sent me a message. You are all drama, Evangelisto. You come in at the last possible hour after the humans have been doing all the fighting and all the work. You angels are just glory hogs. That's one thing that disgusted me about the ways of your kind. You send in the frailest of all creatures to do your work. Women! It's been women here all this time. You've let women do your work. How does that feel? You still okay with your boss's plan as He hides behind women with knives?" There was an edge to Loden's voice.

"He's shaken," thought Evan. "Bingo."

Now that pride had surfaced to his face, Loden's angel of light disguise looked cheap and tawdry, preposterous when compared to a true angel, like a costume you picked up at a thrift store after Halloween.

"I summoned you," Evan corrected. "And you came. Because really, Loden, you are basically the Swastik's errand boy. But, in full disclosure, there's been a child here too. Not just women. A little boy nearly obliterated your entire battalion in this region. So, when you tell your boss the story of how women came to this battlefield, as if it were a badge of honor, be sure to give the full report about those worrisome piles of carnage you've all been wondering about. That was done by a six-year-old little human child, under your watch."

Loden could no longer maintain the control that kept him in disguise. With a ripple, he morphed into his hideous Jader self. His whole body turned red, and his smile only got harder and more brittle with anger. Evan had accomplished his mission and in honor of His King, he would leave before a fight broke out. He would save a battle for when the Word was given and the host swarm down from above. He needed to get back to the angels.

They'd been watching, listening to reports, guessing on what strategy Yahweh would use to win this battle. They knew that He never lost a battle, and never would, no matter how bad it looked or seemed. They've had many millennia to learn to trust their boss. Not once since the Great Revolution had they regretted that trust in Him.

Evan evaporated into the air without glory, without fight, and without pride. He did the work of His God. But just before he left, he whispered the word "Yahweh" just for fun.

The group of Jaders fell to the ground screaming and covering their ears. Loden was the first down, and he grabbed the nearest Jader by the hair, pulling him close to run him through with his sword. He stabbed over and over until there was very little form and shape left to his fellow demon. The other demons watched their leader's frenzied attack as they also tried to recover from the sound of that hated name. Their rage to Yahweh was subdued by their desire to stay alive. Let Loden vent, but if he grabbed for them, they were going to leave him, dead, in this ghastly and disgusting green place, command or no.

Loden's rage was unceasing. He paced, gripping onto the sword still dripping with pus and blood. His nostrils flared, and he muttered angrily, his crimson red skin now filthy, still clearly hostile.

"Oridon's errand boy? Really? Oridon, who hasn't even been to one meeting in his own cave?" Loden walked the perimeter of the oasis, but when he came near the rock on the southern side, he took as wide a path as possible around it. Something about that rock made him squirm and while he would never tell anyone, he was afraid of it. He was afraid of a rock. That thought made Loden even angrier at the imbeciles he worked with and for, and at being summoned by the angel, Evangelisto. The history between the two was bad and would always be bad. He paused, thoughtfully. They sent Evangelisto to give him a message to deliver. His brain shifted. They sent Evangelisto, an archangel.

Loden stopped his frantic pacing and looked over to the group of Jaders. They still hovered and cowered, together in their panic. Disgusting cowards.

"Have you no pride?" Loden roared at them. "Stand up! Evangelisto, the archangel, was just sent to report to me on what the future holds."

He put his filthy sword away. Now his evil mind was on full throttle. His eyes sparkled and his smile, while still fierce, switched from rage to a knowing smirk. He wiped froth from his mouth and walked over to the rock and climbed on it, no longer afraid. He looked over the small oasis and onto the desert dunes in the background. Purples and pinks were beginning to swirl in the sky.

Loden figured it out, finally understanding some of the pieces that had been a mystery. An epic battle was coming. Briners or Lappes had been sending the Watchers. An archangel was just sent to challenge him to a duel. Something bigger is going on here than this battle over one little marriage. But no need to tell anyone else this just yet. If Fairen finds out, he will try to remove Loden himself, taking the glory as leader of the

Jaders. Should he tell Oridon? No! that's what the enemy said to do, so no, he wouldn't obey the enemy's voice.

"Think, think, think," Loden muttered to himself. Keep this information to himself. He can lead the Jaders (without Fairen) to handle the women. Wait. He already did that. He infected the one. What they need is to capture the child or scare him away for good. That would leave a couple of bimbos and the jerk husband who is just a newbie. So, if Evangelisto comes again, (who knows really, they are such liars!) it will be Loden and his crew who meet him for a Jader victory in an epic battle. His name will finally be etched onto the walls of the caves. He might even get promoted from a principality to a power and claim Oridon's cave as his own.

Loden jumped down off the rock and marched over to his Jaders, who seemed to have finally recovered from the mention of the hated name. They waited anxiously, their leader again calm and controlled.

"Tell no one about meeting the enemy here. No one. Your allegiance is to me, your Jader leader, not to a bloody Swastik. Betray me and you are dead." Loden looked calm and composed when he spoke in low tones, but they knew he was dead serious.

No one said a word as they marched off into the desert, into the cool of the night.

When the air had stilled, and the whole desert was in darkness, the portal once again opened and out came Kendall. He had awoken and wanted to pray for his mom and dad again. Something was wrong with mommy. She was afraid, but she wasn't crying anymore. She slammed things, and she seemed angry.

Between the portal and the rock was the body of a demon and a pile of something that looked all mashed up. Kendall *walked around it to get to the rock, his favorite place. He skillfully climbed up, which had taken some time to learn. He'd come enough and practiced enough that now he was like a little goat climbing up the sides, knowing where the edges protruded just enough to grab with fingers or toes.*

He made it to the top and sat down crossed legged. Sometimes the rock brought him shelter when he came during the day, when it was too sunny and hot. Tonight, it brought him perspective. Once his eyes adjusted to the dark, he could see the desert dunes. In that quiet, peaceful moment at the oasis in the middle of the night, Yahweh spoke to the child.

The girls sat in the friend booth and watched as Evie went about her usual morning duties. She hadn't in fact ignored them, but she hadn't exactly greeted them with coffee either.

"Do you think she's still mad?" Sam asked Vicki.

"Can't tell," Vicki answered while studying Evie. "Could be mad, could be just in a mood. Here she comes," Vicki's voice dropped to a whisper as she came towards them.

Evie stopped at their booth, but busied herself with her pen and notebook, avoiding eye contact with either of them. Sam's eyes darted from Evie to Vicki as no one spoke.

"Hey," Vicki finally said. "You look really busy this morning!"

For a moment Evie didn't respond, then she sighed, "Yes, I am. What can I get you two?"

Vicki continued to study Evie's face while Sam looked like she was watching tennis, as her eyes moved back and forth between the two.

"Stop!" Vicki silently mouthed to Sam.

"Bacon," Sam said. "I'll have bacon." Both girls turn to her and drop their jaws.

"You have got to be kidding me!" snapped Evie. "Bacon? How stupid do you think I am? You'd use bacon to manipulate me?! No. You are not getting bacon. You don't deserve bacon. You deserve egg whites. And flax seed."

"How about coffee? Do I deserve coffee?" Sam asked.

Evie rolled her eyes and all but stomped to the kitchen.

Vicki turned to Sam. "What is wrong with you?"

"What?" Sam's voice was innocent.

"That's what I said. What is wrong with you?"

"It worked, didn't it?" Sam smugly replied.

"It depends on what you were going for! If you were trying to make her more mad, yes. That worked."

"No. I was trying to make her say something. Anything. Once she says something, she'll say something else, then before you know it, we'll be talking!"

"You're messed up, you know that?" Vicki sat back in her seat with her arms folded. "What would you have done if she'd actually taken your bacon order?" she continued.

"Scratched her name off my BFF bracelet."

Vicki laughed. "Okay, well, let's hope it doesn't come to that.

Evie came back to the table, dropped off a carafe, and glared, before turning around and walking back to the kitchen.

"Do we dare hope?" asked Vicki.

"Please be coffee..." Sam begged, and then watched Vicki pour hot coffee into her mug.

"See! I told you it worked! I asked if we deserved coffee, and she brought us coffee! It's a good day, a good, good day, whoo hoo." she smiled, singing the Tiko hit.

Vicki rolled her eyes and tentatively took a sip from her own mug. "Huh. Tastes like a fresh pot," she said, while closing her eyes and relishing the warmth. "So now what? We got coffee, but she's also good and mad, and we've not even had a chance to talk."

"How about we wing it?"

Vicki stared at Sam. "No, we don't wing it. That's a terrible idea. We need to think about this!"

"Too late," Sam said as Evie approached the table with their plates. She practically dropped their plates in front of them.

"Egg whites for you," she said to Sam. "And omelet, cheese, hollandaise and bacon for you," she said to Vicki.

Vicki stared at her plate, looking for greater meaning. Sam looked at Evie and said softly, "Thanks."

Evie sighed. "Slide over."

Sam grabbed her plate with one hand and her coffee with the other and moved over.

"Evie," Vicki began.

Evie held up her hand. "No. Just eat and let me talk for a minute." She looked at Sam and said, "No singing, humming, tapping."

Sam muttered something under her breath and then started eating.

"Listen," started Evie. "I need to say this. I'm mad at you two and I don't think I'm wrong to be. You guys crossed a bunch of lines, and I don't think you understand. I feel like you should, but maybe you can't." Neither of them said anything, so she continued, "None of this is relatable unless you've been here. And with your perfect guy and perfect house and perfect marriage," she nodded to Vicki, "and your perfect single life," she nodded to Sam, "I don't think you can get where I'm coming from."

Vicki gasped as she leaned back in the booth and Sam's fork stopped midway to her mouth as she froze. Evie continued, "I'm happy for both of you. I am. But you can't expect to jump in and make things perfect for me. And that's what you did. You thought you had it all figured out, and you jumped in and took over, trying to make it whatever you decided it should be. Even after I told you how I felt."

"Girl," Sam said quietly, "You don't know what you're even saying." She dropped her fork down on her plate and pushed away the food.

"Yes, I do!" Evie's voice was rising. "I do know what I'm saying! You had no right to get involved!"

"Get involved? Evie! We have been praying for you! With you! You came to us and asked us to help! Remember?" Vicki finally spoke.

"I remember telling you I was done in the battlefield, and I remember you sitting in my house telling me that you had taken my son and my husband and had been praying with them about me. That's what I remember."

"Woah." Sam raised her hands in front of her. "We didn't take Kendall, Ev! We got there, and he was already there! You saw yourself that he had already been there! We found him; we didn't bring him!"

Evie looked at the table for a moment before saying, "I thought about that. But I don't think all that killing was him."

Vicki started to reply, but Evie stopped her. "No, I don't. I know he was there. But what has been happening there, couldn't have been him. He's six. More than ever, he needs me. Not an escape, not a dream, but me."

"Yes, he needs you," Vicki said soothingly. "He needs his mama so much. No one can ever take your place, Ev. We talked to Mrs. Taylor about it—"

Evie interrupted her, "This just gets better and better," she laughed bitterly. "Who is we, or should I even ask?"

"Bryce wanted to talk to her," said Sam.

Evie looked at her hands for a moment before saying, flatly, "You know what? I don't want to know. I don't care. If you all want to be the new prayer team, have at it! Back-to-back, sword to sword," a sob caught in Evie's throat. "Go ahead. If the three of you want to hang out there, have at it. But I'm not going back. And neither is Kendall."

CHAPTER THIRTEEN

*F*airen liked to come early and alone to this battlefield of sand and dunes. This was not his favorite habitat, but there were many things he could tolerate here. He liked the heat and the pulsing of the high noon sun. He liked the pungent and fermenting smells of demons sweating. But none of that could be found in these cooler hours of early morning. So why was he here so early, missing his favorite things? Fairen was going to find a portal to the other side.

He had searched every battlefield for the last one hundred years or so for a portal. He'd never found one, but he was positive that this time, he was going to. He was sure the stories were real. He had heard of demons that went to a special place and disappeared, never to come back. What was that? It must be a portal to the other side where the humans lived. It was considered paradise to demons. All this time, humans have been coming back and forth to this spirit world, the entry flashing and the location changing. But there must be a pattern, a code to it, and if he could figure it out, he was leaving this side and moving onto the next. He could only imagine the life of finding a host or two. This was his goal and his highest agenda.

Fairen stood near enough to the green oasis to spit on it. He wasn't going any closer to it. The repulsive freshness and greenness of the oasis were completely out of place in this barren sand. With the activity around this place lately, he planned to just stand and observe. That's how he would finally find out about the portals.

His palms were sweaty, not from the slowly rising heat waves, but from the hope of finally seeing a portal open. Where would it be this time? He had been tracking human movements and they were appearing closer and closer to this oasis. Fairen kept squinting his eyes, trying to distinguish what was a heat pulse and what was a portal opening.

When it was obvious that no portal was opening, Fairen decided to return to the caves. He'd come back later to find the way to the other side before this became a stronghold and breeding ground. Once the breeders came in, the portals never opened again.

The Watcher stood so perfectly still that Fairen never saw it. Forbidden from fighting, maiming, and killing, the Watcher trembled with desire and temptation to creep up behind the unsuspecting Jader and rip his throat out with his teeth. But he was forbidden, restricted by a curse to use only his gifts and his talents. A debt owed for millennia kept all the Watchers under the burden of this silent, hidden life. This Watcher hated every single species that was involved in that contract that kept him under such bondage. But a deal was a deal and until he found a way out of it, he would keep watching, completing his job like any other demon of his caliber. No one knew how powerful the Watchers really were. But one day they would. And then he would be free to rip the throats out of every Jader he saw.

But for today's mission, he was going to report this particular Jader, who seemed to stand and stare at nothing. Fairen, he is called, coming here alone in the early hours to do what? Meditate? Soul search? The Watcher stood to full height from his crouching position. His skin was like a camouflage suit, not a sheet he could take on and off, perfectly able to blend in and hide. Only a trained or astute observer could ever spot a Watcher. And no one ever spotted this one. He was too good at its job.

It was then that he heard the thrumming sound. He could feel the solid ground of the oasis where he had been hiding tremble ever so slightly. A portal was opening. Where? The Watcher scanned all around, even looking behind him. He could normally stay unmoving for hours, but the impending portal caused fear to grow deep inside himself. What might come out of that portal? He began to sweat giant beads of toxic liquid on his forehead and upper lip.

He also began twitching, his body acting as if he was short circuiting. These jerky movements would blow his disguise! Untold years of discipline and hatred gave him the strength to calm down. He breathed slower, attempting to suppress the flinching and twitching; slowing down his heart before it exploded. Fear was still there, but that calmed alongside his breathing. No way was he leaving just yet. A Watcher could not resist observing the things that came through those portals. He applied all the skills and techniques he had ever learned and acquired, read the area he was by, including the backside of the large rock on the oasis, and fine-tuned his covering. He sprouted a deeper shade of grey mottled with browns and blacks on his upper torso and pulled on some more shades of green on his waist and legs. There were more colors of green than he had ever used before. 'Lush' was the disgusting word that came to mind.

No one would ever see him. No one could ever see him. He was the best Watcher ever created.

Vicki strode through the portal and found herself close to an oasis, a green, luscious, heavenly oasis at the top of a desert of sand and dune. There were palm trees of various heights and size. There was a huge rock that looked both foreboding and like a shelter offering shade. A fountain of water bubbled within the pond near the center. It was picture perfect and the pull to walk towards that little bit of heaven on this battlefield was irresistible. If Vicki had entered this place in the middle of a battle that had already begun, she would not have even noticed the oasis or considered stopping to rest. One didn't usually come to the battlefield to rest. One came to make war. But part of war is being logical and strategic, and right about now resting on an oasis, which was clearly created by and a gift from Yahweh, was the smartest thing Vicki could do. Vicki had pulled her sword out before she had crossed over into the portal of prayer but now that she could see that there was no enemy near, she slowly put her sword back into her sheath.

She walked quietly on the sand, reached the oasis in less than ten steps. Her long blonde hair blew in the gentle breeze and the beautiful, bronzed warrior of God breathed a sigh of relief as she walked straight towards the sparkling pond. She knelt and scooped up some of the refreshing drink into her hand.

Since breakfast with Sam and Evie, Vicki had been in distress. She came through the portal to kill something, but after seeing the oasis, she didn't feel like doing anything other than sitting in the shade of that rock and resting.

"Perfect life, perfect marriage, perfect husband," Evie had said. If only she knew. Vicki understood it was the infection talking. Clearly, it had reached her brain and her mouth. Because no one has a perfect anything. But hers was so far from perfect, it was laughable. How many battlefields had she traveled to and spent months and years in because of this 'perfect' marriage? The only thing perfect in her life was Yahweh.

Vicki thought about these things as she walked and rested in the oasis. The temperatures were blissfully cooler here even with the sun still beating down on the green, unfaded grass, damp with a cool mist. She enjoyed the warmth from sun, without the scorching heat, and the sound of water, relaxing and comforting. She sat down there, leaning back against this rock, and rested, from her 'perfect' life. She snorted.

Vicki stretched out her legs in front of her. Her leather skirt and vest made a soft sound as she leaned against the rock, closing her eyes. How awesome was Yahweh that He always dressed her in an outfit that was perfect for her? There was that word again. She listened to nothing but the sound of water. She heard nothing, but she felt a disturbance, an unease. She stayed as still as possible, and maintained her steady, relaxed breathing. She could feel the eyes of something on her. Something was watching her, and it was close. The hair on her neck now stuck straight up. It was an enemy; of that she had no doubt.

But how had it remained hidden when she arrived? She had scanned the entire area. She had seen the whole oasis and knew it had been empty when she stepped through that portal. "Yahweh, make my faith sight," she said in her heart. She slowly opened her eyes, lifted her head, and turned to the left. She stared straight into the eyes of the most hideous creature she had ever seen on this side of the portal.

He screamed as the human looked straight at him, as if he had been seen. He jumped in shock and ran behind the rock, hunched over, trying to become smaller. Where could he go? There's no cover in this place. His choices were to either climb the rock or start running. Running was the only good option. He was fast, so thought he had a chance against a slow, stupid human. But she had just spotted him. No one had ever...another scream tore from his throat. There she was, standing on this side of the rock, staring at him. Not only had she spotted him, but she'd also tracked him.

He had to get out of here. No Watcher had ever been captured. Death would be better than that humiliating reality. He didn't even know where he was going, but the Watcher took off running as fast as he could. He expended some energy blending himself into the sandy dune color he was running against. After running a long distance, he turned to look back at the human. She still stood there, looking right at him. He yelled again, this time in sheer panic. How could she see him? He had to get himself to the Briner he was bonded to and tell him about Fairen, but no way was he telling him that he had been spotted, that the Watcher had been watched. He would rather kill himself than reveal this information, but he needs to kill that human. He should have done that rather than panic. But the panic was not his fault-this had never happened before. There was no training for this. So best to just be invisible and run to the Briner and tell him what he wants to know. Later he will go back to that oasis to wait for that human and kill it. No one need ever know.

"What the heck?" thought Vicki. She should have been alarmed at the hideously hunchbacked, buck toothed, wart skinned creature, but the frightened look of the creature made her more curious than anything. It had been standing so close to her, looking at her so intently, and when she investigated its eyes, she could feel the desire to harm her, the sheer malevolence of the monster. But it had turned towards a dune and took off running. She could tell it was wearing some sort of camouflage and could see it adjusting its color until settling on a sandy color. She was sure it was trying to be invisible, but unsuccessfully. By the time it got to the top of the dune, it looked back at her. She had been standing there watching it and when it looked back at her, it made a chilling cry of agony, jumped as if startled, and took off running further into the desert. She wasn't going to chase it.

She had come and found an oasis. She wasn't leaving it to chase a war. Let the war come to her. Until then, she was going to enjoy this place of rest in a world of fighting and hostility. The only thing that would make this place better was if her friends would show up. That would be perfect.

Bryce had been sitting at his little table in his little room for so long his coffee had grown cold. He wasn't the type to write down lists, but he liked to silently go over details in his mind until he figured out what his next step should be. He had been hired back to work last week, and he had today off. He was glad to be working again. Working was good, really good, one, because he needed the money and two, because he couldn't spend the money he had.

He'd been going over it all in his head and had finally reached some conclusions. Something wasn't right. Before he had been arrested, he had put his cash earnings into a bank account Evie didn't know about. He'd saved every penny. After the arrest, he answered every question they had, gave up every name, every stop, every vehicle he had seen. Everything. But one thing they hadn't asked him about was the money. He didn't know much about legal practices, but he'd watched enough TV to at least expect they would be interested in the money he earned from a money laundering operation. But they hadn't been. Or at least they didn't seem to be. They hadn't gone to his and Evie's home, they hadn't looked at his bank records that he knows of, and they didn't even ask him what he had done with it. It seemed deliberate that they didn't go after that.

There were more unanswered questions than there should be at this point. It had seemed so simple. So why was it not over? Was he being watched, and by who? He thought back to his conversation with Bartrug. That conversation had terrified him. Why was a special task force watching him? What did they think he had? Who were they? And could he trust that Bartrug was who he said he was? His instinct told him yes, but he no longer was sure his instincts were reliable. The way things stood with Evie, he was pretty sure he wasn't going to be able to protect her. He wasn't even sure she needed protecting, but as much as he didn't want to admit it, something told him that she did. If they were watching him, they were probably watching her. He needed help. He needed Evie, and he wanted her safe. He needed to keep his family close. He seemed to be filled with needs.

And now he needed clothes. He still had all his things at the house. When he asked Evie about them, she said she had put all his stuff in the basement. She had told him he could come around eleven. He knew she would still be at work, which means she wanted him to collect his things when she wasn't there, which seemed reasonable. But darn, he was just too busy drinking coffee to make it at eleven. He will have to go at one when she most likely will come home. He didn't have the answers he needed, but he did have the next step.

He refilled his coffee, pulled out his little orange book, propped his legs up on the other chair and tried to see if coffee and the Psalms would ease his mind until he went back home.

He'd arrived at the house and let himself in. As expected, Evie wasn't there yet. It seemed so different, odd, to be in the house alone. Until now, he'd only been here when Evie and the kids were. That had felt familiar to him, the noise, the typical routine. Being here alone reminded him even more of what he had lost. It used to be his home. Now he felt like an intruder.

He stood in the kitchen and looked around. It was tidy, of course. Evie liked everything put away, in the place she designed for it. She had always complained that he would never know where the salt was when he needed it, as he never put it back in the same place twice. That was true, but he had also begun to move it just so she'd get annoyed. Then he could kiss her 'til she laughed. He grinned to himself as he moved the salt to the opposite corner. Old habits die hard.

He left the kitchen, walking into the living room. He stood still and tried to feel something. Anything. But this wasn't home. Home was where Evie and the kids were. He didn't want this without them, and if he was telling the truth to himself, he really didn't want them to want it without him, either. Not that he had control over that right now. He knew she had said his clothes were in the basement, but while he was here alone, he had some things he wanted to see. Jayne and Kendall's bedroom, for starters.

He stepped into each room, looking at their beds, their toys. Picking up their "specials" as they called them. Most of them he could identify, and it made him smile. There were a few he didn't recognize. "Looks like they gained a few memories without you," he mumbled to himself. Their rooms felt peaceful, and that peace passed through him as well. "God, will I ever be part of this again?" he asked. He shut their doors behind him and stood facing the other door. Their door. He opened it slowly, as if either a terror or anticipation of sun breaking through was on the other side, he didn't know which. The sleigh bed they'd bought the first year they were married was still there. The blankets and pillows had been changed. It was more feminine than he remembered. But he remembered this room well. So much love, loving, laughing, even crying had been in here. The memories flooded through him.

They had spent their honeymoon in this room, locked away from the world. They only left it for Evie to prepare food to eat. She had eagerly planned every meal and delighted in that part of their honeymoon. He had wanted to whisk her away some place exotic, she had wanted to claim this place as theirs. She was right, of course. He wouldn't trade that week for any beach in the world. He remembered her walking out of their bathroom one morning two years later, while he was still half asleep in bed. Through cracked lids, he could see her smile like a cat who had caught a mouse. She had crawled up on the bed over him, smiling down with her hair all around them and whispered, "Hey, baby daddy!" It took a few moments to stop looking at her long enough to register what she had said. She dropped a white stick on his chest, rolled over to her back, and just laughed with joy.

He could smell her still in this room. Her scent. Her hair. She lived in the whole house, but this room was hers altogether. What she called their "oasis". Funny, the oasis they shared now was something very different, out in the middle of a desert war zone. How many times had he seen her sleeping here? Waiting for her to wake up so he could kiss her, sometimes not waiting. He smiled to himself. Loving her had been so easy. And it was still easy.

He'd been lost in his thoughts for too long, he realized, when he heard the door to the kitchen shut. He turned around and stood frozen in his spot, in the bedroom, until he saw her come around the corner and into the doorway.

"Gotta admit, this is kind of creepy, Bryce," Evie said as she stepped into the room. They stood staring at each other, each waiting for the other to say something.

Bryce wanted to assure her he wasn't being creepy, but he didn't know how to, so instead he moved to leave the room. Evie felt the awkwardness and dropped her purse on the bed, planning to tell him to leave. They each took a step and ended up in front of each other.

He could see from her expression of confusion that her mind was spinning as she stood silently, staring at his chest. Bryce, hands in his pockets, was looking down at her, and he just couldn't help himself. He smiled. He knew she felt it as she looked up. The tension felt beautiful as he dipped his head towards hers.

Bryce figured she might clobber him, but this was going to be worth it. He didn't want to scare her. Didn't expect passion. Just wanted to feel her lips. His movement was so slow, and when his lips touched hers, and she didn't flinch, he let himself just enjoy that moment. Nothing fancy, just his lips pressing against hers. It felt like every nerve in his body was roaring to life, yet he forced himself to keep his hands in his pockets and keep his kiss gentle. With actual physical pain he made himself pull away. He stood close, just breathing her in. Her eyes were huge, her lips soft, and then she blinked. It was almost comical as she shook her head and stepped back.

She found her voice. "Uh, okay. Hmm. So, you're done here?"

Bryce couldn't help himself as his smile widened.

"I don't mean done here, cause obviously we are done here, I mean done here," she said as she waved her arms around to indicate the house.

"Nope," replied Bryce. "Just getting started." He moved away from her, walking around her to head to the basement, feeling her eyes on him as he left.

In the basement, he found the plastic bins marked with a "B". He didn't realize he'd had so many clothes until he started opening them and found it wasn't just his clothes she had boxed up and stuck down in storage, it was everything. Pictures, old cards, bedding. "Bedding?" he thought. "She had to get rid of our bedding?!" There were his clothes, and he noticed every piece had been folded. "Maybe that's a good sign? They weren't still dirty and wadded up." Shoes, his razor. "So much for a good sign," he sighed.

Bryce brushed back his hair back in frustration, as he realized that he didn't want to do this now. "Just get what you need today, and you can deal with this later," he thought. Going through the clothes kind of felt like shopping, alone, at a thrift store. Before he could get depressed standing there, he began tossing things he needed onto the floor and left the others wadded up in the bin. He found t-shirts, jeans, socks, even underwear. He rifled through the bins, looking for his jacket and found it in the bottom of the fourth one. He smiled as he lifted it out. Man, he loved this jacket. Perfect brown leather. Aged to perfection.

He put it on and was thankful she hadn't pitched it just because he had loved it. The fit was perfect, and he zipped it halfway and dropped his hands in his pockets. He felt the paper in the pocket and pulled it out to find an old receipt. Looking it over, he saw it was for gas and then saw the date. The night before the arrest. Reaching his hand back in the pocket for the other item he had felt, he pulled out a small piece of plastic-a thumb drive. "What in the world..." he thought to himself.

A sliver of fear went through him as he stood there holding it and staring into space, trying to remember something, anything. He went through every detail he could remember. He didn't remember specifically getting gas anywhere, but that didn't surprise him. Who remembers getting gas? He was working every night, sometimes all night, those last few months before the arrest. He also was working his day job. Could this be something from there? He didn't know. After a moment, he felt stupid. It's a thumb drive. Why the paranoia? He dropped it back into his pocket, gathered his clothes, and headed upstairs.

He found Evie in the kitchen making coffee, and she turned to see him when he entered the room. He noticed at first the warmth in her smile and her eyes seemed to soften, even if the warmth didn't last. It was like she realized she was smiling at him and instantly shut it down.

"Got everything?" she asked, shortly. "Well, I decided I could get my razor and bedding later," replied Bryce with a hint of a smirk.

Evie almost seemed embarrassed. "Yeah? Well, I needed a razor, and yours was just sitting there unused, so…" she said.

"Ha, touché!" he responded. "Hey, do we still have that laptop?"

"I have my own personal laptop. Why?"

"Is it new?"

"I got it a few months ago. Why?"

"What happened to the old one we had?"

Evie sighed, "Bryce, why do you care about our old laptop? Do you want it back?"

"I don't care! I'm just wondering! Do you still have it?"

"No."

"How did you get my emails?"

"On my new laptop. Why?"

"What did you do with the old one?"

"Okay! Enough! Why the questioning? Why do you care?"

"I'm just wondering!"

"Really? Just wondering? Does it matter what? Do you think I bought a new one with your money? Is that what this is about?" Evie could feel her frustration turning into anger.

Bryce wasn't sure how asking a simple question could have possibly turned into a yelling match. It was a simple question. Still holding his clothes, he asked, "Can I sit down?"

"No."

"No?"

"Yes, you're correct, no you can't sit, I have stuff to do. Taking inventory of my belongings isn't one of them."

Bryce couldn't help but look confused, but knowing she was ticked was not on the list of confusing matters. "Okay, sorry. First, it has nothing to do with what is yours or mine. Don't make it something it isn't. Second, I only asked because I found a thumb drive in my old coat pocket, but I didn't remember buying it or what I had it for. I thought if you had the old laptop, I could use it or borrow it to check it out. If not, no big deal."

"All of this because you have a thumb drive?! I don't know, maybe it's mine!"

"Ok, makes sense. Thanks." he said and just stood there.

"Are you going to show me?"

"Well, sure," he said while holding his pile of clothes. "You can put your hand in my pocket and get it, or I can set my stuff down and get it for you. Your choice." he smirked.

Evie rolled her eyes. "This is so dumb," she said, while motioning to the table. He smiled his best smile, casually walked over, dumped his clothes all over her table, and reached into his pocket. He pulled it out and held it in his hands to show her.

"Can I have it, please?" Evie asked.

"Is it yours? Do you remember it?"

"How would I know? It's a thumb drive. This is so stupid. Seriously, what is the big deal? Can I just plug it in my laptop and see?!"

Bryce paused. He didn't know. It all just felt weird. Why would he have this if he never used it and why can't he remember it if he did use it?

"Bryce?" Evie asked, breaking the silence.

"Huh? Oh, yeah, I guess that makes sense."

Evie went behind the kitchen island and pulled her laptop out from a drawer and brought it to the table. Pushing his clothes to the side, she set it down and started it.

"Good grief," she said. "Why didn't you just say mention this to begin with?" She took the drive from his hand and connected it. Bryce moved behind her and look over her shoulder. He could smell her hair and was torn between moving away to avoid the torture or staying to enjoy it.

"It needs a password," said Evie.

"A password?"

"Yes, a password. A word that allows you to unlock a device, document, whatever."

"I know what a password is. Do you know what it is?"

"No! I don't have anything that needs a password. So, it's not mine."

The silence extended while Bryce just looked at the yellow box on the screen.

"It's not mine," she repeated. "So where did you get this?"

Bryce looked at her. "I don't know. It was in my coat pocket that was in the basement."

A flash of fear crossed Evie's face.

"Bryce, is there any reason this is something to be concerned about?"

Bryce reached around her and pulled the thumb drive out before dropping it back in his pocket. "I don't know. Probably not."

"When does it stop, Bryce? It just keeps getting more ridiculous."

"Since I don't know what 'it' is, I don't know what you're talking about. I'm sure it's nothing. Thanks for letting me get my stuff. I'll call the kids tonight." He gathered his clothes back up and walked to the door. He opened the door and opened it with his free hand.

"Wait..." Evie said as she watched him walk out.

CHAPTER FOURTEEN

The beauty of the desert battlefield now had lost all its charm and mystique. Not that it had much with the waves of heat and the sand in every crevice of the body after a fight. Thank goodness things didn't carry through the portal to the other side, else Sam would need to be in the sand removal business. There comes a point in every prayer battle where the novelty has worn off. The initial excitement has been replaced with a certain weariness. One isn't coming through that portal with bounce, anymore, but with obligation and duty. Sam thought this must have been what it was like for the children of Israel as they marched around the walls of Jericho. Yeah, the first full day of walking silently was awesome, and the hearts were probably filled with high expectation. But after a few days, miles and miles in the blistering heat and the sun, and everyone would be weary with heat and the routine of it all.

Sam stood by the portal and looked over the wasteland of desert and saw the oasis a mile away. To even get to this place of rest, one could encounter a horde of demons, or maybe just a single vicious one popping up from the sand. One had to tread through the sand valley of death. If someone had asked her in weekly Bible study about her faith and the size and strength of it, she'd have to say it was small, and weak. It wasn't sickly, and she wasn't poisoned like Evie, but man, she was starting to get tired.

She prayed until she fell asleep and prayed when she woke in the night. She prayed while she worked, made meals, drove her son around, went to church, took a bath. When there was a battle going on, it was a constant war on her mind and heart. The constant state of prayer meant you were aware of burdens, of suffering, of pain, of the enemy, of one's own pride and issues. And speaking of one's own issues, Sam thought about her son, Jack. Would she end up on a battlefield all her own over him? If so, please Yahweh, no sand. As a matter of fact, the lovelier you make it, the easier it is to come! Brilliant! Why hasn't Yahweh thought of that? You want people to pray. How about we make the setting a little easier to handle?

Oh, goodness. She knew she sounded like she had sand up her butt. But she was tired and irritated. Sam started to walk towards the oasis. She might as well get somewhere as she processed all of this. She was not poisoned, but she was tired. And if she was honest, she was a little miffed at Evie, who at this point had everything in her grasp that Sam had always wanted. But Evie was going to throw it all away, the husband, a whole family, a solid pack of girlfriends. Sam was here, fighting for Evie to have all these things, when what she wanted was a chance to fight for herself.

As Sam trudged through the heavy sand, she saw a ripple nearby. She stopped, waited for it to come as near as the reach of her sword, and harpooned the body part that was just under the sand.

As she pierced it and drew it up to look at her kabob, she thought it looked like half of a hobbit foot. What was with these things? Why were they always finding bits and pieces of body parts? She put her sword to her shoulder like a bat and swung hard and the foot flew high and far.

Every dune crossed, every step taken, each piece of sand displaced as Sam moved through the desert landscape was moving her towards the oasis. She had come here to fight so many times for Evie, but she hadn't yet come here to rest or worship. It was the easiest thing to forget that the battlefield is not just filled with demons and powers of the air, but it can be an incredible place to meet with Yahweh. For people who love a cause, or love to fight, one of the hardest things to learn and remember was this idea of a holy hush, a pause in the fighting, a meeting with the Most High King. Every battlefield had a secret, or in this case, not so secret, place to meet with Him. This battlefield of the desert had an oasis.

Sam had been to a couple of different places, each offering a secure location given to the warrior to worship, and sometimes recover. Yeah, that's been needed a few times. Sam remembered back to a time when she was in a jungle. She'd searched for days for the secret place and couldn't find it. It wasn't until she was lying flat on her back with a long necked, hairless, gray Snapper standing over her about to rip her heart out. She'd seen it then as she was being dramatic and looking up to meet her Maker. A treehouse. It was a turning point in the battle, that's for sure. Since then, she'd learned that these little sanctuaries weren't retreats, or signs of weakness. They were necessary for the warrior to heal, recover, rest. A proud warrior would never stay here long. It required a certain humility to stop fighting and let the glory of victory wait.

Sam stepped onto the oasis and walked to the middle of it. She looked up to the sky, extended her arms out wide, and spun around several times. She stopped mid-twirl in front of the little *spring and knelt to scoop some water into her hands. A drink from the springs of God. Nothing is as refreshing as this, she thought. She dried her hands on her leather skirt and went to sit against the large rock. With her back against the stone, she could see palm trees. The grass was as green as emeralds, and the sky as blue as Jack's eyes. This moment of tranquility and peace was the gift Sam needed. The battle will always be there and would wait for her. Right now, she was thankful for the gift of alone time with Yahweh. All she had to do was wait for Him. She closed her eyes and accepted the rest offered to her right in the middle of a war zone.*

Loden and his entourage arrived near the oasis. The foot that had reached them had given them the code "E & F". While not a nuclear code, it did stand for effectual and fervent, and that means trouble. Someone was here and someone was serious. Even days before, Loden would have passed this off to Fairen or some other subordinate to check into. But now that he knows Watchers are here and that something bigger than he realized is happening, he was going to handle things himself. And he was going to get the glory when the glory was to be got.

He raised his hand to signal the other Jaders to stop. They stopped right behind him and looked around, raising their faces to the air and sniffed. Like one small army in perfect unison, they caught the smell of a human-a female human. The natural reaction was to smile, and the Jaders began making a thrumming noise which could be called excitement. The Corgs were disgusting and base with their lust, while the Jaders saw themselves as much more sophisticated.

Loden locked in on the smell of the human and started walking towards the giant rock on the oasis. He had great radar. "E & F my eye," he thought. The only decision he had to make was to choose between using his AOL costume or just showing as his own magnificent self. But before he could even decide, there was a flash of bright light before them all, blinding and extreme, as if the sun dropped right down in front of them.

Within seconds the Jaders had braced for war and the sound of swords being pulled out of scabbards told Loden all he needed to know. They were going to fight.

Loden's eyes cleared to show Evangelisto standing before him in the most amazing armor Loden had ever seen. He was instantly filled with jealousy and hatred. Maybe if their armor had been this nice when he was from above, he wouldn't have had to leave. If he had been given what he deserved and been shown some respect, he could be wearing that incredible outfit right now. But he remembered all the disrespect he was shown and all the slave labor he was forced to do, all because Yahweh— "Ah!", screamed Loden. He dropped his sword and grabbed his head in pain.

"I have to say that may be a first, Loden," said Evan. "You truly shocked yourself by merely thinking about Yahweh." At the name of God, the whole entourage fell to their knees in pain and grabbed their heads. It didn't feel fair, but they could win an entire battle by simply saying the names of Yahweh. Why more humans didn't do this was beyond Evan. Surely, they knew, right? They had to know the power in the names. The book told them. He was sure of it. But here his mission was clear. He was to engage and fight. He didn't need to annihilate them, but only to lessen their numbers and put a healthy fear and humility into their sorry and vile hides.

"Okay, enough with that. I, Evan, do come to you today to stop your mission. Whatever you were going to do, and wherever you were heading, I must insist that you change your plans and head back to your cave," Evan commanded.

"I don't think so, throne slave," snorted Lodan as he crossed his arms and widened his stance. "We will go right by you, and we will go over to that stupid rock and we will have a little fun with that human I smell. After we're done with her, we're gonna call in the Corgs and let them have their fun with her. So just move out of the way and no one need get their second-hand, metal uniform, banged up."

Evan looked Lodan directly in the eyes and declared, "You will not go near her. She's resting, enjoying a gift of time and relaxation. You can either turn around and go back to your borrowed cave, or you can stand here until the darkness descends. But you will not advance one more step towards the saint. She rests." With that, Evan reached with two hands over his head and grabbed the giant broadsword hanging from his back. He extended his arms all the way up and pulled the sword in front of him, into the stance of a warrior who while knowing an eternity of battles and fighting, had also won every single one. "What are you going to do, Loden?" he asked.

Loden's mind was busy calculating the choices and the risks, trying to compute the most advantageous way for himself. He wasn't concerned about his team, nor his mission or any purpose higher than his own interests. He concluded that a battle here and now, killing this stupid angel and tormenting the human female, was indeed the best plan and option.

His only reply to Evan was to pick up his sword off the ground, quickly moving to charge toward him. The other Jaders did the same, fearfully copying their leader. They remembered the last time he turned red with anger.

With a mighty roar, the Jaders moved into three rows before Evan. It was a military move and meant to wear out the opponent. Evan saw their plan and shrugged. "Okay," he thought. "If Yahweh sustains me, I will fight them for as long as they last."

Loden was the first to test the sword of the angel. The steel hit hard enough that the angel's and the demon's hands shook. They pushed into each other's swords, their faces closer and closer. Loden was strong, Evan knew, and his depravity was making him stronger. Evan always forgot just how strong the wicked ones were, fueled by hostility and darkness. But Evan wasn't worried. He was alert to the enemy, but not frightened. He leaned into the fight and pushed Loden off balance. Loden stumbled back but caught himself before he fell.

"Charge!" Lodan yelled to his troops. Gone was the plan to assault Evan one demon at a time. His own injured pride had started to turn him pink and with enough rage, he could overtake this angel on his own, and win the right to Oridon's cave.

The first row moved towards Evan, who began swinging his sword like an axe. Up and down, left to right and back again, his sword never stopped moving. It was a beautiful dance.

"I said charge, you imbeciles!" screeched Loden to the remaining two rows of Jaders. The small horde stepped over the remains of their former companions and stood in sand wet with blood. The third row followed but were unable to get past the second row. It was a fight just to get to the fight.

Time moved slowly, as each demon faced the angel, in their own vanity and pride thinking they could be the one to take down this host from heaven.

Loden jumped into the fray at random, periodically making it two on one against Evan.

Evan, covered with demon blood, sweaty and slippery, worked with all the strength and energy he had. It wasn't easy. These Jaders were level four demons. But he wasn't ready to call it hard when the Creator and Giver of Life gave him his very being. This fight was his purpose and part of what he was designed to do. It felt good to fight, good to swing his heavy sword, and good to be on the side of all that was right and holy. These Jaders were mutants, and once you drew their blood, their skin turned crimson, and they were filled with rage. Once they were red, they just looked odd.

Evan dodged the sword coming at him, leaning to his right. At the same time, Loden came at him on his right and for one moment, Evan was reminded that his strength is finite, and pride has no place in the service of Yahweh. His humility returned at this close call, and he finished off nearly all the Jaders. The two that remained were Loden and his lackey.

As the demons fell and Jader body parts dropped onto the sand, the sounds of battle, metal clanging, grunts and groaning, screams and cries receded. Loden was so enthralled with the beauty of his own fighting style that he did not realize there were only two demons left. The other Jader realized it before he did.

"I yield!" the Jader yelled.

Loden stopped mid strike. "What did you say?" He yelled, giving vent all his rage, and turning the darkest shade of red yet. Everyone stopped. Evan held the yielding demon by the hair, his hand ready to shove his sword through the demon's belly.

"You yield?" Evan questioned.

"I do," he said. "Spare me and I will do whatever you say."

Loden couldn't believe his ears. He looked from Evan to the groveling demon. In an instant, he saw the whole entourage fallen, chopped into bits and pieces on the ground. All that remained was this one lone coward and himself. There was no way he was going to let this stupid demon live to tell his own lying side of this story.

Evan pushed the demon away. He fell to his knees, beaten and submissive on this desert battlefield. Evan then looked around and took in the fallen horde, himself. He looked at Loden and didn't expect to see fear or humility at such a defeat, but he was not prepared for the hatred emanating off this Jader. Right then Evan understood, better than ever, just how powerful Loden could be. His rage and self-deception fueled him rather than drained him.

Loden rested his eyes on the defeated demon and walked over to him. He grabbed him by the hair and lifted his head. He raised his sword and stabbed him in the face repeatedly until the demon's head fell off. Evan watched, seeing in action how this fallen kingdom was so divided against itself. "They turn on each other all the time," he thought. "They never even care for their own group."

"Well, it's just you and me, Loden," Evan stated. "As I said, you're not disturbing the human. She is resting, and if she sees your ugly face, she will no doubt treat you harsher than I have. How about you just move along now? I won't tell anyone that you just lost a whole horde of level four demons to one mere angel. It will be our little secret."

Loden certainly couldn't risk this news getting out. How was he going to explain a whole battalion, a whole horde, lost? The Swastiks keep inventory. They keep track of these things. Yet who will bring the news? There are no witnesses. He could come up with a story. The Ventars could help him. Or he could blame them. He needed to get back to the cave. Fairen has men who could become his men, for the right price.

Loden calmed his breathing and stepped over the last fallen demon. He came face to face with Evan. "Until next time," said Loden.

"Okay, then," Evan said with a half shrug. "The only thing you're missing is the dramatic music. It was a fair fight, Loden. You lost fair and square. There's no shame in that. You and your one hundred and," he took his finger and counted bodies, " seventy-five, you think? Yes, fair fight. I am covered in the blood and guts of my enemies. My muscles feel stretched and well worn," he said while stretching out his legs and arms.

Loden stared, gathering himself, fading back to pink. He put back on his AOL costume, looking clean and beautiful. He would travel this way, his beauty giving him the confidence he needed to get his story right. Loden turned around and started walking, alone, a lone man in the desert.

If he didn't know it was a vile demon, the scene could look sad, thought Evan. How he wished he could have killed him today in this spot. But He trusted Yahweh and believed now was not the right time. He completed his mission. He had let the saint rest.

He left the battle scene and walked quietly over to the rock, keeping his sword and armor from clanging. He walked slowly around it until he could take a glimpse at the woman. There she was, leaning up against the rock, still sleeping peacefully, like an angel. He chuckled. The actual angel was doing anything but sleeping peacefully.

Evan lifted his eyes to heaven and mouthed a prayer which echoed the ancient Psalmist: "Praise Jehovah. He indeed giveth His beloved rest."

In an instant, he was gone.

Sam woke from her nap, feeling rested and revived. Her weary spirit felt refreshed. All that bothered her before, every issue that stirred her heart with angst and grief and worry, felt soothed and trusting. She could trust a God who, in the *middle of a battlefield, gave her an oasis to rest. She stood and stretched, looking around the beautiful oasis to see the desert sunset about to flood the sky with color. As she moved to the edge, she heard the thrum of the portal. She wasn't even going to have to walk a mile to get back to a portal from this rest. Yahweh thought of everything. Before she stepped through the portal, she knelt, laid down her sword, and raised her hands. She gave thanks and adoration to the God who allowed her to rest in this uneventful place. Then she stood and stepped back into the visible world.*

Bryce's mind felt like it was running at racing speed. Possible scenarios played out in his mind, ranging from the thumb drive having a favorite collection of music on it, to remembering what Bartrug had said about names, addresses and numbers of deep-state members. Just because he didn't remember getting the thumb drive, putting it in his pocket or using it didn't mean anything. The mind was weird like that, remembering the smallest, most insignificant moments while forgetting entire days he thought were burned into his memory forever.

He pulled into his parking lot and saw Bartrug's motorcycle near the light pole. Bartrug leaned on the seat, legs outstretched, and arms crossed, watching him as he pulled in. Bryce resisted the urge to point his truck directly at him and hit the gas.

He parked next to him and sat in the truck, waiting. Cody pushed off the bike and walked to the passenger side. Bryce waited before unlocking the door, and Cody got in.

"Really, no need for small talk," Cody spoke first. "Why am I here?"

Bryce's jaw clenched as his mind reviewed all possible outcomes of this meeting. He had called Bartrug right after leaving Evie, asking him to meet him here, certain that that was the right thing to do at the time. Now, however, he felt like he had overreacted.

"But what if it's not an overreaction?" he asked himself.

He sat, his mind full of doubt, leaving Cody's question unanswered. "Ya know what?" he asked impatiently. "How about next time you call me and say you need to talk to me, you actually talk?" He opened the door to leave.

"Wait." Bryce spoke quietly.

Cody paused, shutting the door again. "Fine but spit it out."

After yet another pause, Bryce finally began. "When I first saw you, you asked me about where something was. I had no idea what you were talking about. Still don't. But I need to know more about what you were looking for."

Cody watched Bryce closely. "I was expecting you to have more information, not want more information."

"Information about what?" asked Bryce.

"About the team you were working with. Suddenly get your memory back, Bryce?"

Bryce looked at Cody, "No. I told you, I don't know what you are talking about."

Cody responded, "Ok, we've established this already. So, what is this about?"

Looking back out the window, Bryce said, "I think I may have found something."

Bryce's struggle was evident in his trembling voice.

"Yeah? That's great. What did you find?" Cody's voice was now cautiously hopeful.

Bryce sighed and resignedly turned to face Cody. "First, I don't know if it's anything. But it's something that has all my spidey senses going off. Second, it's something I don't remember, and before I go any further with it, I wondered if it was connected to you."

Cody was silent for a moment. "How about you let me see whatever "it" is and I'll figure it out?"

"Yeah, I figured you say that. Here's the thing, it might be nothing. Then I'll admit, this is a waste of time. But if it is what you are looking for, I have some questions of my own."

"Like?"

"Like, what is this? How am I even involved? Why am I involved and what happens next?"

"Okay, well, before we can answer any questions, I repeat, how about you let me see it and I'll figure it out?"

"I'm not just giving it to you."

"Giving what to me, Bryce? You know I don't need your permission, right? Whatever it is, I can just take it."

Bryce snorted, "I also figured you'd say that. Let's just say I'm not stupid. I didn't bring it with me. I want to know what it is, and I want to know if it's something important."

Cody laughed. "OK, let's try this. I almost feel like you're being honest. Obviously, you have found something that you suspect is what I am looking for. How about if we take this one step at a time, yeah? Step one, you have to let me actually see it. Then we can go from there. I'll include you as much as I can. I give you my word on that."

"Do you have a computer?"

"Obviously."

Bryce made his decision, saying, "Okay, how about ya tell me where your room is, and I'll meet you there?"

Cody stared at Bryce for a moment, before nodding. "All right, we'll try this your way."

"So, there's more than one dive hotel in the county," Bryce thought as he pulled into Cody's parking lot. Looking around, he couldn't help but feel a little better about himself.

"Nice place you have here," he said as Cody got off his bike. "Real sense of ownership!"

Cody smirked at Bryce as he locked his gear in his saddle bags and smiled, "Ah, a bit smug, are we, Bryce? Here's the thing, want to know the difference between my place and your place? This isn't my home. It's just my cover." He winked at Bryce and sauntered away.

Bryce couldn't deny it. "Good one. You're quicker than I expected," he said as he joined Cody.

They almost looked like brothers walking across the parking lot, same height, same stride, and same confidence. Cody unlocked the door, and they walked in. Bryce noticed the made bed, the tidy room, clean dishes on the kitchenette counter. "Okay, and he's not a slob," thought Bryce.

Cody pulled the laptop off the nightstand and sat it on the small dinette table. "Computer. What is it you need?" he said to Bryce.

Bryce pushed away one last doubt and pulled his hand out of his pocket, turned his palm up, and held out the thumb drive.

Cody looked at it, then looked at Bryce. As he reached for it, Bryce closed his fist. "First things first."

"Seriously?" Cody asked. "Now isn't the time to play games."

"I'm not playing a game, but I don't know what this is and I want to be sure we agree on the boundaries."

Cody snorted, "Boundaries? You need to be reminded that I could take that from you!"

"You could try. And if you failed and had to use your weapon, you might be able to get it. But what if you find this was a test that you failed, and now had only an empty thumb drive? Along with a discharged weapon? So much paperwork," Bryce said confidently.

Cody put his hand down. "Fine. What are your 'boundaries'?"

Bryce set the thumb drive on the table. "I went to my house to get some of my old clothes and in the pocket of this jacket was this thumb drive. I don't know where it came from, and I don't know if it's nothing or something. I remember you saying you were looking for something and I don't know..." he paused, "I thought this should be checked out."

"So did you check it out?" asked Cody, standing still.

"I tried. It needs a password," answered Bryce.

"Seems like you'd remember password protecting a thumb drive," said Cody.

"Seems like it. Here's the thing. If it's nothing, fine, I overreacted. But if it's something, I need to know what happens next. If it is important, or incriminating in some way, I want to know, and I want to know in advance what the response is going to be."

"Ahh, protecting yourself, I see," smirked Cody.

"No. I'm protecting my wife and kids."

"Okay, brother. I get that. The best I can do is try to figure out what it is first. I will keep you informed, and I will continue to watch your family."

Bryce reached down to the thumb drive and slid it across the table towards Cody.

Evie found herself growing more annoyed with everything. Literally, everything. She decided, after what seemed like a long and tortuous dinner where the kids hated every food that they normally loved, followed by an evening of laundry and dishes, that it was best if they called it an early night. Of course, she had to wait until after Bryce called.

She had listened to each of the kids retelling their day like it had been an adventure to Disney. They had laughed together, animated, perfectly charming, as they described their time with Bryce. She was ticked off, not with them, but with him. She knew she was overreacting, but she felt like a burn had ignited and was turning into wildfire in her heart. How was any of this fair? How was he being the hero to her children fair? And now he was suddenly the good guy to her friends? It wasn't fair, plain and simple. He had robbed her of a normal life when he made his choice to keep secrets and get involved in something illegal. He destroyed their family, and whatever lies he told himself to make it sound like he meant well really didn't matter. Now that he was back, she could only feel like an idiot for even entertaining the thought of seeing their family pieced back together. Who would want that?! A botched up, stitched up, ragged family?

She sat on her bed staring, her thoughts going crazy, unable to explain why the anger felt so deep, why it felt like it was penetrating her every cell. If she closed her eyes, she could almost feel it traveling in her blood stream. A part of her knew she should feel alarmed. This didn't feel good.

For a moment she thought she felt a whisper, "Evie." She knew that sound, and knew that voice, and usually responded with joy. But this time, she just didn't care.

Sam sat on her couch deep into the Bermuda Triangle, otherwise known as social media, when she felt that familiar urge. The little, almost annoying, invasion into her thoughts, that she had learned to pay attention to. It was easy when it was the middle of the night, and she would awake with a thought or person pressing on her mind. She knew it meant to pray. It was harder to recognize during the waking hours. There were always many thoughts rambling through her mind at any given moment.

Sam was accomplished at prioritizing. She didn't juggle her lists of things to do, she sorted them. Move some things to the top, bump some things to the bottom.

Right now, she was enjoying a moment of freedom from her list. So, when a thought arose that had nothing to do with the memes or cute videos she was focused on, her first reaction was to push it aside and continue enjoying this burden-free time.

But again, there came that small whisper, "Evie." As she was scrolling through her feed, it was more felt than heard, soft but urgent. Sam looked away from her screen, paused, and knew it for what it was. The shofar was blowing. It felt different during the day, soft, distant, but she heard it, nonetheless. She called Vicki.

"Hey, Sam. Evie?" asked Vicki.

"Yep, shall we pray now or plan a later time?" asked Sam.

"Now...but what a crappy time of day for this! Let's hope it's a quick in and out, and see how it goes," answered Vicki.

"Sounds good. See ya there." Sam hung up. "Here's hoping this is just another sit at the oasis call," she thought to herself, knowing full well that the shofar didn't blow in the middle of the afternoon very often.

"Please be simple," she thought to herself, just before the portal opened.

CHAPTER FIFTEEN

Vicki was kneeling before the throne of God. Her head was bent, and tears rolled down her cheeks, pouring onto the sparkling floor. Her eyes were closed hard, trying to stop dripping all over the King's throne room. Why did she cry every time she came here? Couldn't she come through the doors with a skip and a song just one time?

She knelt before the throne of grace. And boy, did she need grace. She'd made so many mistakes, threw gasoline on so many fires, let bitterness take root, repaid evil for evil. She rarely got it right in an argument or 'altercation' with her husband. Vicki was sure of the promise that He that was in her was greater than anything she faced, but she didn't have one personal victory in recent memory to prove that to be true. She was so tired of fighting, so tired of caring and every time she promised herself that she would just stop caring to try to avoid the pain. She came here to tell God what she was going to do, but each time she ended up in a puddle on His floor. He always melted her heart.

As she sat here, mermaid style, eyes closed, she heard the tinkling of the little glass bottles hanging from the rafters of silver. Clink, clink, clink. There were different tones based on how full the bottles were. She felt movement near her, opened her eyes and looked to her left, where a man stood dressed in leather armor. He had a giant broadsword strapped to his back and Vicki could see the handle extended over his head. "No, not a man," she thought. A warrior. One of the fighting angels. Yeah, he was large and powerful. He saw she was looking at him and froze like a deer trapped in the headlights.

"Ma'am. So sorry. Sorry, Ma'am." he spoke quietly while he bowed at the waist and pulled a pouch from his belt. He started to open it and Vicki thought he was taking out something to throw at her. She startled and slid away from him. Raising a hand to stop her, he bent low to the ground and gathered her fallen tears into a little glass bottle. It took all of five seconds. He stood up and corked the small bottle, bending his head back to look at the dangling and chiming bottle collection that hung from above. Then he chucked it up as far and as fast as he could.

Vicki gasped, startled that the tear collecting thing was real, and that she had never thought about how they were supposedly collected. Even if she had, she never would have imagined a beautiful warrior angel in leather armor bowing in the throne room of grace and bottling the tears before hurling them up to the ceiling. Was someone up there catching them and tying them to cords? So much to learn. Her eyes went from the ceiling back to the warrior. He still was looking up, his hands on his hips and his legs wide. Only when he seemed satisfied that the new tear bottle wasn't going to come crashing down, he looked over at Vicki.

"Ma'am". He saluted her and backed out, bowing at the hip again before blending into the white and glowing distance. He was gone and Vicki was alone again before the Father.

"So, you really do collect our tears. I thought it was just poetry." Vicki looked up into the direction she assumed was the throne. The light was brighter that way. The presence of love was strong here in this spot. Sometimes there was peace, overwhelming and powerful. Peace wasn't always a given, but the love was. One thing Vicki knew without a doubt, was if she would just come and enter the throne room, even if she crawled in, there was a cocoon of love waiting for her. She never left this room with regrets over coming but felt sure that she was loved. Her eyes went back to the musical bottles, and she was sure that several thousand of them were labeled The Vicki Collection.

She closed her eyes and adjusted her legs into a kneeling position. She reached behind her and pulled out her sword. Her own sword was not nearly as big as the tear drop warrior's, but it was still powerful. She had been given this very sword in this very room by the Most High God who sat on the throne. With two hands, she raised it high into the air. Vicki lifted her head, closed her eyes again, then bowed forward. She adjusted the sword to hold it sideways in both hands, cradling the weapon, the Sword of the Spirit. And then she laid it on the ground between her and her King.

"Yours. My sword is yours. My strength is yours. My loyalty and fealty belong to You. I will fight no one in my name or by my strength. I will hurt no one who is not Your enemy. Please teach me, show me who is who. Who do I fight? Who is Your enemy and who is mine? Until I know, I yield to You." Vicki spoke these words out loud but with little strength, just louder than a whisper, only Yahweh able to hear her.

The gentle wind moved, and the tinkling glass began a song. The tones and pitches, the tempo, it was a most beautiful and tranquil sound to fall over the room. Lights, sparkles, chimes, Vicki wondered how people ever stay awake in here to pray. Vicki herself has been jerked awake many times by the drool dripping off her face. "Hey," she thought. "I sure hope someone didn't bottle my drool, thinking it was tears. Does the warrior know the difference? And what was with him anyway?" Vicki would have thought white robed, child-sized angels would be tear collectors.

As soon as she had that thought, the very same warrior came back running, shouting fiercely as he got closer.

"Run! Run!"

The angel ran past Vicki with his sword pulled out, heading towards the door. Vicki jumped up when he had first come running, but she had not moved away from her spot before the throne. She watched as he ran past her, but her sword was still on the ground, laying as an offering to her King. He came running back and stopped near her. He looked upset. "I said run!"

That's when she heard the Shofar, calling loud and clear, as a heavy gust of wind moved the tear bottles. The Shofar's call and the clanging tear bottles together filled the throne room, sounding like warning cries. Immediately Vicki moved to pick up her sword, and ran towards the door, pushing past the warrior.

"Hey!" he yelled.

She didn't care who he was. She knew her friends were in trouble. Vicki and the angel crashed through the portal side by side. They entered the desert battlefield with their swords drawn, held high over their heads. There wasn't any activity or battle at the entry site, but up ahead Vicki could see a large group in full battle. She didn't know yet who it was that called for help, but as this was Evie's personal battlefield it would be a good thing if Evie was here. It would mean she was praying.

"Let's go!" shouted the angel man as he passed her. This irritated Vicki. He acted like he was in charge and was familiar with this place and her people. He was already running, and Vicki had to work extra hard to stretch her legs to reach him.

"I'm Vicki," she said, quite proud that she wasn't huffing and puffing as she said it.

"I'm Evan, servant of the Most High."

They crested a dune and there it was, a battle worthy of the Shofar call. There was no time for more words as Vicki and Evan came upon the back side of the horde.

"Son of a Snapper," Vicki muttered.

"Level three demons. Nerod sends his horde. This will be hard, human. May the Most High be with you."

Vicki felt a tremor of fear pump through her. She hated Snappers. The alien-like looks of these demons really freaked her out. Their long necks, gray skin, and wide mouths looked other-worldly. She'd met them before on her own battlefield and Yahweh had saved her many times from their attacks on her. She decided to be grateful they weren't Jaders. She just needed to remember the Snappers' long, stretchy necks made their bite a real threat.

They had stopped running as they began their descent from the dune. It was not clear who exactly was under attack. There was no crying or calling, no voice to be heard. Even the Snappers were somewhat quiet, as she could only hear their chewing, gnashing teeth. Vicki and Evan would need to fight *their way to the center of this mob to see who was under attack. Vicki stabbed a hairless, gray Snapper through the back and pulled the sword up, splitting the creature into two pieces. It fell to the ground without a sound. Vicki could see Evan doing the same, quietly puncturing and pulling, and slowly a pile of Snappers grew beneath their feet. Evan kept pace with Vicki as she moved around the outer band of the mob. She wanted to simply roar out Yahweh's name and scatter the demons, freeing whoever was under attack, but quiet and deadly seemed to be what was needed here. Vicki intuitively knew this.*

The Snappers, in their frenzy, did not notice their comrades on each side of them falling to their eternal death. The desert wind had begun blowing and sand began swirling around the carnage. Vicki was making quick work of dropping Snappers. She pierced one, and it screamed. That startled Vicki, and she yelled out in fear. The wounded Snapper twisted its long neck to look at who had stabbed it. The demon looked right at Vicki. Its large eyes filled with tears, no blood. It looked as if it was going to cry. It was hard to tell facial expressions with these noseless, earless demons.

Vicki was caught in the gaze of the demon and did not notice the slow extension of its neck growing towards her. The eyes. She couldn't stop looking at the pool of black eyes. The demon had slowly moved its head right in front of and near Vicki's face. Now it was opening its mouth.

"Wow, that's a lot of teeth," was all Vicki thought. And then the demon head fell off from its body and dropped onto her feet. The hypnotizing moment was over. Evan stood in front of her, swinging his sword wildly. The rest of the demons from the horde were even more frenzied, now aware of their enemy behind them but still intent on destroying whoever was at the center of this pile.

"A little help, human? Think maybe you can stop making lovey eyes with the Snappers?"

Now Vicki was angry. A friend was under this heap of alien monsters. She'd almost been bitten, and an angel had saved her.

"Ahh!" Vicki screamed at the top of her lungs, righteous anger filling her, angry that these hideous and vile creatures attacked and would destroy the children of God if they could, angry that beautiful moments in the throne room were interrupted for the children of God to come to places like this. She was angry that Evie had all she ever wanted within inches of her face, but because of the poison she was refusing to pray on the battlefield, prayers that would actually change things. She was avoiding these prayers, these battles to fight back the monsters from hell who hated Yahweh and anyone in His image. Righteous anger was unleashed and put to good use on the battlefield of prayer.

After Vicki chopped off several more Snapper heads, she paused and leaned back, bent at the knees. Her face looked up to the heavens, arms open her sword hanging from her hand. The sand swirled around her. In a beautiful and holy moment, surrounded by Nerod's Snappers, piles of death and a warrior angel in front of her killing everything in its reach, Vicki cried and screamed out.

"Yahweh!"

The air exploded. She stood up, filled with power and strength that only comes from the name of the Most High. Many of the Snappers on the outer edge had exploded. The ones further in who didn't were filled with rage from their pain. Their focus changed from the child of God in the center of the attack to the one who dared cry out that name.

"Oh, boy," thought Vicki. "Here we go!" The Snappers turned, zombie-like, toward Vicki. The power of the name of the King zapped their energy. They wouldn't be stunned for long, but it was all that was needed. Vicki swung her sword efficiently, beautifully, like a choreographed dance.

One by one, the demons approached her, only to get their heads cut off. Evan worked from the back of the horde that was turned towards Vicki, trying to get to the center and find the one who had blown the Shofar. He was now forced to climb over the slippery gray naked bodies of Snappers. It could always be worse. Corgs. Corgs would be worse with their maggots everywhere.

Vicki continued eliminating demons. Within minutes, the Snappers regained some energy and focus, the effects of the name of the Most High wearing off. Several of the Snappers extended their necks to look around at what was once thought to be a clear victory. The scene had changed. This was a loss for Nerod's Snappers. They looked at each other, some narrowly escaping Vicki's sword only by retracting their necks. Communicating without words, the demons that remained began to back away from the giant circle of carnage piles. They looked like they were floating over the sand, and they moved so quickly away from Vicki and Evan that it startled them. Suddenly, there were no demons left to fight. The Snappers were fleeing.

Vicki knew they were now safe, but she could not see anyone standing at the center of that pile. Whoever had called must be buried. Fear and panic moved Vicki to run and climb over the piles of decaying gray matter, ignoring the blank eyes that stared up at her. Wait, were the eyes following her?

"Evan! Help!" Vicki stood at the bull's eye of the battle, digging through bodies. Where was she? Why isn't she standing? Is she fallen? Wounded? Oh, no no no. She felt something hard under her hands. As she was clearing Snapper parts, she felt solid wood. "What the...?"

Evan, beside her now, used his strength to pick up large portions of bodies and fling them to the outer edge of the battle circle. There! Something large and wooden, and another smaller object. Evan and Vicki cleared the last demon away and stood looking down at two shields, one giant and one small.

Fear filled Vicki's heart. She didn't know who was fallen under these shields. They must have been hurt in the battle. Grief threatened to overtake her. Is there anything more heartbreaking than to find a child of the King wounded and destroyed in a battlefield of prayer, fallen under the enemies of God? Will Evan catch the tears she weeps here in a little bottle? Can he throw it high enough to reach The Vicki Collection of tears dangling in the throne room?

But a movement startled Vicki, bringing her back to the scene before her. The shields were moving! First the big one moved to the side, and then the little one moved as two humans stood up. Bryce and Kendall.

They were safe. They were laughing and high fiving. Vicki and Evan just stood and watched the fist-bumping and dancing of father and son. Evan stabbed his sword into the sand and leaned on it. He smiled and laughed at the joy between Bryce and Kendall. Vicki needed a moment. She stood affectionately with her hands on her hips, having dropped her sword on the ground, before she bent over at the waist, hands on her knees. Yeah, she just needed a moment.

"Shields of faith, guys! Shields of faith." Bryce's voice rose as his relief and excitement grew. "They're a real thing. Like we were completely safe. Well, we couldn't move, could we, Kendall? I mean, we had to stay there and not move, but we were like turtles, weren't we, Kendall?" Bryce grabbed his son in a side hug and rubbed his hair.

"Yeah, like turtles! We're like Ninja Turtles, Dad!"

Evan burst out with a loud, booming laugh. At that comparison, Vicki had to laugh too.

"I'm glad to see you both safe. But answer me this, who blew the Shofar?" Vicki needed to know.

They wouldn't be able to leave the battlefield until the one who blew the Shofar declared victory or retreat. Ground was either gained, held, or lost. But when you sent a call for battlefield prayer warriors, you waited until the person who did the calling knew they were safe. Then you made your way back to the portal, and back to bed, or cooking, or work, or to the movie you were supposed to be watching with your husband.

"Shofar? We didn't call you. We don't have a Shofar," Bryce said, seeming confused.

Evan and Vicki exchanged a look between them. It wasn't over. Someone was still here.

Vicki had a surge of panic pour through her. Sam or Evie. One of them had been fighting alone for quite a while. They called for backup and backup had come, but not to them. What Vicki wanted to do was pick up her sword and run. But instead, she fell to the sand. She was down on her knees and hands, head dangling down, rocking back and forth. She was so tired. Then she caught sight of the pieces and parts of the Snappers lying around the cleared part of the center circle. She couldn't stop and couldn't afford a nap. Evan reached out his hand to her. She accepted, and he pulled her up.

"Daughter of God, Warrior." Evan bowed before her. "Shall we go forth?"

"We shall go forth," Vicki replied, and then laughed. If there was ever a proper time to say 'go forth' she guessed this was it. She spoke it a little stronger this time. "We shall go forth!"

Bryce and Kendall picked up their shields and drew their swords. Evan pulled his sword from the sand. As one small unit in the army of Yahweh, they turned away from the direction of the portal and towards the interior of the sandy battlefield. It should have been a picturesque moment, but they had to climb over the piles of dismembered, gray Snappers, some of them whose big black eyes still followed them. They reached the end of the battle circle and stood with the fallen prey behind them. One child, one man, one angel, and one woman stood facing the sandy horizon wondering which direction to run in.

And then the Shofar blew again.

It had been a long, long day, Evie thought to herself. She'd got everyone out the door on time, worked her shift, kissed Bryce, got weirded out by Bryce, cooked dinner, put the kids to bed, and now just wanted to have some moments that were quiet.

She was tired, annoyed, concerned, and angry. But mostly just tired. "How sad is it," she thought, "that I wish everything could go back to the way it was when Bryce was gone?"

When he was gone, she and the kids had been okay. Not great, but okay, good, on the way to great. Now it felt like everything was in upheaval. She had been pretty good at self-reflection and introspection. She was a reasonable person most of the time and maybe just a little proud about being able to set her feelings aside so that she could effectively assess the needs of her family.

She picked up her mug of chamomile tea and let herself relax into her cushion so that she could think for a quiet minute. Mostly about that kiss. For a moment, she thought she should call the girls about it, but then realized that was probably just a reaction of habit. She didn't really want to call either of them. They were part of the complication. She replayed the moment, remembering, with a soft smile.

What the heck was that about?! Bryce had been very clear about his intentions. But what about her own desires? She remembered the leap her heart had taken, and it had taken a few seconds for her brain to catch up. Did she like it? She tilted her head to the side. "Of course, I liked it. I'm a woman. He's a man, and it's been a long time since a man had kissed me." For the briefest of moments, she felt her heart stir, just before her mind stepped up. No. That was a perfectly normal, physical reaction in an adult woman who had been abandoned for a long time. "Don't romanticize it, Evie," she said to herself. "Don't make it what it's not."

Evie sipped her tea and felt a familiar nudge. The soft touch within her spirit. She knew without question that it was calling to her, seeking her attention. She knew what it was, and she also knew that she just couldn't.

She didn't want to pray about this.

She couldn't explain why, she just didn't. What she needed was to organize her thoughts, make sure she was looking out for herself, allowing enough self-care. She thought bitterly, "No one else is going to take care of me, but me."

She pushed aside all other thoughts, reached for her planner on the coffee table, and begin to fill in the hours for the next day. "I need to be less hormonally responsive and a lot more organized with my time. Productive." As she spent the next hour making food plan lists, errand lists, children's book lists, every list she could think of, she consciously directed her remaining energy to everything but the quiet voice that had almost drawn her attention.

Standing in the checkout line, Sam's arms were full. She remembered how Evie always told her that she'd have more time if she just planned a menu and shopped for the week. Problem with that was there was no possible way on this planet that she could decide today what she wanted for dinner tomorrow. Some people are just destined to be at the grocery store every day of their life, forever in line.

She got to her car and set her grocery bag in the passenger seat. Her thoughts went to Evie again. Over the past couple of years, she had gotten better at sensing the difference between her own thoughts and a nudge of the Spirit. There was a difference between having something on her mind and having something laid upon her mind. The more she exercised responding to the Spirit's call— the call of the Shofar—the better she got at recognizing it. The quicker she got at responding, the stronger she got on the battlefield.

She used to be really good at promising to pray for someone or something, only to realize later that she never had. She didn't mess around with that anymore. If she felt a burden, she stopped immediately and prayed. Of course, there were still other times, when people asked for prayer for some event or just everyday things, and she learned to write those down. Evie had advice for that, too. "Make little lists, Sam. Check 'em off one by one."

Those were important, they were just different than from the drop everything, you are needed now type of prayer. She took a second after putting on her seatbelt to sit quietly for a moment. Does this feeling have urgency behind it? "No, but it does feel like it's not coming from me," she thought. "And it's definitely about Evie. Well, I hope Vicki doesn't stand around the desert waiting for me. I'm gonna be a bit late." She headed towards Evie's house.

Sam saw Evie look through the window as she pulled into the driveway. Then she saw the kitchen light shut off. "Ha," Sam laughed, "Not that easy, girlfriend." Sam got out of her car and waved towards the window, knowing even in the dark, Evie would be looking to see what she did. She walked up to the door and didn't even bother knocking. Just stood there. After a full minute, Evie opened the door and looked at her.

"Do you see my lights are off?" Evie asked.

"I see there are no lights on, if that is what you mean," said Sam.

"You do realize when the light is off, it means I'm done visiting for the day, right?" Evie snapped.

"Actually," Sam replied, "Since it's not Halloween, I didn't think it meant anything."

Evie stared at Sam for a moment and then opened the door further. "You're not funny."

"I'm a little funny," Sam smiled as she walked through the door and flipped on the light in the kitchen. "I sure could use some tea," Sam added, doing her best to sound hopeful.

"Tea? Wow, really, Sam? You don't drink tea."

"Sure, I do, you just hadn't noticed."

"Really? What kind of tea do you drink?"

Sam only paused for a moment. "I basically like all teas. Hot teas, cold teas, medicinal teas, Irish teas, High tea, pretty much all teas."

Evie stared at Sam while she filled the electric tea kettle and turned it on. Sam was starting to feel just a bit awkward as Evie simply stared at her. It felt like a mom glare.

"So, how about I just sit down here?" Sam said as she pulled out the kitchen chair and slowly sat down. "This is nice!"

Evie rolled her eyes and grabbed the chamomile tea and two mugs. "Ok, Sam. This is fun and all, but maybe you should just say what you're here for?"

"I just missed you!"

Evie plopped in the tea bags and poured the hot water. "Huh. Weird."

"C'mon Ev, I was at the grocery store and was thinking about you, so I stopped by. That's it."

"What did you get?"

"At the store?" she paused. "Okay, um, I got a block of tofu, a tomato, a bag of deli rolls and a cucumber."

Evie just stared at her. "Figures." Evie pulled out her own chair and sat down.

Sam rolled her eyes, picked up her tea, sniffed it, brought it to her mouth, then sniffed again. "Mmm, I love tea."

She smiled across the table at Evie, who sighed. "Whatever. Was there something specific you wanted to talk about? Or just tea?"

"No, not really. Just wondered how you were?"

"I'm good. Why wouldn't I be?"

"See? That's not like you! You're not usually snippy!"

"What am I usually?"

"Nice! You're the nice one."

"I see." Evie rolled her eyes again and leaned back in her chair. "Here's what I think. I think, me being the 'nice one' has made it really easy to also be the dumb one. And I don't like feeling dumb."

"Why do you feel dumb?"

"I feel dumb because I've wasted too much time on a husband who I don't trust. I wasted way too much prayer on it. I feel dumb because I dragged my friends into it and I shouldn't have. I feel separated from my kids over it. I'm now on a way different page than my friends, who, sorry, just don't understand me. So, yeah, being nice isn't working for me right now."

Sam looked at her tea and prayed quickly to not mess this up. "I'm sorry it's like that for you, Ev. You're the sweetest, kindest person I know. Even if this is how you feel, I felt honored to be included in every way you have let me." She paused. "I don't think I have to tell you how much your kids love you. You are their mom. Nothing and no one can change or take away from that. And I think you feel like Vicki and I have worked against you, and I'm sorry for that. I think I can include Vicki when I say we are for you." She reached out and touched Evie's hand. "For you, Evie."

When Evie didn't respond, Sam asked quietly, "The Shofar has blown, and you haven't been there, Ev. Can you tell me why?"

Evie looked up quickly, waited for a moment and said, "I haven't heard it."

"Oh." Sam paused. "Have you felt it?"

"Felt the call to pray? No. No, I haven't," Evie said. "You sure it wasn't Bryce who called you to pray?" Evie sounded cynical.

"I'm sure," Sam said softly.

"So, you're telling me that I'm cut out of my own battlefield? The one I invited you and Vicki to? The same one that you invited Bryce to? Who, in turn, invited Kendall?"

"Not to split hairs, but Bryce didn't actually invite Kendall, Ev. Kendall had been there before I was even there. Remember?"

When Evie didn't answer, Sam asked, "What is it you don't like about Bryce praying about this, about you and him? Why is it sitting all wrong with you?"

Evie could feel herself getting agitated, but she also recognized the honest and fair question. "I don't know, okay? I just don't know. None of it feels right. I want it to be done. I want it over!"

"Can you honestly say you have no feelings for him? No desire to see if there is a possibility or hope of restoration? Cause, Ev, he does have those feelings for you."

"Honestly? I think it doesn't matter what I do or do not feel for him. And even if it did, at this point, I feel more anger than anything."

"Angry at what?"

Evie thought about it for a moment, looked at Sam and said, "Everything. I feel angry about everything."

Sam felt a swell of compassion for her friend. She knew, more at that moment than any other, that there was going to be no easy way to get past this. Evie needed more than just a friend to sit and drink tea with.

Sam spoke gently, "I can't say I know exactly how you feel. Personally, I'd love to have a man fighting for me."

"You say that, but it's all great until he doesn't."

"But," Sam continued, "I can say that more than anything, I am praying for you. I love you. No matter what."

Evie had a million thoughts swirling in her mind. She didn't respond, but sat staring at the table, unmoving.

Sam's own thoughts were firing on all cylinders. "Okay, what do I say now? Little help here, Lord? I don't want to tick her off! Wait, are you saying I should tick her off? No, that doesn't sound right. What to do? What to do?"

Sam asked trepidly, "So, do you think you'd like to join us in prayer? I sensed the call a while back."

Evie's eyes flashed to Sam. "Who is 'us'?"

Sam froze. "I didn't mean us us. I meant in general, me. Join me. Like, just pray. Together, like we do, you and me."

Evie leaned back in her chair and fixed Sam with a stare. "I need a simple yes or no here, Sam. Are you still meeting with Bryce to pray about me?"

"Ok, Lord. Here goes..." thought Sam. "Yes," she said.

Evie drew a sharp breath in, "Is Vicki?"

"Yes."

"Is Kendall?"

Sam paused, searching Evie's face, looking for any kind of good sign and finding none. "Yes, I think so."

"You think so? So, yes?"

"Yes."

Evie laughed. "I guess I should have known! Was it really too much to ask for all the adults to leave my kid out of this?"

"Evie, it's not like that. Seriously! You know how this works. We don't bring Kendall! We never sat down and said, 'Hey Kendall, you should pray for your mom and dad to get back together!'"

"You know what, Sam? I don't care! Do you understand me? I. Do. Not. Care. This is straight up none of your business anymore. None."

"Why are you mad at me? Because I prayed when God called me to? Listen to yourself, Evie! Something is wrong! Can't you feel it?"

Evie laughed, shortly. "So now there is something wrong with me, Sam? Get out. I'm done."

"I'm asking you to pray with me. Right now. Right here. It's ok if you're mad. We can fight that out. But please..." Sam held out her hand.

Evie looked at Sam's offered hand, stood up and said, "I'll make this super simple. I'm done praying with you, and with Vicki. This is between me and God. You can go home and pay attention to your own crappy life."

Sam gasped.

Evie continued, "This is my business. And I'm settling it for good. I don't need you or anyone else standing over my shoulder while I do it."

"What are you doing to do?" asked Sam.

"I'm going to claim it as done. Case closed. And if you value our friendship at all, I won't see you when I get there."

CHAPTER SIXTEEN

Loden hustled through the tunnels of Oridon's cave. He moved in the darkest shadows, clinging to the cave walls as tight and as low as he could. The cavern was filled with the noise of weapons banging, heavy footsteps, sounds of running, and heavy, laborious demon breathing. This filled Loden with dread because he knew this fortress did not hold Jaders. He had lost his whole horde. If it was Swastiks, he was screwed. If it was Swastiks, does that mean Oridon is back? And if Oridon was back after being gone for decades, that means this is unlike any war or battle he has ever been in.

That should have been obvious when he lost his whole army in a battle of hundreds to one. But that reality hadn't sunk into his devious and dark mind until now. He knew that Oridon only returned after expending Jaders. They were used as bait, expendable. In this moment of realization, his hero worship of Oridon was turning to hatred. And a new plan developed.

He would stay hidden for a little while longer. He would become a Watcher.

Loden hid in a dark corner across from a room where both sounds of pleasure and torture emanated. Someone was experiencing delight, and someone sounded like they wanted to die. The door opened and Oridon walked into the hallway, zipping up his pants, buckling his sword into place. His eyes were filled with black, no white in them at all. He stood eight feet high, and what little flesh could be seen through all the scars, tattoos, and runes, was the color of human flesh. The body was not only marked but pierced. Bones, metals, rings, hoops, and bars were stabbed through every visible body part. The weight of the metal alone must have weighed a ton.

Oridon didn't look any bit as pleasured as he had sounded, and the demon on the other side of the door now begged for death. Once you were had by Oridon, the demons mistakenly thought eternal hellfire would be better. Oridon turned and walked down the hall.

He yelled in a thunderous voice, "Make ready for war!" Loden heard the battle cry of a mega horde, followed by footsteps of demonic soldiers leaving to go to the battlefield. Silence followed, and Loden welcomed it. It gave him time to think. But the silence was short-lived. The door opened again and Loden heard someone dragging themselves through the doorway.

A hand reached out and grabbed a stone, pulling itself forward. Another hand, followed by its head and body, moved through the doorway into Loden's vision. There is no love lost between demons and there is certainly no pity. But fear of what Oridon would do when he was seeking pleasure caused Loden to rethink his schemes. If this broken demon was the result of Oridon's pleasure, what destruction would he cause when he sought pain or suffering?

The body was now out into the hall, pulling, moving, crawling forward, leaving trails of blood and stench, their insides *falling out. The mangled demon headed right towards Loden, as if it saw him or knew him. But that was impossible. Yet Loden could see this dying creature, so maybe it could see him. The creature moaned in desperate agony. Loden crawled towards the demon. Who was this? All his Jaders had died. But as soon as Loden reached the creature, he knew. He recognized this shattered comrade.*

"Fairen? What has that Swastik done to you? How dare he harm one of my own Jaders! Who does he think he is to do this to me?"

Just like that, the demon, as demons do, moved from one emotion to the strongest emotion of all, vanity. This was about him, not the destroyed comrade at his feet. Everyone was his enemy, even those in their Dark Kingdom. Fairen let out cries and more guttural moans in answer. Why was Fairen here and not at battle with him? Why was he not dead with all the other Jaders? How had he not followed him into battle to face the human enemy at the battlefield desert?

"Well, well, if it isn't the traitor, Fairen? I went to war for our king, and you stayed here pleasuring the scumbag Oridon. How did that work out for you?" Loden moved in to whisper into Fairen's bruised and bleeding ear. "Are you sorry now? Well, I will tell you this, not as sorry as you will be in the next few minutes." And in the darkened corners of shadowed halls, Loden unbelted his own pants and then afterwards sent Fairen to his eternal doom.

Evan, Kendall, Bryce, and Vicki could hear the Shofar being blown. They followed the sound as best they could, trodding through deep, monochromatic sand. It was hard to move swiftly when crossing dunes, but it seemed speed was important. All four of them were driven with urgency in their hearts. Evie needed them. She was here! She finally came back to pray for her marriage and her family! They moved as fast as they could, helping each other when they tripped and faltered in the sand. They were hot, and the sun shone directly overhead with a burning heat. The horn sounded closer now. They were moving in the right direction.

They topped the crest of the desolate dune, and everyone stopped moving. Vicki sucked in air and gasped.

Kendall stood staring. "Dude."

"What the...." Bryce almost swore in front of his son but stopped in time.

And Evan just stood there, laughing.

At the bottom of the dune was a white, glowing woman. She was like a mythic Amazon, and seemed to glow with white hair, Grecian styled goddess clothes, and gorgeously tanned skin. They could tell she was strong by the way she was spearing the Corgs like shish kebobs. She blew the Shofar with her right hand, and with her left hand, she used the Sword of the Spirit, executing Corg after Corg. This woman didn't look like she was in dismay or about to fall under this attack and lose. Why was this beautiful specimen blowing the most sacred of weapons?

Vicki felt annoyed. She could have been home and present with her husband right now. She could have been focused on her own marriage, but she heard, and answered, the Shofar's call. This had better be good. The four strolled towards the woman. As there was no obvious threat, they paced themselves, letting her kill the final Corg.

"Let her wade through the disgusting maggots to come to us," thought an irritated Vicki. She looked at her prayer team. Only

Bryce seemed as irritated as she was. Evan appeared in full appreciation of this woman. Did he know her? Kendall smiled his biggest smile. He had his Christmas morning face on. Yep, Kendall definitely knew her.

Vicki was moving past irritation, into full blown jealousy for her best friend Evie. This was her battlefield. How dare this gorgeous woman come here to show off and call all the strong men to her side? Just who did she think she was?

"Mrs. Taylor!"

Kendall ran towards the woman with both arms open. The wind billowed in her long white hair, and the strong, beautiful woman ran towards him with a look of joy on her face. She swept the child up into her embrace. She twirled and laughed with joy. And was she crying?

Wait, what? Old Mrs. Taylor? Vicki was sure her face was full showed her confusion. The old woman no longer looked old, but like a youthful warrior. Mrs. Taylor looked over the head of the child she held, right at Vicki. She winked.

As the others reached her, Mrs. Taylor put down the warrior child and patted him on the head. There was silence for a moment. Vicki and Bryce were stunned into silence.

Bryce was the first to speak. "Wait, old Mrs. Taylor? The oracle? The old lady in the chair who can't even walk?"

"Mind your manners, human." It was the first time Vicki had ever heard Evan speak in a harsh tone towards them. "You are in the presence of a saint. You don't need to bow your knee to anyone other than the Most High, but you had better remove any trace of aggression from your tone or I will remove it for you."

Evan moved his glare from Bryce to Vicki. She held his gaze until he could see that there was no harm in hers. Reality was sinking in now. Evan could see the understanding toppling over her confusion. Evan moved towards Mrs. Taylor and picked up the hand that held the Shofar. He took it out of her hand, then pulled her hands to his lips. He kissed the old saint with love and affection, as if they were old and dear friends, meeting once again.

Vicki was then able to discern all that was happening before her eyes. Vicki looked from Evan to 'old Mrs. Taylor'. Her eyes filled with tears, and she could do nothing else but rush towards her aged mentor and spiritual teacher. This was the real Mrs. Taylor. Vicki held her tight, smelled the familiar scent of peppermint. She kissed her cheek and didn't ever want to let go.

Vicki had so many thoughts and questions, but she remembered the Shofar.

"Mrs. Taylor, why have you been blowing the Shofar?" Vicki asked.

Mrs. Taylor looked over the hill to her left. She raised her sword in that direction. "They are coming. All of them," she spoke without any fear in her voice.

All four followed her eyes and stood in front of her, as if to protect her. It would take some time to remember that in the battlefield she was not the fragile and weak old woman they had known. Their attention was now directed towards the skyline, and Bryce looked nervously in that direction. Evan was clenching his teeth. Kendall had his hand over his eyes and was squinting. Vicki was filled with fear and dread as her gaze focused hard on the dune.

But then Mrs. Taylor spoke again, "Over there, look over there. Evie comes."

They prepared themselves for a fight, facing the dune where Evie was expected to arrive. Swords were out, and they stood firm and steady as they waited for their friend, mother, and wife.

Evie appeared on the horizon of the tallest dune. Her silhouette looked angry and unyielding. They could see another figure running behind Evie. She seemed more panicked in her body language. They didn't look like the ideal image of warriors, bound together as a unified army of two. This looked more helter-skelter with one angry woman and one a bit fretful.

They realized the figure behind Evie was Sam. Sam waved her arms back and forth over her head at them. They each waved back, not sure what was going on. Evie was the first to move off the top of the sand pile. She marched towards them, Sam trying to catch up to her.

That's when they heard the enemy. The sand vibrated with the footsteps of a coming army of evil. They saw the demons crest the first dune the prayer warriors could see, and then the next dune, and the next. These demons were big, bigger than Evan, and bigger than their Amazon Mrs. Taylor. They had a Goliath. And there was no doubt he was the boss. But Evie wasn't marching toward the enemy. She was marching towards them. Sam was stumbling behind her, trying to keep up with her.

Vicki looked around with a quick glance. The demon army was moving slowly, almost like they were stalking their prey. They were slow and purposeful. Vicki looked back at Evie and Sam. Evie was not slow and steady. She was hot and furious. And she drew her sword from her back sheath and raised it. Towards the prayer warriors.

It was a strategic military movement, an army of demons walking towards them from an outside circle, with two more saints coming their way in the inner circle. Their timing would be nearly in sync.

"Come on, Evie girl. Come on. Hurry it up just a little," Bryce was talking to himself, but he was worried the horde would get *there at nearly the same time and would separate Evie and Sam from them. That was the worst-case scenario.*

Vicki moved towards the girls, but Evan spoke with authority, saying, "Hold your place, humans." Vicki's knuckles were white from gripping her sword, and beads of sweat dripped down her face. The stress of watching Evie and Sam lumber through the sand with an army of demons approaching was more than Vicki could take. Evie wasn't even aware of the demons. All she seemed to notice was the little prayer army. The walk was not cooling her anger down. Sam finally outpaced Evie and passed her. She ran towards the little group with a look of terror all over her face. Something was wrong, wrong with Evie, wrong with this setting.

Sam was now close enough to be heard, and she shouted, "Someone get me a bloody portal! Bryce, get Evie into a portal now!"

Bryce started to run, obeying Sam. He staggered around, looking for the portal he thought would be right here, simply because they needed one.

"Evan!" he shouted at the angel. "Give us a portal, now!" Bryce seemed as big as Evan. Power rolled off him. A man on the battlefield to protect his wife is one of the most empowering gifts one could ever be given. He was no Goliath, but Bryce appeared like a gladiator. His love for Yahweh and his love for Evie fed his spirit and grew his faith. When faith grows on the battlefield, the body changes. And he was becoming the Hulk. Which seemed dangerous right now because he was mad at everyone. He wanted a portal and there wasn't one.

Evan stepped towards Bryce, "Child of God, protect your wife!"

Then they all heard it, the growling of a thousand Swastiks. It sounded like bears vocalizing, then chomping their teeth. Their heads were held upwards, turning back and forth as if they had meat in their mouth they just ripped out of their prey. And here they came, running now.

Sam was with the group only seconds before Evie arrived. She had been frantically calling out for a portal, searching everywhere. Mrs. Taylor had remained still and in the back of the group. Sam hadn't even noticed her. Bryce was in the front, holding out his arm towards his wife, wanting to catch and hold her before the battle started. Evan was focused on the approaching demons.

Kendall was busy looking at maggots, but he sensed a change in the atmosphere and looked up, "It's Mommy. She's here! Hi, Mommy. We're here with you today!" He didn't seem to be aware of the impending battle. All he saw now was his mother. "Daddy, why does she look angry?" asked Kendall.

Bryce didn't have time to answer because Evie was within sword distance. He knew this because she was coming at him with her sword. She swung to take off his head, but Bryce ducked just in time.

"Mommy, Mommy, no! Don't hurt Daddy!" Kendall cried out to his mother. Evie heard his voice and looked towards him. The sight of her son on a prayer battlefield should have softened her heart, but all could see it only made her wrath worse. She quickly looked at them all. In her anger, she skimmed over Mrs. Taylor, not even noticing there was a huge glowing young woman in their group. She was too angry to see anything but the color red.

The sounds of the demons grew closer, their growling now almost a roar.

"Every single one of you can leave now! Do you hear me? Get off my battlefield! It's mine and I'm shutting it down. Don't you ever come here again. Do you understand me?" she shouted. Spit

flew out of her mouth. She was red with heat and aggression; her heart was pounding, and the pulsing of her blood could be seen in her neck veins.

Bryce had gotten behind her after her first swung at him and saw her look at Kendall. He had thought seeing most of her family here would have melted her heart. He had thought they would stand here in this impending battle and fight with each other for their marriage. Now he remembered she was poisoned. The poisoned pulsed through her body, spreading until she was doing things, saying things, and behaving in a way she never would have, either here on a spiritual plane or in the world of flesh and bone. It was then he knew. He knew he loved Yahweh more than Evie. He knew he trusted Yahweh more than he trusted his wife.

And he knew what he had to do.

From behind Evie, Bryce spoke in a soft and beautiful voice, "Evie, I love you." And Bryce took his sword and stabbed Evie through her back and right through her heart. He held her up with his arm as his other arm held the sword pierced through her body.

Evie looked down at her chest. There was a sword sticking through it. And her husband had done it.

"What have you done?" she asked in a trembling voice. Sam was in the back, still looking for a portal, when she saw Bryce rise behind Evie. Sam saw the look of love on his face when he ran his sword through her, and she screamed with a cry that ripped the air. Thunder boomed from the darkening sky. Kendall looked at his mother, watched the blood of his mother run and drip off the end of the sword. He looked into her eyes, filling with tears and his filling with anger.

Vicki gasped with shock. What had Bryce done? "He killed Evie, he killed Evie," she kept repeating over and over as she *looked at her friend. Vicki couldn't move. Her legs wouldn't obey her command to move, but her arms reached out to her beloved friend.*

Bryce called out to the still and quiet Mrs. Taylor, "Here!"

Mrs. Taylor came running and took hold of Evie. She held her up while Bryce ripped out the sword. The wound was great, and right through the heart. Once the sword was ripped out, Evie fell into Mrs. Taylor, who lowered her onto the ground, holding her upright in her arms like a child.

All eyes then went to the forgotten demon army, about to descend on them. The demons had stopped in their tracks when they saw the man plow his sword right through the woman they were sent to kill. There was a moment of confusion. What were they to do now? The Swastiks looked to their leader, who was looking directly at the group of humans. His mind swirled with options. As it stood now, the mission was accomplished, was it not? The woman was dead. The others would not be able to fight, given their stupid human weakness called emotion. Right now, the demons can claim the victory. They could turn and walk right back up the dune to his cave. The Swastiks could be deep into their devilish victory celebration within the hour if they left now. But what fun would that be? Besides, did he not smell the presence of an angel in that little nest of human scum? So, battle it was.

"Swastiks!" he shouted. "Raise your swords and take their heads!"

Every Swastik roared and raised their swords in a cry, and they ran to the battle.

Only five of the seven would fight. Mrs. Taylor was holding her friend and singing into her ear. She was crying, and the poisoned blood from Evie's chest was pulsing and pouring all over her beautiful white gown. Evie looked into the face of the one who held and comforted her. She knew she was dying, and now it all seemed so silly. Her cold and poisoned heart had been broken in two, pierced by the sword of the Spirit of God, pushed through her bones and heart by her own husband. She looked into the woman's eyes and when she did, she recognized her old, aged friend.

"Mrs. Taylor! What have I done?" Evie sputtered with such sorrow. She looked around her to see Sam and Vicki, Bryce and Kendall, Evan. All of them circled around her, still protecting her. They were going to die here, all of them, because of her, for her. Her broken heart could not take it. She closed her eyes and fell into a state of unconsciousness.

The circle around her was tight, shoulder to shoulder, swords drawn. Kendall stood next to his dad, still shaken at what he had just done. But Bryce was not sorry and was determined to end this now.

The first rows of demons moved in. The Goliath was holding himself in the back. He wasn't going to be the front line. While each saint fought row after row of demons, they kept watch on the giant. He was moving around the circle, gauging each fighter as if he was watching an audition, and picking out whom he was going to fight.

Kendall bent lower to the ground, focused on stabbing demons in the knees. He didn't have to worry about looking at them until they fell in front of him. The ones that didn't die right away would stare intently at him, drawing him to look at them. He could feel the pull of their gaze. It was tempting. But then he remembered his mother laying on the ground behind him. He would show no mercy, and he would not look. He raged at each evil creature that came in front of him.

Vicki and Sam sliced the Swastiks with their swords as tears streamed down their faces. They didn't have to worry about looking into the demons' eyes because they couldn't see through their tears. They saw silhouettes and shapes and fought their enemy with that ability alone. They were standing in the valley of death and had never once wondered what the shadow was from. It was from Swastiks. The giant demons towered over them casting an evil, terrifying shadow.

Bryce was filled with doubt, now second guessing the stabbing of his wife. What had he done? Why did he think that was the right thing to do? In what world would stabbing your wife through her chest, from behind, be okay? He was filled with agony and grief, yet there was still a peace he could not understand, given the fact that she was laying in her own blood on the ground behind him, and demons straight from hell were surrounding them. His precious son, fighting next to him, was toppling demons. The doubt was strong, but it was not poisonous. He had not been touched by a demon hand or sword. His faith was strong. And faith in Yahweh grew you, it didn't break you.

Bryce attacked each demon, the sword itself growing larger and more powerful. Evan gave away no emotion. He was given a mission by Yahweh, and he would complete it. He was not doubtful of the victory as long as the humans kept their trust in Yahweh, even if their hearts were breaking. He had seen their reactions when Bryce had stabbed Evie through the heart. He hadn't seen that coming. He thought he knew humans and right now he was going to have to admit he didn't. But he did know battle, and he knew that giant demon circling around them. Evan saw his face and remembered his name. Oridon, Swastik leader. They had never before met on the battlefield. But it seemed today was the day.

The sky which had thundered at Evie's falling was now dark. Time seemed to stand still, and nothing seemed to change in this wearisome and dreadful battle. Piles of demon bodies were being sucked into the sand as they fell. They were pulled in by the legs slowly, sucked down like quicksand. Less than a hundred Swastiks remained, and the giant was ready to make his move. He had picked out the warrior whose style he likened as near to his own. He had chosen carefully, studying each sword, each technique. He had found the one worthy of battle.

As he began to walk forward, a hand emerged from the sand to deliver a message. Oridon wanted to dismiss it. He had waited all this time to fight! But he bent down to pick up the hand and held it up to his ear. His face paled. His wrath was not hidden. He turned his eyes, now glowing red, and stared at the stupid humans. Oh, the hatred he had for them. But rules were rules, and commands were commands. And he had just been issued a command to stand down. Unreal.

"Hold!" he shouted in his guttural, demonic voice. And as much as he hated to say the next word, he hated what would happen to him if he didn't. "Retreat!" Oridon took one last look at his worthy opponent. "Soon," he thought. "Soon I will spill your guts onto the ground." But for now, he turned around and ran up the dune, followed by every last Swastik.

The warriors stopped in confusion when the demons suddenly turned and ran away. They thought they were regrouping and strategizing, but now they were escaping up the hill. Any other time, this would have been met with victory cries and cheers, shouting to Yahweh. But no one had forgotten what was on the sand behind them. Their beloved friend, pierced through the heart, bleeding out poisoned blood. They turned around to see Mrs. Taylor holding Evie so gently. Now that the roar of the demons was gone, they could hear her singing tenderly to Evie.

The old hymn "My Jesus, I Love Thee" had a sorrowful tone. Evie was gray and lifeless. Bryce was the first to move to his wife's body. He gently took her from Mrs. Taylor's lap, holding her on his own now. Kendall fell next to his dad, hugging his father and mother tightly. The little warrior was covered in blood, just like his mother, but unlike her, it was not his own. It was the blood of the enemy that had come to kill his mother, his family, and his friends.

Kendall was tired. For the first time since coming to the battlefield, Kendall was weary of fighting. The small warrior laid his head on the chest of his father and kissed the head of his mother.

Vicki and Sam dropped their swords and crawled towards the little family that was theirs by Yahweh's blood. The women cried and put their arms around Bryce, Kendall, and Evie. They never thought it would end this way. But miraculously, they were not angry at Bryce for this. They had seen Evie and knew what the poison had done to her. There had been no stopping her, otherwise. The Sword of the Spirit was not used on demons alone.

The arms of Mrs. Taylor did not stay empty long as she wound them around the huddled women, gathering each one closer. Glittering tears flowed down her beautiful cheeks. Evan walked over and Vicki watched him take a small vial from his belt and to collect the tears that fell.

He put a cap on the vial and attached it to his belt again.

"Sons and daughters of Yahweh, it is time to go home." Evan spoke, and a portal appeared right next to him. It was low to the ground, and all they had to do was crawl in. They had no energy left in them to even stand. No one wanted to move away from Evie, but the battle was done here. The greatest army they had ever seen had retreated. There would be no stronghold built here. They were sure of that. Sam was the first to move out of the

group hug. She crawled forward into the portal and slid away from everyone's view. Next was Vicki, who gave one last hug to Mrs. Taylor before going.

"'Bye Mommy. I love you," said Kendall as he moved away from the body of his mother.

He dragged himself to the portal and never looked back. He paused to looked up at Evan, who stood next to it the portal. "Bye Evan. I love you, too."

Who collects angel tears? They don't often cry, but Evan was not able to stop one big tear from falling into the sand as he said goodbye, and Kendall entered the portal headfirst.

Bryce held Evie as he entered the portal. He didn't say goodbye to Mrs. Taylor or to Evan. He didn't have anything to say. He didn't know what anyone thought about what he had done. What did he face on the other side of this portal? Would it be worse than the horde of demons he faced here? He didn't know, but he knew he was taking his wife back home.

Mrs. Taylor was the last to leave. "Old friend, remember the time you stabbed me clean through my heart with your sword?" Mrs. Taylor spoke to the angel of the Most High.

"Yes. And I remember you needing that as much as our Evie did today. Are you still mad at me?" Evan asked with a twinkle in his eye. He knew the saint harbored no bad feelings towards him. That is not possible after the sword pierces the heart.

"Well, I will tell you this, you little pipsqueak. When I meet you on the other side of this life, we will have a good long talk about it. Goodbye for now, old friend. Thank you for your service to our King." The tall, young woman entered the portal to take her back to the land of her birth, but not the land of her heart.

Vicki lifted her head and opened her eyes, while saying, "Amen." She sat in her seat for a moment, trying to make sense of what had just happened. It only took a moment before she jumped off the couch and grabbed her cell phone.

It barely even rang once before Sam picked up and led with, "What. Just. Happened?"

"I have no idea. Was it real?? Did he stab her?" asked Vicki.

"Yes, he did," answered Sam.

"Did they retreat?" asked Vicki.

"Yes, they did," answered Sam.

Vicki paused and the silence was so full and so loud as both of their minds just replayed everything all over again.

Finally, Vicki cut into the quiet, "What are you doing?"

"Sitting on my front step waiting for you to get here," answered Sam.

"Be there in five," said Vicki as she pulled out of the driveway.

Bryce's heart was pounding so hard that he was sure it could be heard.

Kendall had jumped up with a loud 'Amen!', then noticed Jayne still napping on the bed. "Oops. Sorry, Jayne," he whispered.

He didn't even look at Bryce. He grabbed his backpack filled with the Legos he had brought and dumped them on the floor. He started playing with them as if nothing had just happened.

"What did happen?" thought Bryce. "What. Freaking. Happened?" he whispered to himself.

"Good job whispering, Dad. Jayne gets cranky if you wake her up," Kendall said encouragingly.

"Yeah, thanks, Kendall," Bryce said still staring at the floor. He looked up at Kendall.

"Hey, bud," he said to Kendall, "are you ok?"

"'Course, Dad," Kendall said.

Bryce stared at his son, content to play with his Legos. His thoughts went wild. "Is he traumatized? Did I just break my kid? I'm an idiot. What man lets his six-year-old pray about his mom, knowing it will be serious, fighting, enemy battlefield praying?!"

"Kendall, can you come here for a sec?" asked Bryce, while choosing his words carefully.

Kendall grabbed two handfuls of Legos, got up and walked to Bryce. He continued building the toys in his hands, not looking at Bryce.

"Hey buddy," Bryce said softly, leaning forward and stilling Kendall's hands with his own. "That was some pretty powerful praying that you just did," he paused. Kendall looked up at him, saying nothing. Bryce continued, "So, I'm not totally sure I understand everything. But I want you to know I understand if you are feeling confused. It'd be okay if you didn't want to pray like that anymore."

"Dad," Kendall said, moving his hands outside of Bryce's, then settling on top to hold his. "It's okay!"

Bryce was looking at his son's hands holding his own, his throat moving as he held back his tears. "Yeah?" he asked. "Because it'd be okay if you were upset or worried about your mom."

A confused look crossed Kendall's face. "I'm not worried," he said as he shook his head.

"No? You didn't think that was a little scary?" asked Bryce.

Kendall's face lit up with a smile and he replied excitedly, "Dad! That was so cool! It was like, real fighting! And that part about Mom, Evan told me not to worry."

Bryce studied his son's face, searching for the right words. "Evan?"

"Evan, Dad!" Kendall sounded exasperated. "You know, angel Evan?"

"You talked to Evan?" Bryce was trying, really trying to sound normal and keep the shock out of his voice.

Kendall sighed, "Dad. Yes. You did too. Don't you remember?"

"Yeah, buddy, I remember. I just didn't think you would. What did he tell you? What did he tell you about Mom?"

"He told me that sometimes God's words make us feel good, and sometimes they hurt, but not to worry because they are always right. And His words are like, magic. He made a funny face when he said that though," Kendall scrunched up his own face while remembering. "They're like magic," he continued, "because the words know what they should do even if we don't. And he said not to worry, because when we love God, sometimes he has to use hard words, but that's because the hard words fix any parts that might have got messed up," Kendall finished. He gave his dad's hands a squeeze, effectively pushing his Legos into the backs of Bryce's hands.

Bryce looked down, then back at his son, smiling, "That Evan is pretty cool, isn't he?"

"He's awesome," Kendall answered. "Can I go play?"

Bryce looked into the face of his son, searching for any traces of hurt, confusion, anything that shouldn't be on a six-year-old's face. Seeing nothing but Kendall's sweet face, he said with a wink, "Sure Son, just try not to wake Jayne."

Kendall smiled his matching smile back, "I'm pretty quiet, Dad."

He watched Kendall walk carefully to his pile of Legos, turn, and grin at his dad and send a thumbs up.

Bryce, thumbed up back, leaned back in his chair and thought to himself, "How much time do I give her?"

His phone ringing broke his silent weighing options. He reached for it and saw the caller. After a pause he answered, "Bartrug."

"Bryce," came the response.

Bryce sighed, "I'm guessing you called for a reason?"

"Yeah. Remember that time you asked me for help? Usually when people ask other people for help, they act like they want the help."

After a heavy silence, while Bryce was considering the coincidental timing, changed his tone and replied,

"Sorry. Been a day here already. I did ask you for help. And I appreciate it. I can assume you got something?"

"Somewhat," Bartrug replied. "You want to meet to discuss it?"

"It's a meeting kind of thing, huh?"

"Doesn't have to be right now, but we are gonna want to talk about this soon."

"Yeah, ok," Bryce said. "I have my kids right now; can you give me something to keep my mind from going crazy? Then we can figure out a time?"

Cody was silent for a moment. "Yeah, sure. So, it took a while, as it had some pretty advanced protection on it. Doesn't seem to jibe with the sleepy town here. But our guy finally got into it."

Bryce's heart was back to pounding, and he took a split second to notice before answering, "And?"

"And it's more code."

"Code?" Bryce ran his hands through his hair. "Hilarious. Did he figure it out?"

"No, he didn't. Apparently, the code is advanced. You know anything about advanced code?"

Bryce snorted, "Yeah. No. I don't know anything about advanced code. But I got to tell you, it's kind of freaking me out. What was it?"

It was Bartrug's turn for the pause, then he replied, "Okay, so, it was just a bunch of letters and numbers, listed, in random order. It's not unbreakable, it's just gonna take a bit. They're working on it, so we'll figure it out. So don't freak out. To be honest, it's something, and it seems obvious it's part of what we're looking for. Maybe it's all moved on, or maybe someone remembers dropping it into your pocket. I don't know. But you should know, I'm gonna stick around a bit longer. Until we figure it out at least," he continued, "In the meantime, you got my number. You call and I'll be there."

"There's a code." Bryce repeated back to Bartrug. "A code some task force has to make a decoder ring for. It was in my coat for months and may or may not be remembered by the people who put it there, you are changing your plan to stay, and I'm to call if there's a problem. And I shouldn't freak out? I'm not really feeling that, Bartrug!" He was starting to raise his voice when he noticed Jayne stirring and Kendall snapped his head towards him and scowled. Bryce took a breath and finished quietly. "Sorry, thank you for the information. Do you think there is a threat for me or my family?"

"Man, I get it. Really. My thoughts right now are, it doesn't appear anyone else is looking for it and if no one is looking for it, there likely isn't a danger. But if it is something someone wants, and they know you had it last, their interest in you could change. So yes, today, I think you're good. I don't know about tomorrow."

"What if it gets out that you have it, not me?"

"I think we should get together to discuss that."

Bryce was quiet for a moment, then asked, "What am I supposed to tell my wife?"

"I'm not married," said Cody, "so take this for what it's worth. But if it were me, I'd tell her the truth. If she's in, she needs to know what to look for. Maybe she'll want out, but even then, she deserves to know that some people may come looking for something someday."

Bryce rubbed a hand over his face. "Yeah, okay, thanks. I gotta go."

"Also," continued Bartrug, "you should know something. About an hour ago, I got the impression you needed help."

Bryce felt a ripple, right before he felt goosebumps, "I don't know how you would know about any of that. And it wasn't the kind of help you'd know anything about."

"I heard the Shofar."

Bryce's mind was racing. "No, it's not possible."

"So, you're saying, again, that you're one of the freaking good guys?" Bryce wasn't sure if he felt shocked or disappointment.

"Mostly," Cody laughed. "Call me if you need anything. Peace, brother."

Bryce heard the phone go dead. "Wow," he muttered, "I'd really rather hate him."

Sam hopped in the car and turned to look at Vicki. Vicki turned to look at her.

"Never have I ever seen that kind of power. Holy. Crap," said Sam.

Vicki smiled at Sam, "Right? I literally feel like I could be high or something!"

"Wait," said Sam, "What do you know about being high?"

"Nothing! It's just a figure of speech!" Sam squinted her eyes while scrutinizing her.

"Oh, good grief," laughed Vicki, "I just feel like something amazing has happened, and I don't know how to describe it! Where are we going, anyway?"

"Mm-hmm. Okay. Whatever," Sam scoffed. "I called Bryce while I was waiting, he asked us to go to his place to watch the kids and give him a head start, then bring them to the house. He wants to go in first, make sure it's okay."

"Great plan," Vicki said as she pulled out of the driveway. "Did you see him out there? He was like the Hulk!"

"How could you not see him? I don't think I can even describe it! Or even better, Mrs. Taylor?"

Vicki squealed with laughter as she put the car into drive and headed to Bryce's place. They both took turns laughing, praising, and reliving every moment.

Evie was sitting at her table when she heard the truck pull in. She'd been expecting him but was so thankful for the delay he'd given. She looked out the window, saw him slowly get out of the truck. She noticed he didn't have the kids. He wouldn't have left them alone, would he?

Hands in his pockets, he walked to the door, paused, and knocked.

"So, this is it," she thought. "The moment. The moment that decides the rest." She walked to the door, opened it, and stood looking at him.

"Evie..." he began.

She turned away, leaving the door open, and returned to her seat. "The kids?" she asked.

"Vicki and Sam are with them, bringing them here in a few minutes," he answered as he stepped into the kitchen.

Evie nodded.

"Evie, can we just talk?" Bryce softly asked.

She lifted her eyes to him, "I think it's better if I say what I need to say."

Bryce felt his heart sink. Right into his gut. Then he felt fear-laced adrenaline shoot up his throat.

Evie took a deep breath, and said, "I knew you had been there, but I didn't realize," she searched for the words to continue, "I didn't realize you belonged there."

"Evie, I'm sorry."

Evie held up her hand. "Please," she said, "let me say this first."

Bryce could only swallow his fear down, praying, "It is what it is, and Lord, whatever it is, you'll go with me."

"I don't know when it happened. I really was praying and asking God to help me. Point me in the right direction. Send an answer," she laughed. "I meant it. I didn't know what the right thing to do was, but I was open to learning."

Bryce nodded, hoping it was encouraging.

"But then I got afraid," she continued, "Afraid of what you had done, afraid of what had changed, afraid of what we might be involved in. I got... angry."

"It's okay," Bryce said softly.

She smiled sadly, "Yeah, probably. I don't think that was wrong. But it felt like the beginning of something. Something got dark. It wasn't just that my feelings for you changed. My feelings for God changed. I was so, so mad at him," she paused. "Then I heard you were there, praying for me. It was so messed up, to hear someone is praying for me and to be so ticked off about it," she laughed. "Then Kendall, I never wanted this for my son. Not my six-year-old son. A child shouldn't have to pray for his dad, and then his mom."

Bryce dropped his eyes, his face washed in guilt.

"But who am I to say what a child can and should pray about? I saw him there, really saw him. And I saw you too." Her voice dropped to a whisper, "You were magnificent."

His eyes shot up to hers.

"You were for me."

"Yes," he whispered back, his voice hoarse.

"You've been for me all along."

"I've been an idiot, but yes." He watched her face, then her eyes filled. He watched as a tear slipped from her eye and slid down her cheek.

"Thank you," she earnestly said.

Bryce felt undone. He slipped from his chair to his knees and reached for her hands. She let him take them. "Evie, don't cry. It's on me. All of it. If you need me to be gone to be okay, I'll go. But if there's any way to stay, please let me." He held her hands in his, resting his head on them.

"This is the moment," she thought to herself. She slipped off the chair to the floor with him, pulling their hands to her lap, she raised one hand to hold his face.

"Stay," she said as she looked into his eyes. She watched his face as the slow grin, complete with dimples, spread across his face.

"So, what you're saying is," he said, "you want me, just like I suspected?"

Her face registered her surprise, and then she threw her head back and laughed.

He saw her hair swinging as she threw her head back, saw her eyes close, saw her face light with joy, felt her hand on his face and he knew. He knew, this was the moment it all changed.

"Thank you, God." He pulled Evie to him, for the first time in a long time, wrapping his arms around her, and feeling her arms wrap around him.

"I know everything isn't automatically fixed," he murmured into her hair as they held each other, "but can we try? Will you let me try?"

Evie smiled. She finally had the answer and she felt it in her heart, her mind, and her spirit. "No, we won't try," she said as she pulled back to see his face. She traced a dimple with her finger. "We go all in. Not just you, not just me, but both of us, all in."

His eyes dropped to her mouth, back to her eyes. Then his lazy smile appeared. Just as she realized his intentions, the door burst open. Before they could register their surprise, they were rushed by Kendall, Jayne and two grown women.

After the laughing, and hugging, Evie drew Kendall to her and looked him in the face. "Kendall, my little warrior, thank you. Thank you for every prayer you spoke for me. I promise you that I will always," she repeated, "always, battle with you any and every time you need me."

"Okay, Mom. Cool!" he answered, happily grinning.

Evie looked over the head of her children to the faces of her friends. Each of their eyes were swimming as Evie whispered, "Thank you. Thank you, a million times."

In that moment, huddled on the floor in a giant hug, they knew He was there, loving, hugging, laughing with them. For them.

"To the Most High God," whispered Vicki.

"To the Most High God," was the echo.

EPILOGUE

Oridon and his troop reached their fortification, the cave which held a deep underbelly of rooms where the darkness was felt. Small torches hung far apart on the walls, the light nearly lost in shadows. He was enraged at the order to retreat, after he had finally found a foe worthy of his hand in battle. He had waited, watched, and had been intrigued to finally find the one marked just for him.

The call to retreat came from a higher level and he knew to obey. He would wait it out and every dream from now until then would involve a slow and painful dismembering of this chosen enemy.

But he must do something about his horde. Furious at his order to fall back, he will need to motivate them to stay in line and not turn on each other. It wasn't easy being a ruler of demons. They could turn on each other tonight, and not one of them would ever walk out of this cave. Well, only one would, and that would be him. Nobody knew this cave system like Oridon.

He had designed every inch of it, taking ideas from other demon fortresses he had been in. But his cave had something unique. The only ones who had known about it were the ones who built it and he got rid of them and buried their carcasses in the last layer of molten lava on the floor. He was the only one who knew where it was, how to enter, and what was inside. He was going to have to reveal his secret for the greater good.

Oridon went to the Great Hall, where his minions would be gathered. Lately, the after-battle meetings were victory parties. They'd enjoyed party after party because followers of that One were so weak and selfish, or shortsighted and stupid. The only downside to the victories was that the higher-ranking demons were not getting called to battle as much. The low-ranking peons were handling most of the work. It was only because a horde of Jaders were destroyed that he was called in this time. They were finally going to give the thirsty desert sand some human blood to drink. Then the retreat was called. He will never forget receiving that message just before his chance to fight.

In the Great Hall, Oridon could see the anger and the frustration on his demon's faces. He would need to give them something to satisfy their lusts, their pride, their desire to inflict pain, their depravity. He would still be their hero and leader if he gave them what they crave.

"Demons!" Oridon bellowed so loud the cave walls shook from the floor to the ceiling. "The victory was yours today, within your grasp." He began walking towards the center of the room, moving between the tables of bone and glass. "You saw the filthy creatures break into our space and defile it with their vanity and pride! They have destroyed everything they touch, and now they come into our world and pick fights with us, the greatest demons ever to dwell behind the mist!"

All black eyes were set on Oridon. He could feel their engagement and connection with him. He knew he was a *spectacular leader. He was their prize. "For your obedience and to compensate for the orders were given from below, I announce to you, for one night only, the opening of the gate!" he bellowed.*

Screams and cheers roared so loud that cracks formed and moved through the tables of glass and bones. Oridon knew this gift would secure their temporary allegiance. It would cost Oridon immensely. One did not open the gates of hell without pursuing the correct channels and following the proper chain of command. But the higher-ups owed him this. They could summon him before the court later. For now, he had to keep morale up and maintain his authority. The screeching of the sacred gates was heard. The demons could hear the sound coming from down the long, dark hall. One by one, they stopped cheering and talking, and stood quietly, trembling with excitement. Some were frothing at the mouth, looks of lust on their faces. Other's sullenness was replaced with rage, as their veins pulsed and throbbed over their necks and heads. What a night of terror and horror this would be. The humans kept in a bottomless pit, grabbed by demons, and pulled through to this cave tonight, would know fresh horror. They would have to be thrown back in before the gates closed. The demons had twenty-four hours to use every dark deed on them.

The gates stopped their slow, clanging opening with a loud and jarring crash. The gate was open. The demons ran at once towards the hall, everyone wanting their turn to reach in and grab a soul who lived here for eternity. They were their slaves now.

As Oridon turned to go to his secret lair, he reached out and grabbed the first demon running by him. He grabbed it by the collar and jerked it towards him. "You're coming with me."

The demon looked at the hero of the hour and said with glee, "Yes, my master." Oridon led him away from the devilish fray and towards his own quarters. "Where are we going, Master?" Oridon could sense the mixed desire of the demon, wanting the night of mischief with his companions, but to be singled and out and chosen by the master was thrilling as well.

"I am going to show you something no one has ever seen before. I chose you because you are superior, you stand out, and I know I can trust you. If you so swear to keep this secret only between you and me, I will invite you to my personal lair these next twenty-four hours for your own night of delights, full of anything you desire."

The black eyes sparkled and glittered. The smell of desire was all over him. He was dripping with gratitude and anticipation. "Yessss, my lord. Anything you command, I will do. I will keep every secret you share with me. I delight in doing your will."

"Follow me." Oridon kept descending towards his own personal space. It was a long walk and the deeper they went into this place, the darker it became. Just before reaching Oridon's door, he stopped. The demon stopped as well, wondering why they didn't walk to the end of this corridor. It was just right there. Oridon turned to the lesser demon and seemed to say with gentleness, "Are you ready?"

"Yes, lord. I am."

Oridon pulled on the nearest sconce of flame, and it triggered a hidden door opening. The eyes of the little demon looked as big as black marbles as it realized how special he was to be chosen to know secrets from Oridon. A hidden room? Oridon walked in and moved aside to let the demon enter. When they were both in the dark room, the door behind them closed, sealing them both in.

"What is this place, Master?" He looked top to bottom as he moved deeper into the room, following Oridon.

"I have a treasure here that helps us have an advantage in battle. It's a secret weapon. I am the only one who has one. This secret must remain between you and me alone, upon pain of death, demon. Do you swear?"

"I so swear." The demon placed his long, creepy hand on his heart to signify his sincere promise.

And then Oridon pushed him to the center of the room. The demon fell into a space on the floor made with a circle of blood. He was now standing inside the circle. He moved quickly to get away, away from the heat beginning to burn his feet. He looked questioningly at Oridon, and as he moved to get out of the circle, he was pushed back by an unseen force. He moved around the blood circle trying to get away from this barrier, but he could not press out of it.

"Master?" he said in fear and panic.

"Wait, faithful servant. The secret will be revealed."

Now that the weight of the demon was in the center of the floor, a lever was triggered, and a stone opened next to its feet. Up came a podium with a book on it. The demon knew immediately what this was and began to scream in terror.

"No! No, Master! Release me! Let me out of here!"

"Not yet. Do this one thing and I will free you. You have proved yourself trustworthy. I will reward you with the highest honor and prize for being my only true and faithful companion. You will be rewarded for this work. Focus. What is your name? "

"Sorvene." He said with a whisper. His eyes would not look away from the book risen from the ground. The podium was at its full height now. The book put out a light that was white and bright. The compulsion to flee away from it and to touch it was both strong for Sorvene. Never had he ever seen The

Book. He had heard of it all his life, but he had never seen one, much less been within a foot of it, able to reach out and touch it. He had heard The Book contained secret information about their eternal enemy. He had also heard the words could be read but couldn't be touched. He didn't know what that meant. The burning sensation at his feet, this heat, was slowly creeping up into his ankles. It wasn't quite yet pain, but it was alarming. The compulsion of The Book was stronger and held his attention.

"What should I do, Master?"

"Open it. I don't care where. Just open it and read me something. It is all in code and makes absolutely no sense, but with your skills, the code will reveal itself to you. I have no doubt about your ability. I have heard of you, Sorvene. I am honored to be here in this secret room with you. Now do as I say and open the book to wherever and read to me what you see."

The praise and flattery fed Sorvene's devilish desire. His boldness grew. His fear was pushed aside by his vanity, and he stepped to The Book. He poked a long finger out and touched it quickly, withdrawing his finger as fast as he could. Nothing. Nothing happened. He poked it a second time, using more of his hand. The burning in his feet stopped. He became emboldened and reached his hand out and grasped hold of it. He flipped open to a middle section and let it fall. The Book now opened and both sides lying flat to reveal the Word.

"Read it to me, Sorvene," said Oridon in a voice quivering with fear.

"Yea, though I walk through the valley of the shadow of death, I will fear no evil, for thou art with me. Thy rod and thy staff they comfort me. Thou preparest a table before me in the presence of my enemies. Thou annointest my head with oil. My cup runneth over."

"Stop!" Oridon shouted. "Stop, Sorvene. That is enough. Now close the book." Sorvene was torn. The Book pulled him. The Words seemed like magic and a spell to him. The burning wasn't felt when The Book was opened. He wanted to look at every page, read every word. "Sorvene, I said, close the book. Step away."

"Yes, Master." Sorvene did as he was commanded, for he was a dutiful demon. Once the book was closed, the fire began to burn in his feet, ankles and now moving up to his knees.

"Master, I burn! Help me!"

"Yes, I know Sorvene. It is the cost of being near and touching The Book. You promised you will tell no one and that the secret of this chamber was safe with you. You spoke the truth. Had you been a better demon, you may have lived today and enjoyed the opened gates of hell. I consider this the survival of the fittest demon. See you in hell."

And then Oridon turned to walk out the hidden door, pushing on a rock in the wall to open the door to the hallway. The demon Sorvene began to burn alive, fire now coming up through the floor. He tried to move toward the book, to touch it and open it, but he could not move as his feet were disintegrating. Flames erupted over his entire body, and he screamed loud enough to shake the floors of the Great Hall above him. The demons felt the floor shake but were so involved in their debauchery to the humans from hell that they barely noticed.

Loden buried himself in the sand. He had crawled all the way to the oasis under the sand. He stopped only occasionally to come above the surface to get his breath and feel like a demon again and not a worm. It had been slow and painful, but now he was finally within view of the place on this battlefield that *he despised more than anywhere. This oasis, with its green plants, the cool, refreshing breeze, and the sparkling water represented everything he hated. He clenched his jaw and gripped the handfuls of sand tightly. Just looking at the garden inside this battlefield made his already hot temperature rise. He was sure steam was rising from his body. He had come for one reason only.*

He was going to scale this monstrosity of a rock and stand at the pinnacle and curse his enemies. Curses to Fairen, for making him have to kill him. Curses to Oridon, who thought he was such a big shot, who wouldn't know a great plan or a true leader when he saw one. And mega curses to the One whose name isn't spoken without pain or peril.

He slowly stepped on to the oasis. Humans found great relief from the heat of the sand. Stepping onto cool, lush grass was supposed to be refreshment and a gift from their master. Loden knew that only weak creatures needed gifts or reassurances from masters. When he was given his new orders and a new horde, they would know one thing: that he was in charge. His seething fueled his walk across the grass towards the rock formation. No demon had been able to climb it. Even in the fiercest battle, only the humans were able to find shelter near it or climb up it. No matter how many times they had tried to get here first or to distract the enemy, not one demon from any level had gotten up this rock. It was a high tower and seemed to be a refuge for the human enemies. The fact even the rocks pampered the humans showed just how unfair the war was.

Enough of this. He was going to climb it. Maybe it welcomed solitary figures of all sorts. He stood in front of the rock, with his head turned up, squinting into the sunshine. The whole side was smooth as glass. There was no place to grab hold of, or to place feet. There were no ledges or ridges. How did the humans climb this? Loden made his way around the other side of the rock when the sound of music and laughter caught his ear. He pushed himself into the face of the rock wall and calmed his breathing. The battle was over. Why was anyone here? He crept toward the sound, the merriment growing louder as he scooted closer and closer to the source. Once at the edge, he knew he had to peek around the corner. To see what was happening. After all, he was going to become a Watcher.

Slow as could be, without a whisper of a sound, the slithery, gray alien like demon put his head just barely around the edge. He saw and he watched. And the hatred boiled and brewed from every pore of his being. He must learn to bury the rage and focus on taking meticulous information, recording everything he could see and hear, learning and remembering every face, taking in all the details.

A long table was set in the shade of the rock, sheltered from the hot, burning sun. A pool of clear sparkling water bubbled and flowed nearby. Large palm trees moved in the gentle breeze. The table held four chairs on each side, with a chair on both ends. There were pillar candles and small candles down the center of the table, surrounded by fresh evergreen boughs and eucalyptus branches. Fresh flowers in vases brought color, and a man and a woman sat at the table ends. They raised their glasses of wine to each other and whispered, 'I love you". There were three women on one side of the table and a small girl. A long-legged bronzed warrior, a small, dark-haired woman, and a beautiful, angelic woman clothed in wisdom. Across from them were four males, one of them a small boy who sat in the middle. He laughed at the conversation with the one who was next to him. There was a man he hadn't seen before, a guy who looked like a lumberjack. He was quieter, not quite as jovial, but he raised his glass with the others when a toast was raised.

This was a feast, a feast of joy and thanks. Loden had heard of these but had never seen one before. Just wait until he tells a Watcher what was happening right under Oridon's nose, in his territory! A party to brag and celebrate their defeat of a demon! Someone needed to know about this. And he knew exactly who. He turned to leave, to go back to the sand, bury himself in it and begin the long crawl to the portal that would take him out of this devil forsaken battlefield. He would tell his tale and he would make sure history knew that he was the one who saved his master's plan. He had been here from day one and he had vital information.

But as Loden stepped onto the sand, he heard the shouts of joy, and he heard the name Yahweh. The name drove him to his knees with such excruciating pain it made him cry. How he hated that name, as well as every single person at that table. Loden made it his personal mission to destroy them if it was the last thing he did.

Evie was in her happy place. A magnificent, if all went as planned, dinner of braised short ribs simmered in the oven. The rosemary mashed potatoes were perfectly fluffed and staying warm. Roasted brussels sprouts with maple syrup and crunchy bacon was sizzling in the oven. Perfectly soft dinner rolls were wrapped in a cotton tea towel. A fresh salad was in its bowl, waiting to be dressed.

She could hear the soft music of the High Kings with their lilting Celtic voices, chosen by Bryce, playing in the house somewhere. Weird choice, she thought, but it made her smile none-the-less. She was on the deck in the back yard, a little in need of repair due to lack of attention and use in the last couple of years. But it was an open space, big enough for a couple of tables to sit end to end, and with the soft sun, cooler temperatures and new color of the trees beginning to show off, it felt like the perfect setting. This was the only night everyone had free, and she wasn't willing to scratch anyone off the list.

Bryce didn't share her vision, but he trusted it. Along with a rug, she had wanted twinkly lights overhead. She knew it would still be daylight when they gathered, but if dinner and talk went long, the lights would add to the beauty she hoped for. Of course, Bryce had grand ideas of how to best add posts to the four corners, and she had laughed at the lofty ambition and convinced him of a quicker and more practical method. After too much discussion of the pros and cons, they had decided to use large black flowerpots, filled with cement and posts set in the center. They were a bit heavy, but they could move them around as they needed to make a larger lit area or smaller if they wanted. She had ordered eucalyptus garlands and included extra to wrap around the pots. The round lights crisscrossed in the middle over the tables. It was beautiful, and she could smell the eucalyptus.

She didn't have a single long table, but she put two six-foot tables end to end, and covered them with white tablecloths. She added extra eucalyptus down the center with ivory candles, and her every day white dishes and eclectic collection of wine and water glasses completed the look. It was perfect.

Bryce's idea for a get together was to get the grill hot and flip some burgers and hot dogs. Although Evie loved an outdoor barbecue, she wanted this to be special, and beautiful in its presentation as well as meaning. This was their group, their people, their friends. None of them had family close by, and they become family for each other. They were worth the effort, and she knew there was something special about gathering at a table. It felt sacred, meaningful, and blessed.

That's what she was, blessed. She felt it in her core. Her family had been placed together and defended by the Most High. She knew sadness for those whose outcome was not the same as hers, despite having fought for it, defended it, and desired it. God, in his sovereignty, only knew why. She chose to trust that He knew what would bring Him the most glory, what would work the best for those she cared for, what would be used to fill their purpose, and while on this earth, she trusted his perfect timing.

She finished lighting the candles, and she heard the doorbell ring. It made her smile because it was proper, which her friends were not. She stepped into the house and heard laughter and hellos. Walking into the kitchen, she saw Bryce and the kids hugging Vicki. Steve had joined her, and he shook Bryce's hand. Evie went to Steve and, with a warm smile, hugged him. "Hi, Steve. It's so good to see you. It feels like forever since I last saw you!" He hugged her back and with warmth said, "It's been too long for sure. I've missed your family." Vicki's smile was blinding in its happiness. She looped her arm through Steve's as they made their way into the kitchen, giving Evie a wink as she walked by.

Soon Sam, her son Jack, and Mrs. Taylor were making their way up the steps. Jack held Mrs. Taylor's elbow as he helped her and her walker up the steps. He took this duty seriously, concentrating on her every step.

He looked up as they approached the door, saying, "Hey. I'm going to need you all to back up so I can help her in."

"Oh! Sorry, of course!" said Evie as she, Bryce and the kids all took big steps back.

Mrs. Taylor just smiled at him. "Thank you, Jack."

Sam stepped up, leaned in, and whispered to Evie and Bryce, "Sorry. It's so weird. He adores her. I don't even know how that's possible!" She shrugged and grabbed Evie for a hug. She turned to Bryce, held out her arms, and said, "Come on, you know you want to hug me!" Bryce, without missing a beat teased back, "Oh, can I? Can I please?" Evie laughed as he picked the tiny powerhouse up and twirled her in a circle.

Jayne squealed, "Twirl me too, Daddy!"

Kendall reminded her, "He twirls you every day, Janey, it's Sam's turn."

"What?" said Bryce. "Every time I twirl another lady, I must twirl you too, Janey. Right?"

They congregated in the kitchen watching Bryce twirl Jayne and hadn't noticed Cody step up to the open door.

As Bryce spun around, he saw Cody and gently sat her down. Bryce stepped to the door and saw him holding onto some flowers.

"Aw, you didn't have to bring me flowers, man. Sweet though," he said.

Cody took a breath for support, and then mumbled, "I didn't know what the right protocol was to do here. These are for your wife."

"My wife? You brought flowers for my wife? Right here in front of witnesses?"

Cody's face went ashen. He looked confused, his eyes darting to Evie and back to Bryce. "Uh, I'm sorry. I didn't…"

Bryce laughed. "Ha! Gotcha!" He grabbed him by the shoulder, ushering him in. "Seriously, you should see your face right now! Come in, I'll grab you something to drink."

"You're hilarious. Freaking hilarious," Cody muttered as he stepped to Evie and handed her the flowers. "Thank you for inviting me. I don't get too many invitations like this."

Evie smiled as she accepted the flowers, and then reached to give him a warm hug. "You've been a friend to us, and I hope this is the first of many dinners together." Turning to the kids, she said, "Let me introduce you. I don't think you've met our children. This is our son, Kendall." Cody stuck his hand out to shake Kendall's.

Kendall put his hand into Cody's and said, "Hi. I'm six. Do you like Legos?"

"Pleased to meet you, Kendall. I'm not sure if I like Legos. I've never played with them before." Kendall's eyes got huge as he looked at Evie in disbelief. "I can show you how if you want?"

Evie laughed and said, "How about a little later? Maybe after dinner?"

Kendall looked at Cody expectantly. "Is that okay?"

"That works for me!" Cody smiled and turned to Jayne, kneeling down. "And who is this pretty lassie?"

Janey stood before him in all of her sweetness and said, "You talk funny. I'm Janey."

"Well, Janey, I'm pleased to meet you. And I do talk funny, but that's so you know who I am when everyone talks at the same time."

Janey stared at him for a moment. "Okay. I think I can find you."

He smiled and stood as he warmly greeted Mrs. Taylor and Steve, and shook hands with Jack, who didn't quite meet his eyes.

Evie said, "I'm not sure you've officially met my friends." She motioned to Vicki and Sam. "This is Vicki."

Vicki stepped up and said, "It's so nice to finally meet you, Cody," and stuck out her hand.

He shook it and said, "Thank you, you, too." He held his hand to Sam who had her arms folded across her chest.

"Didn't know you and Bryce had become friendly."

After a pause, Cody continued to hold his hand out to her and said with a smile, "Well, now you know." Sam raised her brows and shook his hand.

Evie took the flowers to be put in water, and the greetings finished, they each made their way to the deck. After all the food had been plated and seated on the table, Bryce cleared his throat.

"Is it okay if I say something before we devour this meal my beautiful wife made?"

Everyone stilled and looked at Bryce.

"I'm not very good at this," he paused and looked at Evie, who smiled encouragingly at him, "but I just wanted to take a second and say this to all of you. Thank you. I don't even know if there are better words. Every one of you means something to me or Evie. You've been here for us in one way or another. I know I kid a lot, but I'm serious now." He took a moment and looked at each of them. "I don't deserve this table. I really don't. But each of you invested in us, either by your own words and actions or by supporting someone who was actively helping." He looked at Steve and Jack, who nodded back to him. "I don't know if we'd be here..." Bryce paused, cleared his throat, and blinked. "I don't know if we'd be here if not for you. I'm the luckiest man in the world and I want you to know I'll do the same for you, anytime, anywhere. I've got your back as you've had mine." He grabbed his glass, lifted it. Each around the table did the same.

"To our friends, you are a gift to us." He looked at each of them. "To my children, you bring me and your mom joy every single day. Thank you for waiting for me." Tears filled his eyes as he looked at Kendall and Jayne, holding their glasses of water in the air.

"To my wife," he looked at Evie, and the tears slipped down his cheeks. "Thank you. Every single day, for the rest of my life, I promise to love you, to honor you and cherish you." Around the table, eyes filled with tears as a holy hush filled their space.

Bryce smiled, laughed a little as he wiped his face and, lifting his glass higher, he said with a raised voice, "To the Most High God!!"

Around the table, cheers broke out as every glass and every voice lifted in unison, "To the Most High God!!"

Their words, filled with joy, with love, with reverence and celebration, lifted and carried to the heavens.

ABOUT THE AUTHORS

The authors, Maureen and Shannon, are not only sisters in the faith and heart friends, but they are sisters by birth. Separated in age by under two years, they share together every memory of their childhood and early adult years. It was in their young adult years that the ministry call on Shannon and her husband's life separated them by 500 miles. It did not, however, separate them in love, contact, or daily updates on their everyday life as they both raised their children and saw them each off into adulthood.

With Maureen raising four daughters and Shannon raising four sons, and the benefits of our current century, they have been so blessed and privileged to be able to keep in such close contact through the years. Yearly family vacations, weddings, quick weekend trips, baby showers, and fun getaways have all been forever planted as wonderful family memories.

Today they are adjusting to life with adult children and have realized there is no such thing as an empty nest when they are so blessed to have their grandbabies live so close. This new season of life made it possible for the two sisters to complete their labor of love, this first book in a short series of inspirational fiction. It's their hope that the series will leave a lasting imprint on the reader's heart and mind and that beauty can be found in each story they tell.